RSC School Shakespeare

Series consultant: Emma Smith
Professor of Shakespeare Studies
Hertford College, University of Oxford

ROMEO AND JULIET

OXFORD
UNIVERSITY PRESS

OXFORD
UNIVERSITY PRESS

Great Clarendon Street, Oxford, OX2 6DP,
United Kingdom

Oxford University Press is a department of the University of Oxford.
It furthers the University's objective of excellence in research, scholarship,
and education by publishing worldwide. Oxford is a registered trade mark of Oxford
University Press in the UK and in certain other countries

Text and activities © Royal Shakespeare Company 2016

William Shakespeare and his world section © Oxford University Press 2016

The moral rights of the authors have been asserted

First published in 2016

British Library Cataloguing in Publication Data

Data available

ISBN 978-019-836480-1

10 9 8 7 6 5 4 3 2 1

Printed in Great Britain by Bell and Bain Ltd., Glasgow

Acknowledgements

Cover and performance images © Royal Shakespeare Company 2016

Cover photograph by Peter Coombs. Other *Romeo and Juliet* performance images by Ellie
Kurttz.

p258 (middle): Janet Faye Hastings / Shutterstock; p258 (bottom): mashakotcur /
Shutterstock; p259 (top right): 19th era / Alamy Stock Photo; p259 (middle right): Granger,
NYC. / Alamy Stock Photo; p259 (middle left): © National Portrait Gallery, London; p262:
DEA PICTURE LIBRARY / Getty Images; p270: Pictorial Press Ltd / Alamy Stock Photo

Contents

Introduction to
RSC School Shakespeare

The RSC approach

The classroom as rehearsal room

All the work of RSC Education is underpinned by the artistic practice of the Royal Shakespeare Company (RSC). In particular, we make very strong connections between the rehearsal rooms in which our actors and directors work and the classrooms in which you learn. Rehearsal rooms are essentially places of exploration and shared discovery, in which a company of actors and their director work together to bring Shakespeare's plays to life. To do this successfully they need to have a deep understanding of the text, to get the language 'in the body' and to be open to a range of interpretive possibilities and choices. The ways in which they do this are both active and playful, connecting mind, voice and body.

Becoming a company

To do this we begin by deliberately building a spirit of one group with a shared purpose — this is about 'us' rather than 'me'. We often do this with games that warm up our brains, voices and bodies, and we continue to build this spirit through a scheme of work that includes shared, collaborative tasks that depend on and value everyone's contributions. The ways in which the activities work in this edition encourage discussion, speculation and questioning: there is rarely one right answer. This process requires and develops critical thinking.

Making the world of the play

In rehearsals at the RSC, we explore the whole world of the play: we tackle the language, characters and motivation, setting, plot and themes. By 'standing in the shoes' of the characters and exploring the world of the play, you will be engaged fully: head, eyes, ears, hands, bodies and hearts are involved in actively interpreting the play. In grappling with scenes and speeches, you are also actively grappling with the themes and ideas in the play, experiencing them from the points of view of the different characters.

The language is central to our discoveries

We place the language in the plays at the core of everything we do. Active, playful approaches can make Shakespeare's words vivid, accessible and enjoyable. His language has the power to excite and delight all of us.

In the rehearsal room, the RSC uses social and historical context in order to deepen understanding of the world of the play. The company is engaged in a 'conversation across time', inviting audiences to consider what a play means to us now and what it meant to us then. We hope that the activities in this edition will offer you an opportunity to join that conversation.

The activities require close, critical reading and encourage you to make informed interpretive choices about language, character and motivation, themes and plot. The work is rooted in speaking and listening to Shakespeare's words and to each other's ideas in order to help embrace and unlock this extraordinary literary inheritance.

Jacqui O'Hanlon
Director of Education
Royal Shakespeare Company

The Royal Shakespeare Theatre

Using *RSC School Shakespeare*

As you open each double page, you will see the script of the play on the right-hand page. On the left-hand page is a series of features that will help you connect with and explore William Shakespeare's play *Romeo and Juliet* and the world in which Shakespeare lived.

Those features are:

Summary

At the top of every left-hand page is a summary of what happens on the facing page to help you understand the action.

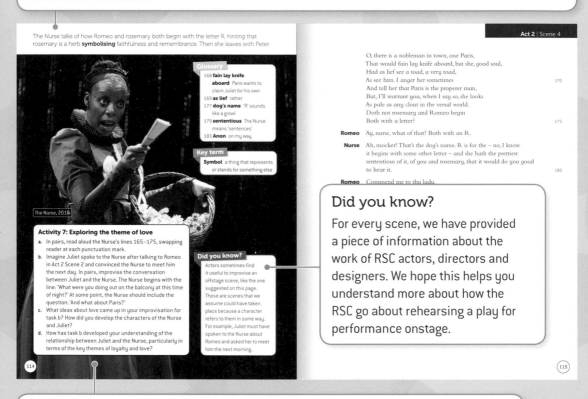

The Nurse talks of how Romeo and rosemary both begin with the letter R, hinting that rosemary is a herb **symbolising** faithfulness and remembrance. Then she leaves with Peter.

Glossary

168 **fain lay knife aboard** Paris wants to claim Juliet for his own
169 **as lief** rather
177 **dog's name** 'R' sounds like a growl
179 **sententious** The Nurse means 'sentences'
183 **Anon** on my way

Key term

Symbol a thing that represents or stands for something else

The Nurse, 2010

Activity 7: Exploring the theme of love

a. In pairs, read aloud the Nurse's lines 165–175, swapping reader at each punctuation mark.
b. Imagine Juliet spoke to the Nurse after talking to Romeo in Act 2 Scene 2 and convinced the Nurse to meet him the next day. In pairs, improvise the conversation between Juliet and the Nurse. The Nurse begins with the line: 'What were you doing out on the balcony at this time of night?' At some point, the Nurse should include the question: 'And what about Paris?'
c. What ideas about love came up in your improvisation for task b? How did you develop the characters of the Nurse and Juliet?
d. How has task b developed your understanding of the relationship between Juliet and the Nurse, particularly in terms of the key themes of loyalty and love?

Did you know?

Actors sometimes find it useful to improvise an offstage scene, like the one suggested on this page. These are scenes that we assume could have taken place because a character refers to them in some way. For example, Juliet must have spoken to the Nurse about Romeo and asked her to meet him the next morning.

114

Act 2 | Scene 4

O, there is a nobleman in town, one Paris,
That would fain lay knife aboard, but she, good soul,
Had as lief see a toad, a very toad,
As see him. I anger her sometimes   170
And tell her that Paris is the properer man,
But, I'll warrant you, when I say so, she looks
As pale as any clout in the versal world.
Doth not rosemary and Romeo begin
Both with a letter?   175

Romeo Ay, nurse, what of that? Both with an R.

Nurse Ah, mocker! That's the dog's name. R is for the – no, I know
it begins with some other letter – and she hath the prettiest
sententious of it, of you and rosemary, that it would do you good
to hear it.   180

Romeo Commend me to thy lady.

Did you know?

For every scene, we have provided a piece of information about the work of RSC actors, directors and designers. We hope this helps you understand more about how the RSC go about rehearsing a play for performance onstage.

115

RSC performance photographs

Every left-hand page includes at least one photograph from an RSC production of the play. Some of the activities make direct use of the production photographs. The photographs illustrate the action, bringing to life the text on the facing page. They also include a caption that identifies the character or event, together with the date of the RSC production.

Activity

Every left-hand page includes at least one activity that is inspired by RSC rehearsal room practice.

Glossary

Where needed, there is a glossary that explains words from the play that may be unfamiliar and cannot be worked out in context.

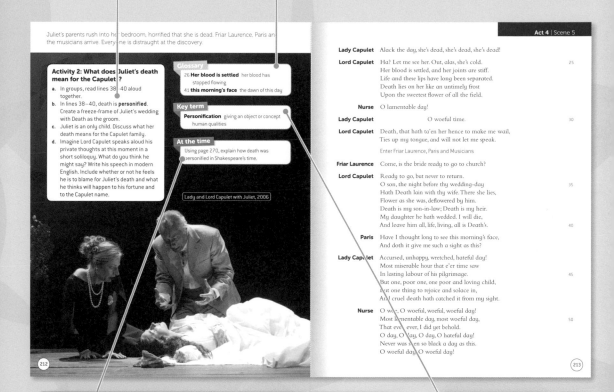

Juliet's parents rush into her bedroom, horrified that she is dead. Friar Laurence, Paris and the musicians arrive. Everyone is distraught at the discovery.

Activity 2: What does Juliet's death mean for the Capulets?

a. In groups, read lines 38–40 aloud together.

b. In lines 38–40, death is **personified**. Create a freeze-frame of Juliet's wedding with Death as the groom.

c. Juliet is an only child. Discuss what her death means for the Capulet family.

d. Imagine Lord Capulet speaks aloud his private thoughts at this moment in a short soliloquy. What do you think he might say? Write his speech in modern English. Include whether or not he feels he is to blame for Juliet's death and what he thinks will happen to his fortune and to the Capulet name.

Glossary

26 **Her blood is settled** her blood has stopped flowing

41 **this morning's face** the dawn of this day

Key term

Personification giving an object or concept human qualities

At the time

Using page 270, explain how death was personified in Shakespeare's time.

Lady and Lord Capulet with Juliet, 2006

212

213

Act 4 | Scene 5

Lady Capulet	Alack the day, she's dead, she's dead, she's dead!
Lord Capulet	Ha? Let me see her. Out, alas, she's cold. 25
	Her blood is settled, and her joints are stiff.
	Life and these lips have long been separated.
	Death lies on her like an untimely frost
	Upon the sweetest flower of all the field.
Nurse	O lamentable day!
Lady Capulet	O woeful time. 30
Lord Capulet	Death, that hath ta'en her hence to make me wail,
	Ties up my tongue, and will not let me speak.

Enter Friar Laurence, Paris and Musicians

Friar Laurence	Come, is the bride ready to go to church?
Lord Capulet	Ready to go, but never to return.
	O son, the night before thy wedding-day 35
	Hath Death lain with thy wife. There she lies,
	Flower as she was, deflowered by him.
	Death is my son-in-law; Death is my heir.
	My daughter he hath wedded. I will die,
	And leave him all, life, living, all is Death's. 40
Paris	Have I thought long to see this morning's face,
	And doth it give me such a sight as this?
Lady Capulet	Accursed, unhappy, wretched, hateful day!
	Most miserable hour that e'er time saw
	In lasting labour of his pilgrimage. 45
	But one, poor one, one poor and loving child,
	But one thing to rejoice and solace in,
	And cruel death hath catched it from my sight.
Nurse	O woe, O woeful, woeful, woeful day!
	Most lamentable day, most woeful day, 50
	That ever, ever, I did yet behold.
	O day, O day, O day, O hateful day!
	Never was seen so black a day as this.
	O woeful day, O woeful day!

At the time

There are social and historical research tasks, so that you can use knowledge from the time the play was written to help you interpret the text of the play. The social and historical information can be found on pages 258–270 of this edition.

Key terms

Where needed, there is an explanation of any key terms used, literary or theatrical.

Introducing *Romeo and Juliet*

The play in performance

A popular success

Romeo and Juliet was written during the 1590s and was first performed by 1597 in London. We know that *Romeo and Juliet* has an enduring appeal for audiences — as the title page of the play's 1597 edition tells us, the play was, even then, a popular success '...*it hath been often (with great applause) plaid publiquely.*'

At the Royal Shakespeare Company (RSC), we have staged countless productions of *Romeo and Juliet* and each time they are completely different. Shakespeare's plays are packed full of questions and challenges for the director, designer and acting company to solve. The clues to finding the answers are always somewhere in the text, but the possibilities for interpretation are infinite.

The Capulet and Montague servants, 2006

Lord and Lady Capulet with guests, 2010

A place of possibilities

One of the most interesting questions a director needs to answer about any scene is whether it is public or private. In *Romeo and Juliet*, we have a very private scene (the first meeting of Romeo and Juliet) happening in a very public context (Lord Capulet's party). That always creates a staging challenge for the director and acting company. Actors and their director try out different ways of playing scenes informed always by the clues that Shakespeare gives them; they effectively become text detectives, mining the language for clues to help inform their performance choices.

We have taken all of the ways of working of our actors and directors and set them alongside the text of *Romeo and Juliet* which, together with the other titles in the series, offers a great introduction to Shakespeare's world and work.

An actor once described the rehearsal room to me as a 'place of possibilities'. I think that's a wonderful way of thinking about a classroom too and it's what we hope the RSC School Shakespeare editions help to create.

Jacqui O'Hanlon
Director of Education
Royal Shakespeare Company

The play at a glance

Every scene in a play presents a challenge to the actors and their director in terms of how to stage it. There are certain key scenes in a play that directors need to pay special attention to because they contain really significant events. Here are some of the key scenes in *Romeo and Juliet*.

The scene is set (Act 1 Scene 1)

Montague and Capulet servants clash in the street; the Prince threatens dire punishment if another such brawl should take place. Romeo tells his friend, Benvolio, of his obsession with Rosaline.

The lovers meet for the first time (Act 1 Scene 5)

Romeo is persuaded to attend a masked party at the Capulet household. Not knowing who she is, he falls in love with Juliet the moment he sees her, and she, equally ignorant that he is a Montague, falls just as instantly for him.

Romeo risks death to meet his love Juliet again (Act 2 Scene 2)

When everyone has left the party, Romeo creeps into the Capulet garden and sees Juliet on her balcony. They reveal their mutual love and Romeo leaves, promising to arrange a secret marriage and let Juliet's messenger, her old Nurse, have the details the following morning.

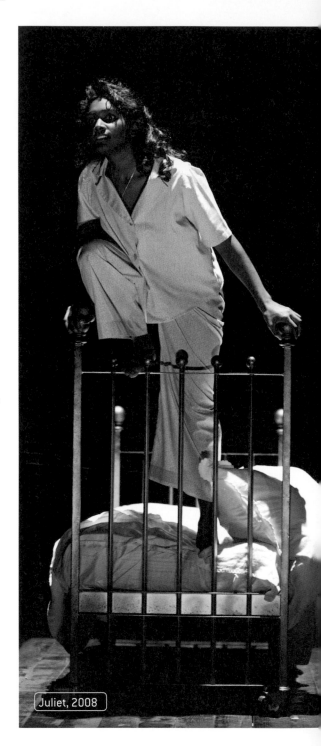

Juliet, 2008

The wedding is held in secret (Act 2 Scene 6)

Juliet tells her parents she is going to make her confession to Friar Laurence, meets Romeo there and, despite some personal misgivings, the Friar marries them immediately.

Romeo angrily kills Juliet's cousin, Tybalt (Act 3 Scene 1)

Romeo meets Tybalt in the street and is challenged by him to a duel. Romeo refuses to fight and his friend Mercutio is so disgusted by this 'cowardice' that he takes up the challenge instead. As Romeo tries to break up the fight, Tybalt manages to kill Mercutio and, enraged, Romeo then kills Tybalt. The Prince arrives and, on hearing the full story, banishes Romeo rather than have him executed.

The unhappy couple are parted (Act 3 Scene 5)

Arranged by the Friar and the Nurse, Romeo and Juliet have spent their wedding night together. They are immediately parted though, as Romeo must leave for banishment in Mantua or die if he is found in Verona. Believing her grief to be for the death of her cousin, Juliet's father tries to cheer Juliet by arranging her immediate marriage to Paris. He threatens to disown her when she asks for the marriage to be at least postponed and she runs to the Friar for advice and help.

Tybalt, Romeo and Mercutio, 2010

The Nurse and Juliet, 2006

The Friar suggests a dangerous solution to the problem (Act 4 Scene 1)

Juliet arrives at the Friar's to be met by Paris, who is busy discussing their wedding plans. She is so desperate that she threatens suicide and the Friar instead suggests that she takes a potion that will make her appear to be dead. He promises to send a message to Romeo, asking him to return secretly and be with Juliet when she wakes, once her 'body' has been taken to the family crypt.

Juliet is found 'dead' (Act 4 Scene 5)

The Nurse discovers Juliet's 'dead body' when she goes to wake her for her marriage to Paris. Friar Laurence is called, counsels the family to accept their grief and arranges for Juliet to be 'buried' immediately.

Romeo learns of the tragedy and plans his own suicide (Act 5 Scene 1)

Romeo's servant, Balthasar, reaches Mantua before the Friar's messenger and tells Romeo that Juliet is dead. Romeo buys poison and leaves for Verona, planning to die alongside Juliet's body.

The tragic conclusion (Act 5 Scene 3)

Trying to break into the Capulet crypt, Romeo is disturbed by Paris and they fight. Romeo kills Paris and reaches Juliet's body. He drinks the poison, kisses his wife for the last time and dies. Having learned that Romeo never received his message, the Friar comes to the crypt to be with Juliet when she wakes. He finds Paris's body and reaches Juliet just as she revives. He cannot persuade her to leave her dead husband and runs away in fear. Juliet realises what has happened, takes Romeo's knife and stabs herself to death with it. The watchmen discover the gruesome sight and call the Prince, to whom the Friar confesses everything. Having heard the full story, the Montagues and Capulets are reconciled. Peace has been achieved, but the price has been the lives of two innocent young lovers.

Lord Capulet, Balthasar, Friar Laurence, Juliet and Romeo, Constable, Lady Capulet, 2010

The Tragedy of Romeo and Juliet

Chorus
Romeo
Lord Montague, Romeo's father
Lady Montague, Romeo's mother
Benvolio, Romeo's cousin
Abraham, Montague's servant
Balthasar, Romeo's servant
Other Montague Servants

Juliet
Lord Capulet, Juliet's father
Lady Capulet, Juliet's mother
Nurse to Juliet
Tybalt, Juliet's cousin
Sampson ⎫
Gregory ⎬ Capulet servants
Peter ⎭
Cousin Capulet
Other Capulet Servants

Prince Escalus of Verona
Mercutio, kinsman to the Prince and friend to Romeo
Paris, kinsman to the Prince and suitor to Juliet
Page to Paris

Friar Laurence
Friar John
Apothecary
Constable
The Watch
Musicians
Citizens of Verona

In the town of Verona, two equally powerful families, who have always hated each other, start fighting again. Two children from the families fall in love, but end up dead. Their tragic deaths finally put a stop to the fighting. This story is what we are about to see performed.

Activity 1: Exploring Shakespeare's rhythm

Read the description of **iambic pentameter** in the key term box.

a. Say out loud: 'and ONE, and TWO, and THREE, and FOUR, and FIVE'.

b. Repeat and clap the iambic pentameter rhythm as you speak.

c. The rhythm is the same as the rhythm of your heartbeat. It also sounds like horses galloping. Stand up and gallop the rhythm, stamping your feet.

d. Read aloud the first **quatrain**, lines 1–4 of the Chorus, galloping at the same time and trying to fit the words to the rhythm.

e. Now read and gallop the second quatrain, lines 5–8. What is the **rhyme scheme**?

f. Read and gallop the third quatrain, lines 9–12. How does the rhyme scheme continue? This particular combination of rhythm and rhyme is called a **sonnet**. Shakespeare is famous for writing sonnets, but it is unusual to find one in a play.

g. Discuss your expectations of the play from what you find out in the Prologue.

The citizens of Verona, 2008

Prologue

Enter Chorus

Chorus   Two households, both alike in dignity,
    In fair Verona, where we lay our scene,
From ancient grudge break to new mutiny,
    Where civil blood makes civil hands unclean.
From forth the fatal loins of these two foes   5
    A pair of star-crossed lovers take their life,
Whose misadventured piteous overthrows
    Doth with their death bury their parents' strife.
The fearful passage of their death-marked love,
    And the continuance of their parents' rage,   10
Which, but their children's end, nought could remove,
    Is now the two hours' traffic of our stage.
The which if you with patient ears attend,
What here shall miss, our toil shall strive to mend.

Exeunt

Two servants exchange comments and jokes about the bad feeling between their households, the Capulets, and the rival family, the Montagues.

At the time

Using pages 262–263, write three or four sentences to describe what it was like to walk the streets of London in Shakespeare's time.

Glossary

1 **carry coals** accept being insulted
2 **colliers** coal sellers (a low status job)
3 **in choler** angry

Activity 1: Exploring language

The jokey exchange between Sampson and Gregory on page 19 can be called **banter**.

Banter often involves cultural references – things the speakers and hearers are familiar with. For example, the audience at the time would have understood what Sampson means in line 10 by 'take the wall' – staying close to the wall and forcing the person passing you to step into the dirty street. They would also have understood what Gregory means in line 12 by 'goes to the wall' – showing weakness.

a. In pairs, read through the exchange on page 19 as if both men are showing off with their witty banter to other people in the street.
b. Read it again as if Sampson is angry and aggressive and Gregory is trying to calm him down by making jokes.
c. Discuss what your view is of these two men. How would you feel about meeting them in the street?

Key terms

Banter playful **dialogue** where the speakers verbally score points off each other
Dialogue a discussion between two or more people

Gregory and Sampson, 2008

Act 1 | Scene 1

Enter Sampson and Gregory with swords and bucklers, servants of the House of Capulet

Sampson Gregory, o'my word, we'll not carry coals.

Gregory No, for then we should be colliers.

Sampson I mean, if we be in choler, we'll draw.

Gregory Ay, while you live, draw your neck out o'th'collar.

Sampson I strike quickly, being moved.   5

Gregory But thou art not quickly moved to strike.

Sampson A dog of the house of Montague moves me.

Gregory To move is to stir, and to be valiant is to stand: therefore, if thou art moved, thou runn'st away.

Sampson A dog of that house shall move me to stand. I will take the wall of   10
any man or maid of Montague's.

Gregory That shows thee a weak slave, for the weakest goes to the wall.

Sampson 'Tis true, and therefore women being the weaker vessels are ever
thrust to the wall. Therefore I will push Montague's men from the
wall, and thrust his maids to the wall.   15

Gregory The quarrel is between our masters and us their men.

Sampson 'Tis all one, I will show myself a tyrant: when I have fought with the
men, I will be civil with the maids, and cut off their heads.

Gregory The heads of the maids?

Sampson Ay, the heads of the maids, or their maidenheads, take it in what   20
sense thou wilt.

Gregory They must take it in sense that feel it.

The Capulet servants confront two Montague servants in the street and they provoke each other to fight.

The Capulet and Montague servants, 2006

Activity 2: Exploring body language

a. In pairs, one of you is a Montague, the other is a Capulet. Stare at each other and hold eye contact for 20 seconds. How does it feel to hold eye contact?

b. Next, bite your thumbs at each other. Try to make the **gesture** as insulting as you can. Why do you think this gesture was an insult? How else might you suggest, through your **body language**, that you are enemies?

Activity 3: Exploring action in the text

a. In groups, decide who will play Sampson, Gregory, Abraham and Abraham's friend (Abraham's friend is part of the action but does not speak).

b. Read through lines 25–43. As you read, think about what actions you need to do so that the lines make sense. For example, when Gregory says 'Draw thy tool' in line 26, Sampson could pretend to get a dagger out. What must Gregory do when he says 'I will frown as I pass by' in line 32? Also, consider that the **tone** you use can make a word mean something else. For example, the **repetition** of 'sir' in this exchange might sound sarcastic rather than polite.

c. Practise the lines a few times to work out how best to act out this confrontation and make the audience think it is leading up to a serious fight.

d. Given the five key **themes** suggested in the key terms, where do you see these reflected in this opening scene?

Glossary

25 **poor John** a dried, salted fish; an insult

30 **marry** by the Virgin Mary; a mild oath

32 **list** please

Key terms

Gesture a movement, often using the hands or head, to express a feeling or idea

Body language how we communicate feelings to each other using our bodies (including facial expressions) rather than words

Tone as in 'tone of voice'; expressing an attitude through how you say something

Repetition saying the same thing again

Theme the main ideas explored in a piece of literature, e.g. the themes of love, loyalty, friendship, family and fate might be considered key themes of *Romeo and Juliet*

Sampson	Me they shall feel while I am able to stand; and 'tis known I am a pretty piece of flesh.
Gregory	'Tis well thou art not fish, if thou hadst, thou hadst been poor John. Draw thy tool. Here comes of the house of the Montagues.

Enter two Servants of the House of Montague

Sampson	My naked weapon is out. Quarrel, I will back thee.
Gregory	How? Turn thy back and run?
Sampson	Fear me not.
Gregory	No, marry, I fear thee!
Sampson	Let us take the law of our sides: let them begin.
Gregory	I will frown as I pass by, and let them take it as they list.
Sampson	Nay, as they dare. I will bite my thumb at them, which is a disgrace to them if they bear it.
Abraham	Do you bite your thumb at us, sir?
Sampson	I do bite my thumb, sir.
Abraham	Do you bite your thumb at us, sir?
Sampson	Is the law of our side, if I say ay?
Gregory	No.
Sampson	No, sir, I do not bite my thumb at you, sir, but I bite my thumb, sir.
Gregory	Do you quarrel, sir?
Abraham	Quarrel sir? No, sir.
Sampson	If you do, sir, I am for you. I serve as good a man as you.
Abraham	No better?
Sampson	Well, sir.

Enter Benvolio

25

30

35

40

45

Benvolio, a Montague nobleman, tries to stop the fight between the servants, but Tybalt, a Capulet nobleman, forces him to fight. Others join the fight, including the leaders of the two households, Lord Capulet and Lord Montague, and it quickly becomes a major incident.

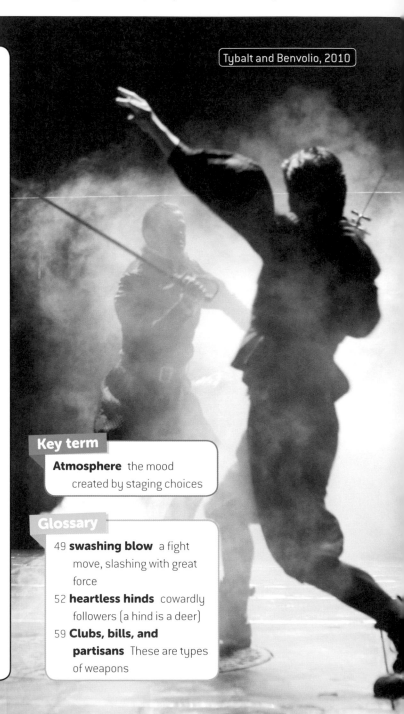

Tybalt and Benvolio, 2010

Activity 4: Exploring atmosphere

a. Read lines 46–65.
b. Look at the photo on this page as an example of how this moment has been staged. What sort of **atmosphere** do you think this scene might create in a theatre?
c. Romeo and Juliet are the main characters in this play, but we do not meet them in this opening scene. In pairs, note down as many reasons as you can think of for why Shakespeare starts the play in this way.

Activity 5: Opening the play

a. In groups, discuss how you would start a production of *Romeo and Juliet*. What would the audience see and hear in the first moments of a performance? How would you present the Chorus or would you choose not to use it at all?
b. Write a description of your ideas or draw a storyboard.

Key term

Atmosphere the mood created by staging choices

Glossary

49 **swashing blow** a fight move, slashing with great force

52 **heartless hinds** cowardly followers (a hind is a deer)

59 **Clubs, bills, and partisans** These are types of weapons

Gregory Say better: here comes one of my master's kinsmen.

Sampson Yes, better.

Abraham You lie.

Sampson Draw if you be men. Gregory, remember thy swashing blow.

They fight

Benvolio Part, fools! 50
Put up your swords, you know not what you do.

Enter Tybalt

Tybalt What, art thou drawn among these heartless hinds?
Turn thee, Benvolio, look upon thy death.

Benvolio I do but keep the peace. Put up thy sword,
Or manage it to part these men with me. 55

Tybalt What, drawn, and talk of peace? I hate the word,
As I hate hell, all Montagues, and thee.
Have at thee, coward!

They fight. More citizens join the fight

Citizens Clubs, bills, and partisans! Strike! Beat them down! Down with
the Capulets! Down with the Montagues! 60

Enter Lord Capulet and Lady Capulet

Lord Capulet What noise is this? Give me my long sword, ho!

Lady Capulet A crutch, a crutch! Why call you for a sword?

Lord Capulet My sword, I say. Old Montague is come,
And flourishes his blade in spite of me.

Enter Lord Montague and Lady Montague

Lord Montague Thou villain Capulet. Hold me not, let me go. 65

Lady Montague Thou shalt not stir a foot to seek a foe.

Enter Prince Escalus with attendants

23

Prince Escalus, ruler of Verona, commands that everyone stop fighting. When they do, he tells them that anyone caught fighting again will be executed. Everyone moves quietly away. Lord Montague asks Benvolio how the fight started.

Activity 6:
Exploring language

a. What differences do you notice between how Sampson and Gregory speak in lines 1–22 (on page 19) and how the noblemen, speak in lines 50–58 (page 23)?

b. In pairs, read lines 67–74 aloud together. What does the Prince want?

c. Read the lines once more, again in pairs, this time emphasising the iambic pentameter rhythm. What effect does reading it this way have? For a reminder of what iambic pentameter rhythm is, see page 16.

d. In pairs, read the Prince's speech, lines 67–89, swapping reader at each punctuation mark.

e. Read the lines again, swapping reader at each punctuation mark, but this time add in at least one gesture for each section you speak.

f. Write at least three paragraphs explaining the following:
  i. what the Prince says has happened in the past
  ii. what the Prince says must happen in the future
  iii. which six key words from the script show how the Prince feels.

Paris and Prince Escalus of Verona, 2010

Prince   Rebellious subjects, enemies to peace,
Profaners of this neighbour-stainèd steel –
Will they not hear? What, ho, you men, you beasts,
That quench the fire of your pernicious rage   70
With purple fountains issuing from your veins.
On pain of torture, from those bloody hands
Throw your mistempered weapons to the ground,
And hear the sentence of your movèd prince.
Three civil broils, bred of an airy word,   75
By thee, old Capulet, and Montague,
Have thrice disturbed the quiet of our streets,
And made Verona's ancient citizens
Cast by their grave beseeming ornaments
To wield old partisans, in hands as old,   80
Cankered with peace, to part your cankered hate.
If ever you disturb our streets again,
Your lives shall pay the forfeit of the peace.
For this time, all the rest depart away.
You Capulet, shall go along with me,   85
And, Montague, come you this afternoon,
To know our further pleasure in this case,
To old Freetown, our common judgement-place.
Once more, on pain of death, all men depart.

Exeunt, except Lord Montague, Lady Montague and Benvolio

Lord Montague   Who set this ancient quarrel new abroach?   90
Speak, nephew, were you by when it began?

Benvolio   Here were the servants of your adversary,
And yours, close fighting ere I did approach.
I drew to part them. In the instant came
The fiery Tybalt, with his sword prepared,   95
Which, as he breathed defiance to my ears,
He swung about his head and cut the winds,
Who nothing hurt withal hissed him in scorn.
While we were interchanging thrusts and blows,
Came more and more, and fought on part and part,   100
Till the Prince came, who parted either part.

Benvolio describes how he saw his cousin, Romeo, out walking an hour before sunrise, but they avoided each other as both were feeling unsociable. Lord Montague says his son has often been seen walking around on his own at night, but during the day he locks himself up in his dark bedroom.

Activity 7: Exploring the theme of family with the Montagues

a. In pairs, choose a line from Lord Montague's speech (lines 117–128). One person from each pair should help the other to create a **statue** or **freeze-frame** of Romeo as Lord Montague describes him in your chosen line.

b. Join with another pair and create a freeze-frame of the Montague family that shows Lord and Lady Montague, their son Romeo and their nephew Benvolio. Your freeze-frame should be based on what you have learned about the characters so far and how they feel about each other.

c. What do you understand about the Montague family now that you didn't know before?

Glossary

103 **fray** fight
111 **covert** hiding place
118 **augmenting** adding to
122 **Aurora** goddess of the dawn
131 **importuned** questioned

Key terms

Statue like a freeze-frame but usually of a single character
Freeze-frame a physical, still image created by people to represent an object, place, person or feeling

At the time

Using page 269, discuss how far Shakespeare's use of the word 'humour' is different from ours (see lines 115 and 127).

Lady Montague, 2010

Lady Montague	O where is Romeo? Saw you him today?
	Right glad am I he was not at this fray.

Benvolio	Madam, an hour before the worshipped sun	
	Peered forth the golden window of the east,	105
	A troubled mind drove me to walk abroad,	
	Where, underneath the grove of sycamore	
	That westward rooteth from the city side,	
	So early walking did I see your son.	
	Towards him I made, but he was ware of me	110
	And stole into the covert of the wood:	
	I, measuring his affections by my own,	
	Which then most sought where most might not be found,	
	Being one too many by my weary self,	
	Pursued my humour, not pursuing his,	115
	And gladly shunned who gladly fled from me.	

Lord Montague	Many a morning hath he there been seen,	
	With tears augmenting the fresh morning's dew,	
	Adding to clouds more clouds with his deep sighs,	
	But all so soon as the all-cheering sun	120
	Should in the farthest east begin to draw	
	The shady curtains from Aurora's bed,	
	Away from light steals home my heavy son,	
	And private in his chamber pens himself,	
	Shuts up his windows, locks fair daylight out	125
	And makes himself an artificial night.	
	Black and portentous must this humour prove,	
	Unless good counsel may the cause remove.	

Benvolio	My noble uncle, do you know the cause?	
Lord Montague	I neither know it nor can learn of him.	130
Benvolio	Have you importuned him by any means?	
Lord Montague	Both by myself and many other friends,	
	But he, his own affections' counsellor,	
	Is to himself – I will not say how true –	
	But to himself so secret and so close,	135
	So far from sounding and discovery,	

Romeo arrives and his parents quickly leave so that Benvolio can try to find out why Romeo seems so depressed. It turns out that Romeo is in love, but the girl he loves doesn't feel the same way.

Activity 8: Exploring the theme of friendship

a. Look at the photo on this page. What might each character be thinking?

b. In pairs, read lines 146–158 with one of you playing Romeo and the other playing Benvolio.

c. Read the lines again, but before you read your own line, repeat the line your partner spoke.

d. Read the lines once more, but this time pause after each line and speak aloud what you think your character is thinking.

e. We don't always say exactly what we mean, but we often show it in our body language. Write a short paragraph explaining what you think Benvolio really wants to say to Romeo at this point as his friend.

Glossary

137 **the bud bit with an envious worm** the worm that destroys a flower from the inside

145 **true shrift** confession

157 **muffled** blindfolded, like Cupid the god of love

Benvolio and Romeo, 2010

As is the bud bit with an envious worm,
Ere he can spread his sweet leaves to the air,
Or dedicate his beauty to the same.
Could we but learn from whence his sorrows grow,   140
We would as willingly give cure as know.

Enter Romeo

Benvolio   See, where he comes. So please you, step aside,
I'll know his grievance, or be much denied.

Lord Montague   I would thou wert so happy by thy stay
To hear true shrift. Come, madam, let's away.   145

Exeunt Lord Montague and Lady Montague

Benvolio   Good morrow, cousin.

Romeo   Is the day so young?

Benvolio   But new struck nine.

Romeo   Ay me, sad hours seem long.
Was that my father that went hence so fast?

Benvolio   It was. What sadness lengthens Romeo's hours?

Romeo   Not having that, which, having, makes them short.   150

Benvolio   In love?

Romeo   Out.

Benvolio   Of love.

Romeo   Out of her favour where I am in love.

Benvolio   Alas that love so gentle in his view,   155
Should be so tyrannous and rough in proof.

Romeo   Alas that love, whose view is muffled still,
Should, without eyes, see pathways to his will.
Where shall we dine? O me! What fray was here?
Yet tell me not, for I have heard it all.   160
Here's much to do with hate, but more with love.

Romeo, 2008

Activity 9: Exploring antithesis

a. In pairs, create a freeze-frame showing 'love' and a second freeze-frame showing 'hate'. Find a way to move slowly from your first freeze-frame into your second.

b. Discuss what physical differences you have found between love and hate through doing task a.

c. Read lines 161–168.

d. Focus on line 166 and create a physical gesture for each word in this line. For example, for 'feather' you might put your hand above your head with your fingers moving gently as though a feather in a breeze. For 'lead' you might clamp your fingers together and bring your hand down as though it is heavy like lead.

e. Rehearse a sequence in pairs, speaking and gesturing each word in line 166.

f. Discuss how it felt moving between the different words in line 166. What do these words suggest about how Romeo is feeling?

Key term

Antithesis bringing two opposing concepts or ideas together, e.g. hot and cold, love and hate, loud and quiet

Glossary

171 **transgression** overstepping a boundary
173 **propagate** increase
177 **purged** purified
180 **gall** poison

Why then, O brawling love, O loving hate,
O anything of nothing first create.
O heavy lightness, serious vanity,
Misshapen chaos of well-seeming forms.   165
Feather of lead, bright smoke, cold fire, sick health,
Still-waking sleep that is not what it is.
This love feel I, that feel no love in this.
Dost thou not laugh?

Benvolio   No coz, I rather weep.

Romeo   Good heart, at what?

Benvolio   At thy good heart's oppression.   170

Romeo   Why, such is love's transgression.
Griefs of mine own lie heavy in my breast,
Which thou wilt propagate to have it pressed
With more of thine. This love that thou hast shown
Doth add more grief to too much of mine own.   175
Love is a smoke made with the fume of sighs;
Being purged, a fire sparkling in lovers' eyes;
Being vexed, a sea nourished with loving tears.
What is it else? A madness most discreet,
A choking gall and a preserving sweet.   180
Farewell, my coz.

Benvolio   Soft, I will go along,
And if you leave me so, you do me wrong.

Romeo   Tut, I have lost myself, I am not here.
This is not Romeo, he's some other where.

Benvolio   Tell me in sadness, who is that you love?   185

Romeo   What, shall I groan and tell thee?

Benvolio   Groan? Why no, but sadly tell me who.

Romeo   Bid a sick man in sadness make his will:
A word ill-urged to one that is so ill.
In sadness, cousin, I do love a woman.   190

Romeo tells Benvolio that he is in love with a beautiful woman called Rosaline. However, she has sworn never to fall in love and so Romeo knows she will never return his love. Benvolio tells him to forget her.

Activity 10: Exploring the theme of love

a. In pairs, one of you reads aloud lines 194–202, while the other listens and repeats any words connected to warfare.

b. Discuss what you think Romeo feels about Rosaline in this speech. What do the words connected to warfare suggest about his feelings for her?

c. In pairs, create a freeze-frame of Rosaline as Romeo sees her, with one of you as Rosaline.

d. Now add Romeo into the freeze-frame. How close should he be to Rosaline? Should he be sitting or standing? How should he look at her?

e. What ideas about love are suggested in lines 194–202?

Benvolio and Romeo, 2006

Benvolio I aimed so near, when I supposed you loved.

Romeo A right good mark-man! And she's fair I love.

Benvolio A right fair mark, fair coz, is soonest hit.

Romeo Well, in that hit you miss. She'll not be hit
With Cupid's arrow. She hath Dian's wit,   195
And in strong proof of chastity well armed,
From love's weak childish bow she lives uncharmed.
She will not stay the siege of loving terms,
Nor bide th'encounter of assailing eyes,
Nor ope her lap to saint-seducing gold.   200
O she is rich in beauty, only poor
That when she dies, with beauty dies her store.

Benvolio Then she hath sworn that she will still live chaste?

Romeo She hath, and in that sparing makes huge waste,
For beauty starved with her severity   205
Cuts beauty off from all posterity.
She is too fair, too wise, wisely too fair,
To merit bliss by making me despair.
She hath forsworn to love, and in that vow
Do I live dead that live to tell it now.   210

Benvolio Be ruled by me; forget to think of her.

Romeo O, teach me how I should forget to think.

Benvolio By giving liberty unto thine eyes:
Examine other beauties.

Romeo   'Tis the way
To call hers exquisite, in question more.   215
These happy masks that kiss fair ladies' brows
Being black puts us in mind they hide the fair.
He that is strucken blind cannot forget
The precious treasure of his eyesight lost.
Show me a mistress that is passing fair,   220

Romeo says he can't just forget about Rosaline, but Benvolio is determined to help him get over her.

Activity 11: Reflecting on Romeo

Look back through Act 1 Scene 1.

a. Draw an outline of a human figure.

b. Inside the outline, write down how Romeo feels, in your own words or in short quotations from Act 1 Scene 1.

c. Around the outside of the figure, write down, in your own words or short quotations from Act 1 Scene 1, what other characters say about Romeo and descriptions of the world he lives in.

d. Imagine you are Romeo sitting in his darkened bedroom, thinking about Rosaline and the fight between the Montagues and Capulets. Write down your thoughts in modern English in a form of your own choice, for example as a diary entry, a blog or a poem.

Romeo and Benvolio, 2008

What doth her beauty serve, but as a note
Where I may read who passed that passing fair?
Farewell, thou canst not teach me to forget.

Benvolio I'll pay that doctrine or else die in debt.

Exeunt

Paris, a wealthy and well-connected man, wants to marry Juliet. Lord Capulet, her father, says she is too young but if she likes Paris, he will give permission for the marriage. Lord Capulet invites Paris to meet Juliet at the annual Capulet party being held that night.

Activity 1: Exploring the theme of love

a. In pairs, read lines 1–17 with one of you playing Lord Capulet and the other playing Paris.

b. Read lines 1–17 again, but this time listen carefully to your partner and repeat any phrases your partner speaks that seem particularly important before you speak your own lines.

c. Discuss what you think each character wants the other to do. Which words or phrases suggest this?

d. Discuss how Shakespeare is developing the theme of love and marriage in the play. Compare the ideas about love expressed by Romeo in Act 1 Scene 1 lines 161–168 (pages 29–31) with how Paris and Lord Capulet talk about marriage here. Write a paragraph or two summarising your ideas.

Paris and Lord Capulet, 2008

At the time

Using page 267, find out how marriage arrangements were different for nobles (important wealthy people) and ordinary people in Shakespeare's time. How are marriage traditions today the same as they were in Shakespeare's time?

Act 1 | Scene 2

Enter Lord Capulet, Paris and a Servant

Lord Capulet But Montague is bound as well as I,
In penalty alike, and 'tis not hard, I think,
For men so old as we to keep the peace.

Paris Of honourable reckoning are you both,
And pity 'tis you lived at odds so long. 5
But now, my lord, what say you to my suit?

Lord Capulet But saying o'er what I have said before.
My child is yet a stranger in the world,
She hath not seen the change of fourteen years,
Let two more summers wither in their pride, 10
Ere we may think her ripe to be a bride.

Paris Younger than she are happy mothers made.

Lord Capulet And too soon marred are those so early made.
Earth hath swallowed all my hopes but she.
She's the hopeful lady of my earth. 15
But woo her, gentle Paris, get her heart,
My will to her consent is but a part.
And she agree, within her scope of choice
Lies my consent and fair according voice.
This night I hold an old accustomed feast, 20
Whereto I have invited many a guest,
Such as I love, and you among the store,
One more, most welcome, makes my number more.
At my poor house look to behold this night
Earth-treading stars that make dark heaven light. 25
Such comfort as do lusty young men feel
When well-apparelled April on the heel
Of limping winter treads, even such delight

Lord Capulet gives a servant a list of guests to invite to his party. However, the servant cannot read. Romeo and Benvolio enter and Benvolio is still trying to persuade Romeo to look at other women. The servant asks them if they can read.

Activity 2: Exploring Shakespeare's clowns

a. Read the servant's speech, lines 38–43.
b. Discuss who you think the servant is speaking to. How is his way of speaking different from the nobles?
   - Servants in Shakespeare's plays were often played by **clowns** who might interact with the audience like a stand-up comic today. The clown's role here is to connect with the audience and make fun of the fact that he cannot read.
c. In pairs, read aloud lines 38–43 again, swapping reader at each punctuation mark. Try to make your partner laugh when you speak.
d. Discuss why you think Shakespeare included the servant in this scene.

Glossary

29 **fresh fennel buds** fragrant yellow flowers (connected to love)
38–40 **Here it is written that...** The servant gives a list of tradesmen using the wrong tools as a comment on the fact he has been given names to read but he cannot read
50 **plaintain leaf** herbal remedy for many ailments
55 **Good e'en** good evening; also used for good afternoon

Key term

Clown an actor skilled in comedy and improvisation who could often sing and dance as well

Did you know?

When Shakespeare wrote *Romeo and Juliet*, the main clown in his theatre company was an actor called Will Kemp. Kemp was very popular with the audience and Shakespeare wrote certain parts with him in mind.

Lord Capulet and a servant, 2008

Among fresh fennel buds shall you this night
Inherit at my house. Hear all, all see, 30
And like her most whose merit most shall be,
Which one more view, of many mine being one,
May stand in number, though in reck'ning none.
Come, go with me. [To Servant] Go, sirrah, trudge about
Through fair Verona, find those persons out 35
Whose names are written there and to them say,
My house and welcome on their pleasure stay.

Exeunt Lord Capulet and Paris

Servant Find them out whose names are written. Here it is written that
the shoemaker should meddle with his yard, and the tailor with
his last, the fisher with his pencil, and the painter with his nets. 40
But I am sent to find those persons whose names are here writ,
and can never find what names the writing person hath here writ.
I must to the learned – in good time.

Enter Benvolio and Romeo

Benvolio Tut, man, one fire burns out another's burning;
One pain is lessened by another's anguish. 45
Turn giddy, and be holp by backward turning;
One desperate grief cures with another's languish.
Take thou some new infection to thy eye,
And the rank poison of the old will die.

Romeo Your plantain leaf is excellent for that. 50

Benvolio For what, I pray thee?

Romeo   For your broken shin.

Benvolio Why, Romeo, art thou mad?

Romeo Not mad, but bound more than a madman is,
Shut up in prison, kept without my food,
Whipped and tormented and—Good e'en, good fellow. 55

Servant God gi' good e'en. I pray, sir, can you read?

Romeo Ay, mine own fortune in my misery.

Romeo reads out the guest list for the Capulet party, which includes Rosaline as well as his friend Mercutio. Benvolio suggests they go to the party even though they are not invited so that he can show Romeo women who are more beautiful than Rosaline.

Romeo and a Capulet servant, 2010

Activity 3: Exploring status

a. In groups, read aloud lines 63–71, swapping reader at each punctuation mark.

b. Based on this description of the guests, create three freeze-frames of the guests arriving at the Capulet party posing for a celebrity magazine photographer.

c. Look at the photo on this page and discuss which line you think is being spoken. Give reasons for your suggestion.

d. How do you think Romeo might feel as he reads out the letter? Does he wish he could go or is he glad not to be invited?

Glossary

81 **crush a cup of wine** drink some wine

82 **ancient** customary

Servant	Perhaps you have learned it without book. But I pray, can you read anything you see?
Romeo	Ay, if I know the letters and the language.
Servant	Ye say honestly, rest you merry!
Romeo	Stay, fellow, I can read.

He reads the letter

'Signior Martino and his wife and daughters;
County Anselme and his beauteous sisters;
The lady widow of Utruvio;
Signior Placentio and his lovely nieces;
Mercutio and his brother Valentine;
Mine uncle Capulet; his wife and daughters;
My fair niece Rosaline; Livia;
Signior Valentio and his cousin Tybalt;
Lucio and the lively Helena.'
A fair assembly! Whither should they come?

Servant	Up.
Romeo	Whither? To supper?
Servant	To our house.
Romeo	Whose house?
Servant	My master's.
Romeo	Indeed, I should have asked you that before.
Servant	Now I'll tell you without asking. My master is the great rich Capulet and if you be not of the house of Montagues, I pray come and crush a cup of wine. Rest you merry.

Exit Servant

Benvolio	At this same ancient feast of Capulet's Sups the fair Rosaline whom thou so loves, With all the admired beauties of Verona.

60

65

70

75

80

41

Benvolio is determined to show Romeo that Rosaline isn't so beautiful when seen in comparison to other women. Romeo remains unconvinced but agrees to go to the party so that he can see Rosaline.

Activity 4: Exploring rhyme

a. In pairs, read aloud lines 82–101 with one of you playing Benvolio and the other playing Romeo.
b. Read lines 82–101 again, but this time whisper them as though the servant is still hovering and you don't want him to overhear.
c. Read the lines a third time, but this time take a few steps away from each other and speak the lines loudly.
d. Read the lines again with Romeo being very serious about his love.
e. Read the lines once more with Romeo more light-hearted and making fun of himself.
f. What did you learn from the different ways of speaking the lines in tasks a–e? Which reading did you prefer?
g. Write two or three sentences explaining what you think worked well and what didn't work so well for the different readings you tried in tasks d and e.
h. What did you notice about the rhyme schemes in both Romeo and Benvolio's speeches? Why might Shakespeare have given them these rhymes?
i. Look back through Act 1 Scene 2. Why do you think Shakespeare sometimes uses **blank verse** and sometimes rhyme?

Glossary

85 **unattainted** unbiased
88–89 **When the devout...falsehood** when my eyes change religion to believe such lies
90 **these who, often drowned** eyes drowned by tears
91 **Transparent heretics... for liars** Heretics could be burnt at the stake for not believing the state religion
96 **crystal scales** eyes
99 **scant** scarcely

Key term

Blank verse verse lines that do not rhyme

Did you know?

Rhythm and rhyme are useful as clues about how a character thinks and feels. When the rhythm and rhyme are regular, it usually means that the character is more sure and clear about what they are saying.

Romeo and Benvolio, 2008

Go thither, and with unattainted eye,   85
Compare her face with some that I shall show,
And I will make thee think thy swan a crow.

Romeo   When the devout religion of mine eye
Maintains such falsehood, then turn tears to fire,
And these who, often drowned, could never die,   90
Transparent heretics, be burnt for liars.
One fairer than my love! The all-seeing sun
Ne'er saw her match since first the world begun.

Benvolio   Tut, you saw her fair, none else being by,
Herself poised with herself in either eye,   95
But in that crystal scales let there be weighed
Your lady's love against some other maid
That I will show you shining at this feast,
And she shall scant show well that now seems best.

Romeo   I'll go along, no such sight to be shown,   100
But to rejoice in splendour of mine own.

Exeunt

Lady Capulet asks the Nurse to call Juliet. They discuss whether Juliet has reached her fourteenth birthday yet.

Activity 1: Exploring the theme of family with the Capulets

a. In groups, read aloud lines 1–13 and then create a freeze-frame of the Capulet family at this moment in the play. Try to show the relationships between Lady Capulet, Juliet and the Nurse.

b. Imagine Lord Capulet came in; where would you place him in the freeze-frame?

c. Still in your group freeze-frame, each person in the group should take turns to speak aloud their thoughts about Juliet marrying Paris from the point of view of their character.

d. What have you learned about the Capulet family from tasks a–c?

Did you know?

In a production, the director sometimes chooses a time period in which to set the play and works with the actors to explore how the relationships suit that time.

At the time

Using page 268, discuss the differences and similarities between how young people were brought up in Shakespeare's time and today.

Juliet and the Nurse, 2006

Act 1 | Scene 3

Enter Lady Capulet and Nurse

Lady Capulet Nurse, where's my daughter? Call her forth to me.

Nurse Now by my maidenhead at twelve year old,
I bade her come. What, lamb! What, ladybird!
God forbid, where's this girl? What, Juliet!

Enter Juliet

Juliet How now? Who calls?   5

Nurse Your mother.

Juliet Madam, I am here. What is your will?

Lady Capulet This is the matter. Nurse, give leave awhile,
We must talk in secret. Nurse, come back again,
I have remembered me, thou's hear our counsel.   10
Thou know'st my daughter's of a pretty age.

Nurse Faith, I can tell her age unto an hour.

Lady Capulet She's not fourteen.

Nurse I'll lay fourteen of my teeth – and yet, to my teen be it spoken,
I have but four – she's not fourteen. How long is it now to   15
Lammas-tide?

Lady Capulet A fortnight and odd days.

Nurse Even or odd, of all days in the year,
Come Lammas Eve at night shall she be fourteen.
Susan and she – God rest all Christian souls –   20
Were of an age. Well, Susan is with God –
She was too good for me. But as I said,
On Lammas Eve at night shall she be fourteen,
That shall she, marry, I remember it well.

After confirming Juliet's birthday to be Lammas Eve (31 July), the Nurse reminisces about Juliet being weaned when she was three years old. She links this to when an earthquake struck Verona and Juliet fell and hit her head.

Activity 2: Exploring the theme of family with the Nurse

a. Read aloud the Nurse's speech, lines 52–59. When you reach a comma or dash, move to face a different direction and when you reach a full stop or question mark, sit down or stand up.

b. Repeat task a with the longer speech, lines 18–50.

c. Discuss what you learn about the Nurse, both from *what* she says and *how* she says it here.

d. Look at the photo on this page. How do you think Juliet feels about the story the Nurse is telling? Give reasons for your suggestion.

e. From what you learned about the Nurse in the tasks above, how do you think the Nurse fits into the Capulet family?

f. Write the Nurse's story in your own words or draw it as a cartoon strip.

The Nurse and Juliet, 2008

'Tis since the earthquake now eleven years,   25
And she was weaned – I never shall forget it –
Of all the days of the year, upon that day,
For I had then laid wormwood to my dug,
Sitting in the sun under the dovehouse wall.
My lord and you were then at Mantua –   30
Nay, I do bear a brain – but, as I said,
When it did taste the wormwood on the nipple
Of my dug and felt it bitter – pretty fool,
To see it tetchy and fall out with the dug.
'Shake', quoth the dovehouse – 'twas no need, I trow,   35
To bid me trudge.
And since that time it is eleven years,
For then she could stand alone – nay, by th'rood,
She could have run and waddled all about,
For even the day before, she broke her brow,   40
And then my husband – God be with his soul,
A was a merry man – took up the child,
'Yea,' quoth he, 'dost thou fall upon thy face?
Thou wilt fall backward when thou hast more wit,
Wilt thou not, Jule?' And by my holidam,   45
The pretty wretch left crying and said 'Ay'.
To see now how a jest shall come about!
I warrant, an I should live a thousand years,
I never should forget it: 'Wilt thou not, Jule?' quoth he,
And, pretty fool, it stinted and said 'Ay'.   50

Lady Capulet   Enough of this, I pray thee, hold thy peace.

Nurse   Yes, madam, yet I cannot choose but laugh,
To think it should leave crying and say 'Ay'.
And yet I warrant it had upon it brow
A bump as big as a young cock'rel's stone –   55
A perilous knock, and it cried bitterly.
'Yea,' quoth my husband, 'fall'st upon thy face?
Thou wilt fall backward when thou comest to age,
Wilt thou not, Jule?' It stinted and said 'Ay'.

Lady Capulet announces that Paris has asked to marry Juliet and that Juliet will have an opportunity to meet him and see if she likes him at the Capulet party that evening.

Activity 3: Exploring relationships

a. In small groups, read lines 65–90 as Lady Capulet, Juliet and the Nurse.
b. To help you understand more about the characters, their relationships and their motives, read the lines again. This time, as you speak and listen, keep choosing between the following movements:
   - Take a step towards another character.
   - Take a step away from another character.
   - Turn towards another character.
   - Turn away from another character.
   - Stand still.
   Try to make instinctive choices rather than planning what to do.
c. In your groups, read lines 65–90 again, but this time try making different choices about how you move.
d. Reflecting on the movement choices you made, discuss what you think Lady Capulet and the Nurse want Juliet to do. What did your choices about movement suggest about how they might persuade her? Were they comforting, aggressive or flattering?

Activity 4: Exploring the theme of love

a. Read aloud Lady Capulet's lines 81–96 and tap your book whenever you say a word connected to books.
b. Why do you think Shakespeare gives Lady Capulet this **extended metaphor**? What does it suggest about how Lady Capulet views love?

Glossary

78 **man of wax** perfect model of a man
85 **lineament** line in a book, or feature of a face
88 **margent** margin

Juliet, 2010

Key term

Extended metaphor describing something by comparing it to something else over several lines, e.g. Lady Capulet compares Paris to a book in lines 81–96

Juliet   And stint thou too, I pray thee, Nurse, say I.   60

Nurse   Peace, I have done. God mark thee to his grace!
               Thou wast the prettiest babe that e'er I nursed.
               And I might live to see thee married once,
               I have my wish.

Lady Capulet Marry, that 'marry' is the very theme   65
               I came to talk of. Tell me, daughter Juliet,
               How stands your disposition to be married?

Juliet   It is an honour that I dream not of.

Nurse   An honour! Were not I thine only nurse,
               I would say thou hadst sucked wisdom from thy teat.   70

Lady Capulet Well, think of marriage now. Younger than you,
               Here in Verona, ladies of esteem,
               Are made already mothers. By my count,
               I was your mother much upon these years
               That you are now a maid. Thus then in brief: 75
               The valiant Paris seeks you for his love.

Nurse   A man, young lady – lady, such a man
               As all the world – why, he's a man of wax.

Lady Capulet Verona's summer hath not such a flower.

Nurse   Nay, he's a flower, in faith, a very flower.   80

Lady Capulet What say you? Can you love the gentleman?
               This night you shall behold him at our feast.
               Read o'er the volume of young Paris' face,
               And find delight writ there with beauty's pen,
               Examine every several lineament,   85
               And see how one another lends content
               And what obscured in this fair volume lies,
               Find written in the margent of his eyes.
               This precious book of love, this unbound lover,
               To beautify him only lacks a cover.   90
               The fish lives in the sea, and 'tis much pride

A servant announces that the party is starting. Lady Capulet and the Nurse encourage Juliet to like Paris.

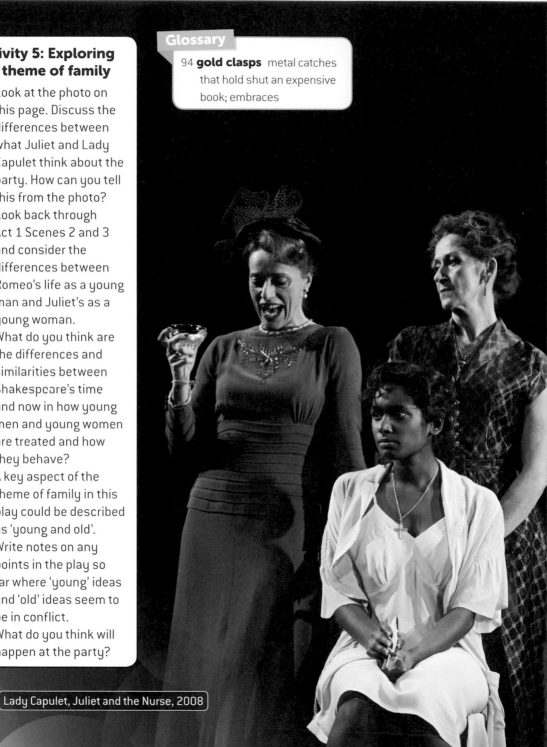

Activity 5: Exploring the theme of family

a. Look at the photo on this page. Discuss the differences between what Juliet and Lady Capulet think about the party. How can you tell this from the photo?

b. Look back through Act 1 Scenes 2 and 3 and consider the differences between Romeo's life as a young man and Juliet's as a young woman.

c. What do you think are the differences and similarities between Shakespeare's time and now in how young men and young women are treated and how they behave?

d. A key aspect of the theme of family in this play could be described as 'young and old'. Write notes on any points in the play so far where 'young' ideas and 'old' ideas seem to be in conflict.

e. What do you think will happen at the party?

Lady Capulet, Juliet and the Nurse, 2008

50

For fair without the fair within to hide.
That book in many's eyes doth share the glory,
That in gold clasps locks in the golden story.
So shall you share all that he doth possess,   95
By having him, making yourself no less.

Nurse   No less? Nay, bigger – women grow by men.

Lady Capulet   Speak briefly, can you like of Paris' love?

Juliet   I'll look to like, if looking liking move.
But no more deep will I endart mine eye   100
Than your consent gives strength to make it fly.

Enter a Servant

Servant   Madam, the guests are come, supper served up, you called,
my young lady asked for, the nurse cursed in the pantry, and
everything in extremity. I must hence to wait. I beseech you,
follow straight.   105

Exit Servant

Lady Capulet   We follow thee. Juliet, the County stays.

Nurse   Go, girl, seek happy nights to happy days.

Exeunt

Romeo, Benvolio and Mercutio are on their way to the Capulet party. Romeo says he is not in the mood for dancing.

Activity 1: Exploring movement

a. In pairs, read lines 9–26 as Mercutio and Romeo.
b. Read the lines again, this time with Romeo sitting on a chair while Mercutio moves around him.
c. Read lines 9–26 again. This time, swap over so that Mercutio sits on the chair while Romeo moves.
d. What have you discovered about the relationship between Romeo and Mercutio when reading lines 9–26 in tasks a–c?
e. Look at the photo on this page. How does it reflect the relationship you found between Mercutio and Romeo?
f. Summarise lines 9–26 into three or four lines of dialogue in modern English that Romeo and Mercutio might speak at the moment shown in the photo.

Did you know?

When actors first start to act out a scene they will often use different techniques or games to explore it. They might limit the amount of space they have to work in, limit the amount of movement a character can make or limit the number of times they can move. Applying limitations to a scene in rehearsal can help actors to make discoveries about their characters and the situations they are in.

Romeo and Mercutio, 2010

Glossary

1 **this speech** Masked intruders to a party were often welcomed when they made a speech complimenting the host
3 **The date is out of such prolixity** such long-windedness is out of fashion
5 **Tartar's painted bow of lath** a pretend bow, imitating those carried by Tartar warriors
6 **crow-keeper** scarecrow
8 **measure them a measure** walk through a dance
19 **bound a pitch** jump to a height

At the time

Using page 264, discuss why the characters are wearing masks at the party.

Enter Romeo, Mercutio and Benvolio

Romeo   What, shall this speech be spoke for our excuse?
Or shall we on without apology?

Benvolio   The date is out of such prolixity.
We'll have no Cupid hoodwinked with a scarf,
Bearing a Tartar's painted bow of lath,   5
Scaring the ladies like a crow-keeper.
But let them measure us by what they will,
We'll measure them a measure, and be gone.

Romeo   Give me a torch, I am not for this ambling.
Being but heavy, I will bear the light.   10

Mercutio   Nay, gentle Romeo, we must have you dance.

Romeo   Not I, believe me. You have dancing shoes
With nimble soles; I have a soul of lead
So stakes me to the ground I cannot move.

Mercutio   You are a lover; borrow Cupid's wings,   15
And soar with them above a common bound.

Romeo   I am too sore enpiercèd with his shaft
To soar with his light feathers and so bound,
I cannot bound a pitch above dull woe.
Under love's heavy burden do I sink.   20

Mercutio   And to sink in it should you burden love,
Too great oppression for a tender thing.

Romeo   Is love a tender thing? It is too rough,
Too rude, too boisterous, and it pricks like thorn.

Mercutio   If love be rough with you, be rough with love.   25
Prick love for pricking, and you beat love down.

Benvolio and Mercutio encourage Romeo to have fun at the party, but Romeo is not convinced he is in the mood for such fun.

Benvolio and Mercutio, 2008

Activity 2: Exploring friendship

a. Look at the photo on this page. How would you describe the relationship between these young men?

b. In pairs, read lines 46–51 as Romeo and Mercutio.

c. Read the lines again, but this time clapping or stamping the iambic pentameter rhythm as you read. For a reminder of what iambic pentameter rhythm is, see page 16.

d. Like the conversation between Sampson and Gregory at the start of the play, the conversation between Romeo and Mercutio on page 55 is banter, but this time between educated young noblemen. Why do you think Shakespeare has Mercutio and Romeo using rhythm and rhyme in this way? What might it suggest about their friendship?

Glossary

27 **Give me a case to put my visage in** give me a mask to cover my face

28 **A visor for a visor** an ugly mask for an ugly face

29 **quote** observe

30 **beetle brows** heavy eyebrows (of the mask)

33 **wantons** lively people

34 **senseless rushes** unfeeling rushes (used to cover the floor)

35 **am proverbed with a grandsire phrase** can quote an old phrase

38 **dun's the mouse** the mouse is brown; Mercutio picks up on Romeo's word 'done' to suggest a policeman might say 'dun', meaning be quiet like a mouse

Give me a case to put my visage in,
A visor for a visor! What care I
What curious eye doth quote deformities?
Here are the beetle brows shall blush for me.   30

Benvolio Come, knock and enter, and no sooner in,
But every man betake him to his legs.

Romeo A torch for me. Let wantons light of heart
Tickle the senseless rushes with their heels,
For I am proverbed with a grandsire phrase: 35
I'll be a candle-holder, and look on.
The game was ne'er so fair, and I am done.

Mercutio Tut, dun's the mouse, the constable's own word.
If thou art dun, we'll draw thee from the mire
Or, save your reverence, love, wherein thou stick'st   40
Up to the ears. Come, we burn daylight, ho!

Romeo Nay, that's not so.

Mercutio   I mean, sir, in delay
We waste our lights in vain, light lights by day.
Take our good meaning, for our judgement sits
Five times in that ere once in our five wits.   45

Romeo And we mean well in going to this masque,
But 'tis no wit to go.

Mercutio   Why, may one ask?

Romeo I dreamt a dream tonight.

Mercutio   And so did I.

Romeo Well, what was yours?

Mercutio   That dreamers often lie.

Romeo In bed asleep, while they do dream things true.   50

Mercutio O, then I see Queen Mab hath been with you.
She is the fairies' midwife, and she comes

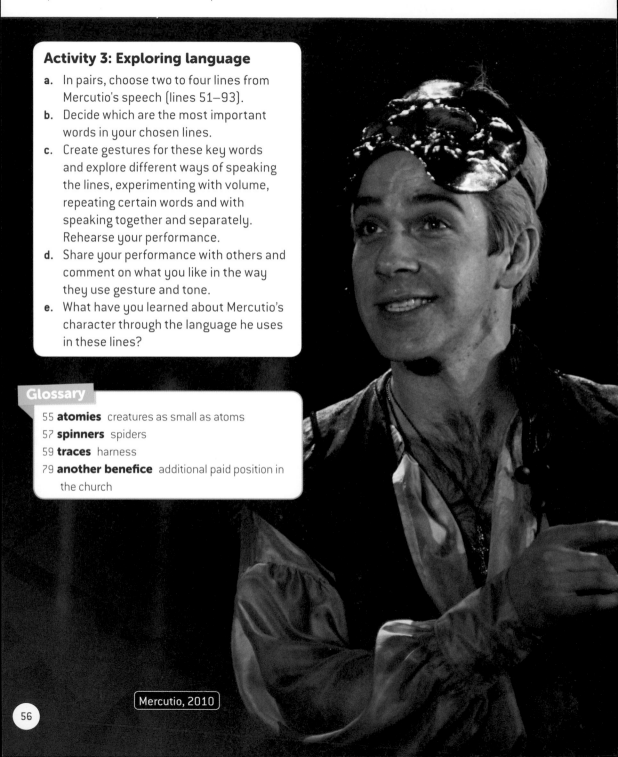

Mercutio describes how Queen Mab, a fairy, rides in a tiny fairy carriage and affects the dreams of people as they sleep. His descriptions of the various dreams become more unpleasant and violent as he speaks.

Activity 3: Exploring language

a. In pairs, choose two to four lines from Mercutio's speech (lines 51–93).

b. Decide which are the most important words in your chosen lines.

c. Create gestures for these key words and explore different ways of speaking the lines, experimenting with volume, repeating certain words and with speaking together and separately. Rehearse your performance.

d. Share your performance with others and comment on what you like in the way they use gesture and tone.

e. What have you learned about Mercutio's character through the language he uses in these lines?

Glossary

55 **atomies** creatures as small as atoms
57 **spinners** spiders
59 **traces** harness
79 **another benefice** additional paid position in the church

Mercutio, 2010

In shape no bigger than an agate-stone
On the forefinger of an alderman,
Drawn with a team of little atomies   55
Over men's noses as they lie asleep.
Her wagon-spokes made of long spinners' legs;
The cover of the wings of grasshoppers;
Her traces of the smallest spider's web;
Her collars of the moonshine's watery beams;   60
Her whip of cricket's bone, the lash of film;
Her wagoner a small grey-coated gnat,
Not half so big as a round little worm
Pricked from the lazy finger of a maid.
Her chariot is an empty hazel-nut   65
Made by the joiner squirrel or old grub,
Time out o'mind the fairies' coachmakers;
And in this state she gallops night by night
Through lovers' brains, and then they dream of love;
On courtiers' knees, that dream on curtsies straight;   70
O'er lawyers' fingers, who straight dream on fees;
O'er ladies' lips, who straight on kisses dream,
Which oft the angry Mab with blisters plagues,
Because their breath with sweetmeats tainted are.
Sometime she gallops o'er a courtier's nose,   75
And then dreams he of smelling out a suit.
And sometime comes she with a tithe-pig's tail,
Tickling a parson's nose as a lies asleep,
Then he dreams of another benefice.
Sometime she driveth o'er a soldier's neck,   80
And then dreams he of cutting foreign throats,
Of breaches, ambuscadoes, Spanish blades,
Of healths five-fathom deep, and then anon
Drums in his ear, at which he starts and wakes,
And being thus frighted swears a prayer or two   85
And sleeps again. This is that very Mab
That plaits the manes of horses in the night,
And bakes the elflocks in foul sluttish hairs,
Which once untangled, much misfortune bodes.

Romeo interrupts Mercutio who then dismisses his description of dreams as nothing more substantial than air. Romeo says he has a bad feeling about going to the party.

Activity 4: Exploring the theme of fate

a. In pairs, read lines 104–111 aloud together.

b. Read the lines again, but this time whisper and emphasise the sounds of the words as you read.

c. Which sounds do you find you are repeating? What do these sounds suggest about how Romeo feels about going to the party?

d. Fate is an important theme in this play. Write a paragraph or two explaining how Romeo feels about going to the Capulet party and whether or not you think he should go.

Capulet servants, 2008

At the time

Using page 265, find out what people believed could influence fate in Shakespeare's time. What do people today believe influences their fate?

This is the hag, when maids lie on their backs,   90
That presses them and learns them first to bear,
Making them women of good carriage.
This is she—

Romeo   Peace, peace, Mercutio, peace.
Thou talk'st of nothing.

Mercutio   True, I talk of dreams,
Which are the children of an idle brain,   95
Begot of nothing but vain fantasy,
Which is as thin of substance as the air
And more inconstant than the wind, who woos
Even now the frozen bosom of the north,
And being angered puffs away from thence,   100
Turning his side to the dew-dropping south.

Benvolio This wind you talk of blows us from ourselves.
Supper is done, and we shall come too late.

Romeo I fear too early, for my mind misgives
Some consequence yet hanging in the stars   105
Shall bitterly begin his fearful date
With this night's revels and expire the term
Of a despisèd life closed in my breast
By some vile forfeit of untimely death.
But he that hath the steerage of my course,   110
Direct my suit. On, lusty gentlemen!

Benvolio Strike, drum.

Exeunt

Activity 1: The party begins

a. Read lines 1–13 and make a list of all the jobs the servants need to do.

b. In groups, one person plays Lord Capulet and the others become either party guests or servants.

  i. The person playing Lord Capulet practises speaking aloud lines 14–27.

  ii. Those playing guests and servants decide for their character:

  - a name and age
  - an attitude (For example, do you feel excited, grumpy, curious, etc.?)
  - an **adjective** (For example, are you important, shy, busy, slow, etc.?).

  iii. The guests then rehearse arriving at the party, while the servants rehearse preparing the party.

c. Now run through lines 14–27. As Lord Capulet speaks, the guests and servants respond to what he says, using the ideas you have been rehearsing.

d. Discuss the kind of atmosphere you want to create for your audience and how you can adjust your performances to create this atmosphere. For example, Lord Capulet could seem warm and relaxed to create a fun atmosphere or tense and stressed to make it more edgy.

e. Look at the photo on this page. How might you describe the atmosphere of the Capulet party in this production? What are the differences and similarities with the atmosphere you created?

Lord and Lady Capulet with guests, 2010

Glossary

2 **trencher** wooden plate

5 **joint-stools** wooden stools

5 **court-cupboard** sideboard

6 **marchpane** marzipan

Key term

Adjective a word that describes a noun, e.g. *blue*, *happy*, *big*

Act 1 | Scene 5

Enter Servants

Servant 1 Where's Potpan, that he helps not to take away? He shift a
trencher? He scrape a trencher?

Servant 2 When good manners shall lie in one or two men's hands, and they
unwashed too, 'tis a foul thing.

Servant 1 Away with the joint-stools, remove the court-cupboard, look to   5
the plate. Good thou, save me a piece of marchpane, and as thou
lovest me, let the porter let in Susan Grindstone and Nell. Antony,
and Potpan!

Servant 3 Ay, boy, ready.

Servant 1 You are looked for and called for, asked for and sought for in the   10
great chamber.

Servant 2 We cannot be here and there too. Cheerly, boys, be brisk awhile,
and the longer liver take all.

Enter the Capulet family and guests including the Nurse

Lord Capulet Welcome, gentlemen! Ladies that have their toes
Unplagued with corns will walk a bout with you.   15
Ah, my mistresses, which of you all
Will now deny to dance? She that makes dainty,
She I'll swear hath corns. Am I come near ye now?
Welcome, gentlemen! I have seen the day
That I have worn a visor and could tell   20
A whispering tale in a fair lady's ear,
Such as would please: 'tis gone, 'tis gone, 'tis gone.
You are welcome, gentlemen! Come, musicians, play.

Music plays and they dance

Lord Capulet sits down with his cousin and reminisces about when they were young men wearing masks to parties. Romeo sees Juliet for the first time. Amazed by her beauty, he plans to touch her hand when she stops dancing.

Activity 2: Exploring the theme of love

a. In pairs, read lines 41–50, swapping reader at each punctuation mark.

b. Now one of you reads the lines as Romeo, while the other listens as the servant. The servant should listen attentively and encourage Romeo with facial expressions and gestures but no words.

c. Romeo reads lines 41–50 again, but this time the servant turns away, trying to get on with his/her work. Romeo must try to get the attention of the servant.

d. Romeo reads the lines one last time and this time the servant can interrupt, making comments or asking questions. Romeo can only answer by repeating a line of the speech or reading the next line.

e. Discuss which version of the speech you think worked best. In what ways is it helpful to talk to someone rather than speak the lines aloud to yourself?

Activity 3: Looking at themes

Write two or three paragraphs explaining how the key themes of love and fate are developed in this section of the play.

Glossary

31 **By'r lady** by our lady; the Virgin Mary

33 **nuptial** wedding

34 **Pentecost** Whitsunday

38 **a ward** a young man, under the control of a guardian

Romeo and a Capulet servant, 2008

A hall, hall, give room, and foot it, girls.
More light, you knaves, and turn the tables up, 25
And quench the fire, the room is grown too hot.
Ah, sirrah, this unlooked-for sport comes well.
Nay, sit, nay, sit, good cousin Capulet,
For you and I are past our dancing days.
How long is't now since last yourself and I 30
Were in a mask?

Cousin Capulet   By'r lady, thirty years.

Lord Capulet   What, man? 'Tis not so much, 'tis not so much.
'Tis since the nuptial of Lucentio,
Come Pentecost as quickly as it will,
Some five and twenty years, and then we masked. 35

Cousin Capulet   'Tis more, 'tis more – his son is elder, sir!
His son is thirty.

Lord Capulet   Will you tell me that?
His son was but a ward two years ago.

Romeo sees Juliet

Romeo   What lady is that, which doth enrich the hand
Of yonder knight?

Servant 1   I know not, sir. 40

Romeo   O, she doth teach the torches to burn bright.
It seems she hangs upon the cheek of night
As a rich jewel in an Ethiope's ear.
Beauty too rich for use, for earth too dear.
So shows a snowy dove trooping with crows, 45
As yonder lady o'er her fellows shows.
The measure done, I'll watch her place of stand,
And touching hers, make blessèd my rude hand.
Did my heart love till now? Forswear it, sight,
For I ne'er saw true beauty till this night. 50

Tybalt sees Romeo and calls for his sword, determined to attack him for coming to the party. Lord Capulet persuades Tybalt to step down from attacking Romeo. Tybalt agrees, but tells us that he will not forget what he considers to be an insult from Romeo.

Tybalt and Lord Capulet, 2008

Glossary

53 **antic face** comic mask
54 **fleer** sneer
54 **solemnity** ceremony
67 **disparagement** dishonour
78 **set cock-a-hoop** create disorder

Activity 4: Exploring how characters get what they want

a. In groups, read lines 62–80, swapping reader at each punctuation mark.
b. Now one person in the group plays Lord Capulet, another plays Tybalt and the others are Lord Capulet's servants. As you read, think about the following for your chosen character:
   - Tybalt's **objective** is to get at Romeo, who is on the other side of the room. His **obstacle** is the servants.
   - Lord Capulet's objective is to persuade Tybalt to stop and walk away. His obstacle is Tybalt's quick temper. He should try different **tactics** to achieve his objective, such as calming, ordering, encouraging, humiliating, etc.
   - The servants' objective is to stop Tybalt by getting in his way, but they should avoid touching him.
c. Read lines 62–80 again with different group members playing Lord Capulet and Tybalt.
d. Discuss which tactics from tasks b and c worked best to make Tybalt stop.
e. Read lines 86–89. How do you think Tybalt feels at this moment?
f. Imagine Tybalt then walks away and talks to a friend. Describe what happens between lines 62 and 89 in your own words as though you are Tybalt telling your friend what happened and how you feel about it.

Key terms

Objective what a character wants to get or achieve in a scene, e.g. Tybalt wants to get Romeo to leave the party

Obstacle what is in the way of a character getting what they want, e.g. Tybalt's obstacle here is Lord Capulet, who does not want to upset the party

Tactics the methods a character uses to get what they want, e.g. Tybalt might threaten Romeo or humiliate him

Did you know?

Actors sometimes use 'blocking' exercises like the one described on this page to get a more physical sense of the obstacles a character faces.

Tybalt   This, by his voice, should be a Montague.
Fetch me my rapier, boy. What dares the slave
Come hither, covered with an antic face,
To fleer and scorn at our solemnity?
Now, by the stock and honour of my kin,   55
To strike him dead I hold it not a sin.

Lord Capulet   Why, how now, kinsman? Wherefore storm you so?

Tybalt   Uncle, this is a Montague, our foe;
A villain that is hither come in spite,
To scorn at our solemnity this night.   60

Lord Capulet   Young Romeo is it?

Tybalt   'Tis he, that villain Romeo.

Lord Capulet   Content thee, gentle coz, let him alone.
A bears him like a portly gentleman,
And to say truth, Verona brags of him
To be a virtuous and well-governed youth.   65
I would not for the wealth of all this town
Here in my house do him disparagement.
Therefore be patient, take no note of him.
It is my will, the which if thou respect,
Show a fair presence and put off these frowns,   70
An ill-beseeming semblance for a feast.

Tybalt   It fits when such a villain is a guest.
I'll not endure him.

Lord Capulet   He shall be endured.
What, goodman boy, I say, he shall. Go to.
Am I the master here or you? Go to.   75
You'll not endure him? God shall mend my soul,
You'll make a mutiny among the guests.
You will set cock-a-hoop. You'll be the man!

Tybalt   Why, uncle, 'tis a shame.

Lord Capulet   Go to, go to.
You are a saucy boy, is't so, indeed?   80

Romeo touches Juliet's hand and speaks to her. They share a sonnet using an extended metaphor comparing Juliet to a saint and Romeo to a pilgrim come to worship her.

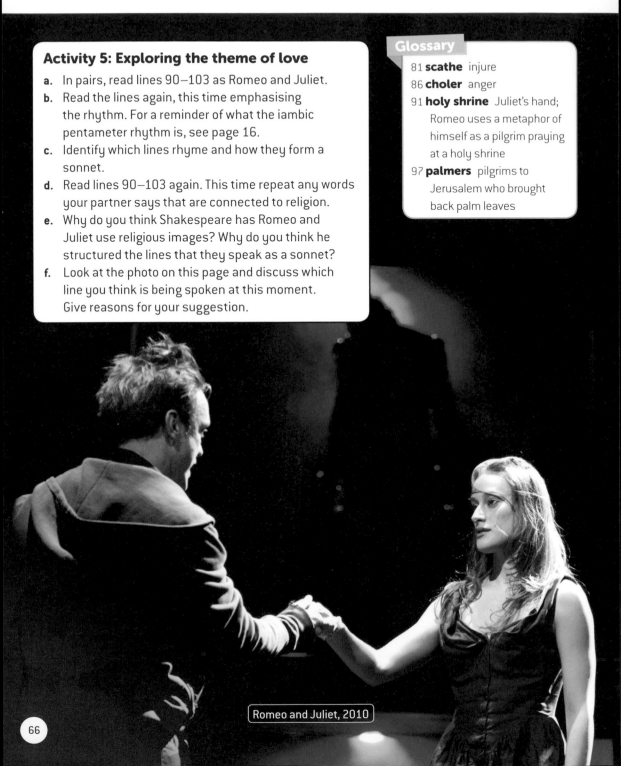

Activity 5: Exploring the theme of love

a. In pairs, read lines 90–103 as Romeo and Juliet.

b. Read the lines again, this time emphasising the rhythm. For a reminder of what the iambic pentameter rhythm is, see page 16.

c. Identify which lines rhyme and how they form a sonnet.

d. Read lines 90–103 again. This time repeat any words your partner says that are connected to religion.

e. Why do you think Shakespeare has Romeo and Juliet use religious images? Why do you think he structured the lines that they speak as a sonnet?

f. Look at the photo on this page and discuss which line you think is being spoken at this moment. Give reasons for your suggestion.

Glossary

81 **scathe** injure

86 **choler** anger

91 **holy shrine** Juliet's hand; Romeo uses a metaphor of himself as a pilgrim praying at a holy shrine

97 **palmers** pilgrims to Jerusalem who brought back palm leaves

Romeo and Juliet, 2010

This trick may chance to scathe you, I know what.
You must contrary me? Marry, 'tis time.

(To the guests) Well said, my hearts! (To Tybalt) You are a princox. Go,
Be quiet, or – More light, more light! – for shame,
I'll make you quiet. (To the guests) What, cheerly, my hearts!   85

Tybalt Patience perforce with wilful choler meeting
Makes my flesh tremble in their different greeting.
I will withdraw, but this intrusion shall
Now seeming sweet convert to bitter gall.

Exit Tybalt. Romeo takes Juliet's hand

Romeo If I profane with my unworthiest hand   90
This holy shrine, the gentle sin is this,
My lips, two blushing pilgrims, ready stand
To smooth that rough touch with a tender kiss.

Juliet Good pilgrim, you do wrong your hand too much,
Which mannerly devotion shows in this,   95
For saints have hands that pilgrims' hands do touch,
And palm to palm is holy palmers' kiss.

Romeo Have not saints lips, and holy palmers too?

Juliet Ay, pilgrim, lips that they must use in prayer.

Romeo O, then, dear saint, let lips do what hands do,   100
They pray, grant thou, lest faith turn to despair.

Juliet Saints do not move, though grant for prayers' sake.

Romeo Then move not, while my prayer's effect I take.
Thus from my lips, by thine, my sin is purged.

He kisses her

Juliet Then have my lips the sin that they have took.   105

Juliet is called away and Romeo learns from the Nurse that she is Lady Capulet's daughter. Lord Capulet says goodnight to his guests. Juliet asks the Nurse to find out who Romeo is.

Activity 6: Exploring Romeo's response

a. In pairs, read lines 109–115 with one of you playing Romeo and the other playing the Nurse.

b. Read the lines again. This time the person playing Romeo should listen carefully to what the Nurse says and repeat any words they find interesting.

c. Discuss whether you think Romeo should say lines 114–115 to the Nurse, the audience, himself or someone else. How does he feel as he says these lines?

d. Read lines 109–115 again, this time ending on a freeze-frame that shows the decisions you made in task c.

Glossary

114 **chinks** wealth
119 **trifling foolish banquet** simple dessert
123 **waxes** grows

Juliet, 2010

Romeo   Sin from my lips? O, trespass sweetly urged.
              Give me my sin again.

              He kisses her

Juliet   You kiss by th'book.

Nurse   Madam, your mother craves a word with you.

Romeo   What is her mother?

Nurse   Marry, bachelor,
              Her mother is the lady of the house,   110
              And a good lady, and a wise and virtuous.
              I nursed her daughter that you talked withal.
              I tell you, he that can lay hold of her
              Shall have the chinks.

Romeo   Is she a Capulet?
              O, dear account! My life is my foe's debt.   115

Benvolio Away, be gone, the sport is at the best.

Romeo   Ay, so I fear, the more is my unrest.

Lord Capulet Nay, gentlemen, prepare not to be gone,
              We have a trifling foolish banquet towards.
              Is it e'en so? Why then I thank you all.   120
              I thank you, honest gentlemen, good night.
              More torches here! Come on, then let's to bed.
              Ah, sirrah, by my faith, it waxes late.
              I'll to my rest.

Juliet   Come hither, nurse. What is yond gentleman?   125

Nurse   The son and heir of old Tiberio.

Juliet   What's he that now is going out of door?

Nurse   Marry, that I think be young Petruchio.

Juliet   What's he that follows here, that would not dance?

When Juliet hears the gentleman is Romeo Montague, she confesses how much she loves him but how difficult she knows that will be.

Juliet and the Nurse, 2010

Activity 7: Exploring Juliet's response

a. In pairs, read lines 125–138 as Juliet and the Nurse.
b. Create a freeze-frame for line 129 and a second freeze-frame for line 135.
c. Rehearse a performance that begins with the first freeze-frame and ends with the second freeze-frame, bringing the characters to life to speak their lines between the freeze-frames.

Glossary

137 **Prodigious** ominous
140 **Anon** on my way

Nurse   I know not.   130

Juliet   Go ask his name. If he be marrièd,
My grave is like to be my wedding bed.

Nurse   His name is Romeo, and a Montague,
The only son of your great enemy.

Juliet   My only love sprung from my only hate.   135
Too early seen unknown, and known too late.
Prodigious birth of love it is to me,
That I must love a loathèd enemy.

Nurse   What's this? What's this?

Juliet   A rhyme I learned even now
Of one I danced withal.

A call for Juliet is heard

Nurse   Anon, anon!   140
Come, let's away. The strangers all are gone.

Exeunt

Exploring Act 1

Activity 1: Preparing for a big scene

a. In groups, look back over Act 1 Scene 4 and each choose one of the more important characters attending the party.

b. Look back over Act 1 and consider how your chosen character might feel about all the events that have happened so far. Act 1 takes place over one day, a Sunday.

c. Now imagine it is just before the Capulet party and the characters you have chosen are in the final moment of getting ready for the event. Make a freeze-frame that shows that final moment.

d. Bring your freeze-frame to life as each character speaks their greatest hope for the party in their own words.

e. Repeat task d, but this time with each character speaking their greatest fear.

f. Support each other in writing a list of three hopes and three fears for each character in that final moment before the party begins.

g. Discuss how those hopes and fears are met by the end of Act 1 Scene 5.

h. Write a **monologue** in modern English in which your character retells the events of the evening from their point of view. Include their feelings about those events and any reflections on what happened earlier on during the day. Also include what your character thinks will happen next. Try to consider the key themes of love, loyalty, friendship, family and fate in your response.

Key terms

Monologue a long speech in which a character expresses their thoughts. Other characters may be present

Plot the events of a story

Lord and Lady Capulet with guests, 2010

Romeo, 2006

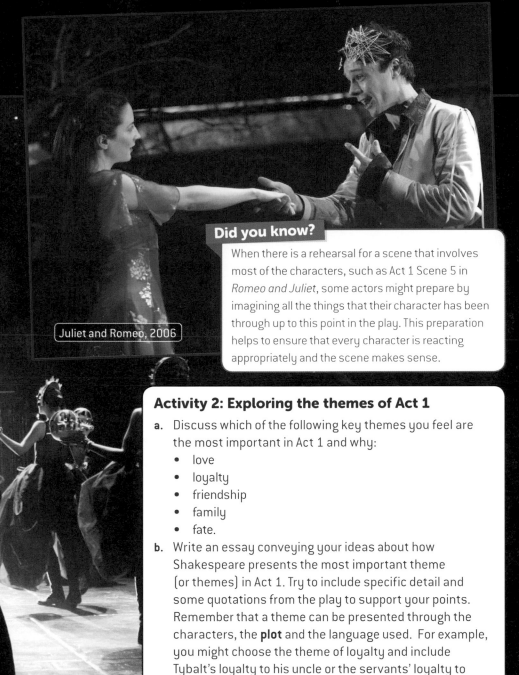

Juliet and Romeo, 2006

Activity 2: Exploring the themes of Act 1

a. Discuss which of the following key themes you feel are the most important in Act 1 and why:
- love
- loyalty
- friendship
- family
- fate.

b. Write an essay conveying your ideas about how Shakespeare presents the most important theme (or themes) in Act 1. Try to include specific detail and some quotations from the play to support your points. Remember that a theme can be presented through the characters, the **plot** and the language used. For example, you might choose the theme of loyalty and include Tybalt's loyalty to his uncle or the servants' loyalty to their masters. You might also explore the lack of loyalty Romeo shows when he shifts his attention from Rosaline to Juliet. Use the title: 'How does Shakespeare present the theme of ___ in Act 1?'

73

Romeo has forgotten Rosaline and fallen in love with Juliet who, unlike Rosaline, returns his love. The hatred between the Capulet and Montague families, however, creates obstacles for Romeo and Juliet, especially as Juliet is given very little freedom outside the house.

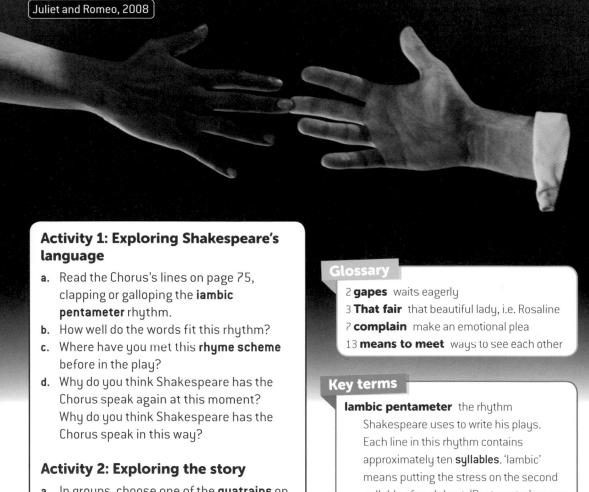

Juliet and Romeo, 2008

Activity 1: Exploring Shakespeare's language

a. Read the Chorus's lines on page 75, clapping or galloping the **iambic pentameter** rhythm.

b. How well do the words fit this rhythm?

c. Where have you met this **rhyme scheme** before in the play?

d. Why do you think Shakespeare has the Chorus speak again at this moment? Why do you think Shakespeare has the Chorus speak in this way?

Activity 2: Exploring the story

a. In groups, choose one of the **quatrains** on page 75. Work out a way to present your quatrain to the rest of the class, acting out what is being described and speaking the lines in a way that sounds natural, rather than emphasising the rhythm.

b. List all the **obstacles** you can think of that Romeo and Juliet face. Write a paragraph or two explaining how you think they will find 'means to meet'.

Glossary

2 **gapes** waits eagerly

3 **That fair** that beautiful lady, i.e. Rosaline

7 **complain** make an emotional plea

13 **means to meet** ways to see each other

Key terms

Iambic pentameter the rhythm Shakespeare uses to write his plays. Each line in this rhythm contains approximately ten **syllables**. 'Iambic' means putting the stress on the second syllable of each beat. 'Pentameter' means five beats with two syllables in each beat

Syllable part of a word that is one sound, e.g. 'dignity' has three syllables – 'dig','ni','ty'

Rhyme scheme the pattern of rhymes at the end of lines of a poem or verse

Quatrain a stanza of four lines

Obstacle what is in the way of a character getting what they want

Act 2

Enter Chorus

Chorus   Now old desire doth in his death-bed lie,
     And young affection gapes to be his heir;
That fair for which love groaned for and would die,
     With tender Juliet matched, is now not fair.
Now Romeo is beloved and loves again,   5
     Alike bewitchèd by the charm of looks,
But to his foe supposed he must complain,
     And she steal love's sweet bait from fearful hooks.
Being held a foe, he may not have access
     To breathe such vows as lovers use to swear,   10
And she as much in love, her means much less
     To meet her new-belovèd anywhere.
But passion lends them power, time, means to meet,
Tempering extremities with extreme sweet.

Exeunt

75

After leaving the Capulet party, Romeo has slipped away from his friends in the hope of seeing Juliet again. Benvolio and Mercutio are looking for him.

Activity 1: Exploring Mercutio

a. In pairs, read Mercutio's speech, lines 7–21, swapping reader at each punctuation mark.
b. Choose two to four lines from the speech.
c. Create **gestures** for the key words in your chosen lines and explore different ways of speaking the words, deciding how to share them between you and experimenting with volume, **tone**, **emphasis** and **repetition**.
d. Look at the photo of Mercutio on this page. How do you think Mercutio is feeling at this moment? Why might he feel this way?

At the time

Using page 265, find out about the stories of love in Shakespeare's time, including the stories about the goddess Venus and Cupid. Why do you think Mercutio mentions these stories?

Key terms

Gesture a movement, often using the hands or head, to express a feeling or idea
Tone as in 'tone of voice'; expressing an attitude through how you say something
Emphasis stress given to words when speaking
Repetition saying the same thing again

Mercutio, 2008

Act 2 | Scene 1

Enter Romeo

Romeo   Can I go forward when my heart is here?
Turn back, dull earth, and find thy centre out.

Enter Benvolio and Mercutio. Exit Romeo

Benvolio   Romeo! My cousin Romeo, Romeo!

Mercutio   He is wise,
And on my life hath stolen him home to bed.

Benvolio   He ran this way and leapt this orchard wall.   5
Call, good Mercutio.

Mercutio   Nay, I'll conjure too.
Romeo! Humours! Madman! Passion! Lover!
Appear thou in the likeness of a sigh,
Speak but one rhyme, and I am satisfied.
Cry but 'Ay me', pronounce but 'love' and 'dove',   10
Speak to my gossip Venus one fair word,
One nickname for her purblind son and heir,
Young Abraham Cupid, he that shot so true,
When King Cophetua loved the beggar-maid.
He heareth not, he stirreth not, he moveth not.   15
The ape is dead, and I must conjure him.
I conjure thee by Rosaline's bright eyes;
By her high forehead and her scarlet lip;
By her fine foot, straight leg and quivering thigh,
And the demesnes that there adjacent lie,   20
That in thy likeness thou appear to us.

Benvolio   And if he hear thee, thou wilt anger him.

Mercutio   This cannot anger him. 'Twould anger him
To raise a spirit in his mistress' circle

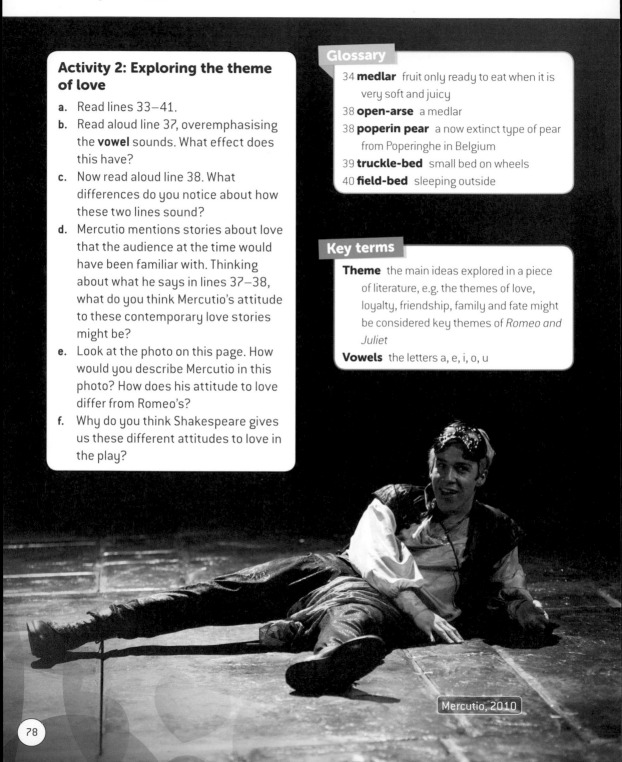

Benvolio and Mercutio realise Romeo does not want to be found and make fun of him for chasing after love.

Activity 2: Exploring the theme of love

a. Read lines 33–41.

b. Read aloud line 37, overemphasising the **vowel** sounds. What effect does this have?

c. Now read aloud line 38. What differences do you notice about how these two lines sound?

d. Mercutio mentions stories about love that the audience at the time would have been familiar with. Thinking about what he says in lines 37–38, what do you think Mercutio's attitude to these contemporary love stories might be?

e. Look at the photo on this page. How would you describe Mercutio in this photo? How does his attitude to love differ from Romeo's?

f. Why do you think Shakespeare gives us these different attitudes to love in the play?

Glossary

34 **medlar** fruit only ready to eat when it is very soft and juicy

38 **open-arse** a medlar

38 **poperin pear** a now extinct type of pear from Poperinghe in Belgium

39 **truckle-bed** small bed on wheels

40 **field-bed** sleeping outside

Key terms

Theme the main ideas explored in a piece of literature, e.g. the themes of love, loyalty, friendship, family and fate might be considered key themes of *Romeo and Juliet*

Vowels the letters a, e, i, o, u

Mercutio, 2010

Of some strange nature, letting it there stand   25
Till she had laid it and conjured it down.
That were some spite. My invocation
Is fair and honest, and in his mistress' name
I conjure only but to raise up him.

Benvolio Come, he hath hid himself among these trees,   30
To be consorted with the humorous night.
Blind is his love and best befits the dark.

Mercutio If love be blind, love cannot hit the mark.
Now will he sit under a medlar tree,
And wish his mistress were that kind of fruit   35
As maids call medlars, when they laugh alone.
O Romeo, that she were, O, that she were
An open-arse and thou a poperin pear.
Romeo, goodnight! I'll to my truckle-bed,
This field-bed is too cold for me to sleep.   40
Come, shall we go?

Benvolio   Go, then, for 'tis in vain
To seek him here that means not to be found.

Exeunt Benvolio and Mercutio

Romeo has climbed over the walls around the Capulet house to catch a glimpse of Juliet. He sees her and declares how beautiful she is.

Romeo and Juliet, 2010

Activity 1: Exploring Romeo's thoughts and feelings

a. Read Romeo's speech, lines 2–25.

b. In groups, choose one of the following sections:
- lines 2–6, 'But, soft,… far more fair than she'
- lines 7–11, 'Be not her maid… she knew she were'
- lines 12–17, 'She speaks… till they return'
- lines 18–22, 'What if her eyes… were not night'
- lines 23–26, 'See how she leans… bright angel'
- lines 26–32, 'O, speak again… bosom of the air'.

c. Create physical gestures for the key words in your chosen lines and explore different ways of speaking the words. Share them between you and experiment with volume, tone, emphasis and repetition until you have a performance you are proud to show to others.

d. In your groups, discuss how you think Romeo feels as he speaks these lines. Which words or phrases help you to understand how he feels?

e. List the words and phrases you have talked about and, for each one, write a sentence or two explaining why it helps you to understand Romeo's feelings.

Glossary

8 **vestal livery** clothing that symbolises purity. Vestal virgins of Ancient Rome never married. Their 'livery' or clothing was white, like the moon

8 **sick and green** 'Green-sickness' was a disease associated with adolescent girls, allegedly cured by marriage. Green was also the colour of envy

13 **discourses** speaks

17 **spheres** Shakespeare's audience believed the stars were held in 'celestial spheres', slowly circling round the earth

21 **airy region** sky

Romeo advances

Romeo   He jests at scars that never felt a wound.

Enter Juliet at her window

But, soft, what light through yonder window breaks?
It is the east, and Juliet is the sun.
Arise, fair sun, and kill the envious moon,
Who is already sick and pale with grief,   5
That thou her maid art far more fair than she.
Be not her maid, since she is envious.
Her vestal livery is but sick and green
And none but fools do wear it, cast it off.
It is my lady, O, it is my love!   10
O that she knew she were!
She speaks yet she says nothing. What of that?
Her eye discourses. I will answer it.
I am too bold; 'tis not to me she speaks.
Two of the fairest stars in all the heaven,   15
Having some business, do entreat her eyes
To twinkle in their spheres till they return.
What if her eyes were there, they in her head?
The brightness of her cheek would shame those stars,
As daylight doth a lamp; her eye in heaven   20
Would through the airy region stream so bright
That birds would sing and think it were not night.
See how she leans her cheek upon her hand.
O that I were a glove upon that hand,
That I might touch that cheek.

Juliet   Ay me.

Romeo   She speaks.   25
O, speak again, bright angel, for thou art
As glorious to this night, being o'er my head,

Romeo continues to admire Juliet from afar as he hides in her garden. Juliet speaks aloud about her love for him and wishes they did not have the problem of being a Montague and a Capulet.

Activity 2: Exploring asides

a. In pairs, read lines 24–40 with one of you playing Romeo and the other playing Juliet.

b. Look at line 37. Who do you think Romeo is talking to?

c. Form a small group of at least three. In lines 24–40, Romeo and Juliet are speaking their thoughts aloud but not directly to each other. One person should play Romeo and one should play Juliet, while the rest of your group are the audience. Now try two versions of these lines:

   i. Romeo and Juliet talk aloud to themselves about each other.

   ii. Romeo and Juliet talk to the audience about each other.

d. Discuss as a group which version of the lines you think worked better in task c and why.

e. Write a paragraph or two comparing how Romeo and Juliet talk about love in lines 24–40 with how Mercutio talked about love in Act 2 Scene 1.

Did you know?

In **asides** and **soliloquies**, actors often directly address the audience, as though the audience is another character in the play.

Key terms

Aside when a character addresses a remark to the audience that other characters on the stage do not hear

Soliloquy a speech in which a character is alone on stage and expresses their thoughts and feelings aloud to the audience

Juliet, 2010

As is a wingèd messenger of heaven
Unto the white upturnèd wondering eyes
Of mortals that fall back to gaze on him   30
When he bestrides the lazy puffing clouds,
And sails upon the bosom of the air.

Juliet   O Romeo, Romeo, wherefore art thou Romeo?
Deny thy father and refuse thy name,
Or if thou wilt not, be but sworn my love,   35
And I'll no longer be a Capulet.

Romeo   Shall I hear more, or shall I speak at this?

Juliet   'Tis but thy name that is my enemy.
Thou art thyself, though not a Montague.
What's Montague? It is nor hand, nor foot,   40
Nor arm, nor face, nor any other part
Belonging to a man. O be some other name.
What's in a name? That which we call a rose
By any other word would smell as sweet,
So Romeo would, were he not Romeo called,   45
Retain that dear perfection which he owes
Without that title. Romeo, doff thy name,
And for thy name, which is no part of thee,
Take all myself.

Romeo   I take thee at thy word.
Call me but love, and I'll be new baptized.   50
Henceforth I never will be Romeo.

Juliet   What man art thou that thus bescreened in night
So stumblest on my counsel?

Romeo   By a name
I know not how to tell thee who I am.
My name, dear saint, is hateful to myself,   55
Because it is an enemy to thee.
Had I it written, I would tear the word.

Juliet   My ears have yet not drunk a hundred words

Romeo directly addresses Juliet. She asks why he is in her garden and how he got there, knowing her family might kill him if they find him there. Romeo explains that love guided him to Juliet and he would rather die than not be able to see her.

Juliet and Romeo, 2006

Activity 3: Exploring 'as ifs'

a. In pairs, read lines 47–69 with one of you playing Romeo and the other playing Juliet.

b. Read the lines again, but this time whisper them as though you are scared of being overheard.

c. Read the lines again loudly as though you are pleased to see each other.

d. Discuss which lines felt better whispered and which lines felt better spoken loudly.

e. Read lines 47–69 again as if Juliet is shocked when Romeo speaks and worried her family will hear him.

f. Read the lines again as if Juliet has already spotted Romeo hiding in the garden and, knowing her family are all asleep, is just teasing him about the dangers.

g. Discuss whether you prefer version e or f, and why.

h. Imagine you are the director for these lines. Write notes on how you would encourage the actors to play the lines based on the discoveries you have made in Activity 3.

Glossary

65 **kinsmen** relatives
66 **o'er-perch** fly over
73 **proof against their enmity** armed against their hate
78 **proroguèd** delayed
88 **Fain** gladly

Did you know?

The phrase 'as if' is often used in a rehearsal room as actors try out different ways of playing a character according to the attitudes that character might have. For example, in the activity on this page, Juliet is played *as if* she is anxious about Romeo being discovered and again *as if* she is relaxed about it.

Of that tongue's uttering, yet I know the sound.
Art thou not Romeo and a Montague?   60

Romeo Neither, fair maid, if either thee dislike.

Juliet How cam'st thou hither, tell me, and wherefore?
The orchard walls are high and hard to climb,
And the place death, considering who thou art,
If any of my kinsmen find thee here.   65

Romeo With love's light wings did I o'er-perch these walls,
For stony limits cannot hold love out,
And what love can do that dares love attempt.
Therefore thy kinsmen are no stop to me.

Juliet If they do see thee, they will murder thee.   70

Romeo Alack, there lies more peril in thine eye
Than twenty of their swords. Look thou but sweet,
And I am proof against their enmity.

Juliet I would not for the world they saw thee here.

Romeo I have night's cloak to hide me from their eyes,   75
And but thou love me, let them find me here.
My life were better ended by their hate,
Than death proroguèd, wanting of thy love.

Juliet By whose direction found'st thou out this place?

Romeo By love, that first did prompt me to inquire.   80
He lent me counsel and I lent him eyes.
I am no pilot, yet wert thou as far
As that vast shore washed with the farthest sea,
I should adventure for such merchandise.

Juliet Thou know'st the mask of night is on my face,   85
Else would a maiden blush bepaint my cheek
For that which thou hast heard me speak tonight.
Fain would I dwell on form, fain, fain deny
What I have spoke, but farewell compliment.
Dost thou love me? I know thou wilt say 'Ay',   90

Juliet tells Romeo she is embarrassed that he overheard her but wants him to know she is serious about her love for him.

Key term

Paraphrase put a line or section of text into your own words

Juliet, 2008

Activity 4: Exploring Juliet's fears

a. In pairs, read aloud Juliet's speech, lines 85–106, swapping reader at each punctuation mark.

b. With your partner, discuss what you think Juliet is worried about in this speech.

c. Pick out three phrases that express Juliet's fears and try to **paraphrase** them.

d. Imagining you are Juliet, write a paragraph in modern English that summarises the fears she expresses in lines 85–106. You might begin 'I know you say you love me but…'.

e. Look at the photo on this page. Why do you think the director chose to use Juliet's bedstead as the balcony? How effective do you think this idea is?

Did you know?

Actors often find it useful to paraphrase Shakespeare's text into words they would use themselves in everyday language. This means the actors have to understand the meaning of every word and phrase.

And I will take thy word. Yet if thou swear'st,
Thou may'st prove false. At lovers' perjuries
They say Jove laughs. O gentle Romeo,
If thou dost love, pronounce it faithfully,
Or if thou think'st I am too quickly won,   95
I'll frown and be perverse and say thee nay,
So thou wilt woo, but else not for the world.
In truth, fair Montague, I am too fond,
And therefore thou may'st think my behaviour light,
But trust me, gentleman, I'll prove more true   100
Than those that have more coying to be strange.
I should have been more strange, I must confess,
But that thou overheard'st, ere I was ware,
My true love's passion. Therefore pardon me,
And not impute this yielding to light love,   105
Which the dark night hath so discoverèd.

Romeo   Lady, by yonder blessèd moon I vow
That tips with silver all these fruit-tree tops—

Juliet   O, swear not by the moon, th'inconstant moon,
That monthly changes in her circled orb,   110
Lest that thy love prove likewise variable.

Romeo   What shall I swear by?

Juliet   Do not swear at all.
Or if thou wilt, swear by thy gracious self,
Which is the god of my idolatry,
And I'll believe thee.

Romeo   If my heart's dear love—   115

Juliet   Well, do not swear. Although I joy in thee,
I have no joy of this contract tonight.
It is too rash, too unadvised, too sudden,
Too like the lightning, which doth cease to be
Ere one can say 'It lightens'. Sweet, goodnight.   120
This bud of love, by summer's ripening breath,
May prove a beauteous flower when next we meet.

Juliet worries that things are moving too fast and says goodnight. Romeo calls her back and asks for her promise of love, which she gives. She then hears the Nurse coming into her room. Juliet has to go, but first she asks Romeo to arrange for them to be married.

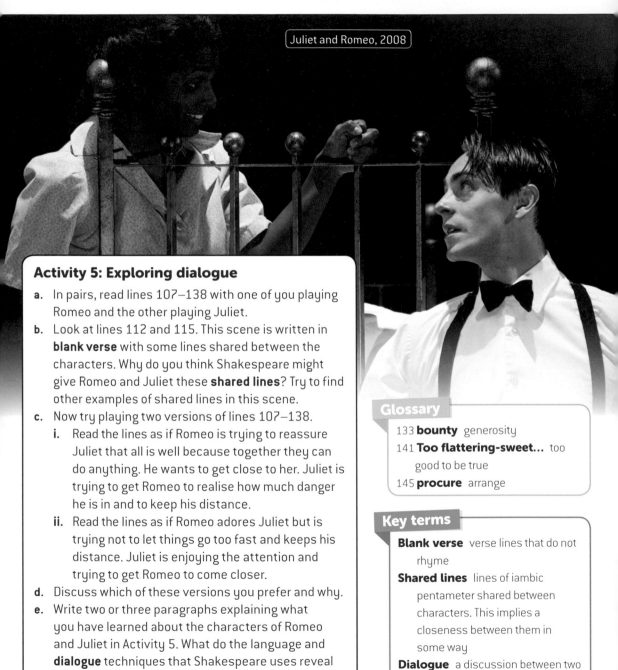

Juliet and Romeo, 2008

Activity 5: Exploring dialogue

a. In pairs, read lines 107–138 with one of you playing Romeo and the other playing Juliet.

b. Look at lines 112 and 115. This scene is written in **blank verse** with some lines shared between the characters. Why do you think Shakespeare might give Romeo and Juliet these **shared lines**? Try to find other examples of shared lines in this scene.

c. Now try playing two versions of lines 107–138.

i. Read the lines as if Romeo is trying to reassure Juliet that all is well because together they can do anything. He wants to get close to her. Juliet is trying to get Romeo to realise how much danger he is in and to keep his distance.

ii. Read the lines as if Romeo adores Juliet but is trying not to let things go too fast and keeps his distance. Juliet is enjoying the attention and trying to get Romeo to come closer.

d. Discuss which of these versions you prefer and why.

e. Write two or three paragraphs explaining what you have learned about the characters of Romeo and Juliet in Activity 5. What do the language and **dialogue** techniques that Shakespeare uses reveal about the two characters?

Glossary

133 **bounty** generosity
141 **Too flattering-sweet...** too good to be true
145 **procure** arrange

Key terms

Blank verse verse lines that do not rhyme
Shared lines lines of iambic pentameter shared between characters. This implies a closeness between them in some way
Dialogue a discussion between two or more people

Goodnight, goodnight, as sweet repose and rest
Come to thy heart as that within my breast.

Romeo   O, wilt thou leave me so unsatisfied?   125

Juliet   What satisfaction canst thou have tonight?

Romeo   Th'exchange of thy love's faithful vow for mine.

Juliet   I gave thee mine before thou didst request it.
And yet I would it were to give again.

Romeo   Wouldst thou withdraw it? For what purpose, love?   130

Juliet   But to be frank and give it thee again.
And yet I wish but for the thing I have.
My bounty is as boundless as the sea,
My love as deep: the more I give to thee,
The more I have, for both are infinite.   135
I hear some noise within. Dear love, adieu.

The Nurse calls

Anon, good nurse! Sweet Montague, be true.
Stay but a little, I will come again.

Exit Juliet

Romeo   O blessèd, blessèd night! I am afeard,
Being in night, all this is but a dream,   140
Too flattering-sweet to be substantial.

Enter Juliet

Juliet   Three words, dear Romeo, and good night indeed.
If that thy bent of love be honourable,
Thy purpose marriage, send me word tomorrow,
By one that I'll procure to come to thee,   145
Where and what time thou wilt perform the rite,
And all my fortunes at thy foot I'll lay,
And follow thee my lord throughout the world.

Nurse   Madam!

Juliet, 2010

Glossary

159 **tassel-gentle** Juliet is comparing Romeo to a falcon tamed through the skills of falconry

161 **Echo** Echo was a nymph who could only repeat what others said. She fell in love with Narcissus and hid in a cave when he rejected her

167 **nyas** young hawk

Activity 6: Exploring tension

a. In small groups, read lines 149–157 with one of you playing Romeo, one playing Juliet and one playing the Nurse.

b. Read the lines again in your groups, but this time Romeo stands ten steps away from Juliet and the Nurse stands between them. When Juliet speaks she should try to get past the Nurse to Romeo, but whenever the Nurse calls or the stage direction says 'Exit Juliet', Juliet has to go back to her starting position.

c. Discuss how task b made your Juliet and your Romeo feel.

d. Paraphrase Romeo's lines from 155–157.

Juliet	I come, anon! But if thou mean'st not well,
	I do beseech thee—

150

Nurse	Madam!

Juliet	By and by, I come!
	To cease thy strife, and leave me to my grief.
	Tomorrow will I send.

Romeo	So thrive my soul—

Juliet	A thousand times goodnight!

Exit Juliet

Romeo	A thousand times the worse, to want thy light.
	Love goes toward love as schoolboys from their books,
	But love from love, toward school with heavy looks.

155

Enter Juliet again

Juliet	Hist, Romeo, hist! O for a falconer's voice,
	To lure this tassel-gentle back again.
	Bondage is hoarse, and may not speak aloud,
	Else would I tear the cave where Echo lies,
	And make her airy tongue more hoarse than mine,
	With repetition of my Romeo.

160

Romeo	It is my soul that calls upon my name.
	How silver-sweet sound lovers' tongues by night,
	Like softest music to attending ears.

165

Juliet	Romeo!

Romeo	My nyas?

Juliet	What o'clock tomorrow
	Shall I send to thee?

Romeo	By the hour of nine.

Juliet	I will not fail. 'Tis twenty years till then.
	I have forgot why I did call thee back.

170

Romeo	Let me stand here till thou remember it.

Romeo and Juliet continue to find it hard to say goodnight to each other. Romeo finally says goodnight to Juliet and decides to go straight to see the Friar to get his help in arranging the marriage.

Activity 7: Exploring motivation

a. Imagine you are Romeo. Make a list of all the reasons you can think of why marrying Juliet is a good idea and a second list of all the reasons why it is a bad idea.

b. Now imagine you are Juliet and repeat task a.

c. Form small groups. One of you plays Romeo and another plays the Friar. The others are the audience. Romeo and the Friar **improvise** a dialogue where Romeo tries to persuade Friar Laurence that marrying Juliet is a good idea, while Friar Laurence tries to persuade Romeo that it is a bad idea. The audience decides who wins the argument and explains which arguments seemed most convincing.

d. Now repeat task c, but playing Juliet and the Nurse, while the other members of the group are the audience.

Activity 8: Exploring Romeo and Juliet's decision

a. Discuss the following questions:

i. Why do Romeo and Juliet agree to get married when they have only just met each other?

ii. How does the time they live in affect their decision to get married so quickly?

iii. What similarities can you think of between how Romeo and Juliet behave in this story and how teenagers behave in stories you know from books, films and TV?

b. Now you have shared and discussed your ideas, write a paragraph or two answering the first question in your own words, including reference to the themes of love and fate.

Juliet and Romeo, 2010

Juliet I shall forget, to have thee still stand there,
Remembering how I love thy company.

Romeo And I'll still stay, to have thee still forget,
Forgetting any other home but this.   175

Juliet 'Tis almost morning, I would have thee gone,
And yet no further than a wanton's bird,
That lets it hop a little from his hand,
Like a poor prisoner in his twisted gyves,
And with a silken thread plucks it back again,   180
So loving-jealous of his liberty.

Romeo I would I were thy bird.

Juliet   Sweet, so would I.
Yet I should kill thee with much cherishing.
Goodnight, goodnight. Parting is such sweet sorrow,
That I shall say good night till it be morrow.   185

Exit Juliet

Romeo Sleep dwell upon thine eyes, peace in thy breast.
Would I were sleep and peace, so sweet to rest.
Hence will I to my ghostly friar's cell,
His help to crave, and my dear hap to tell.

Exit Romeo

Friar Laurence describes how dawn is breaking and says he is out collecting plants and herbs to use for food and medicine.

Activity 1: Exploring the Friar

a. Read lines 15–30.

b. In pairs, focus on lines 23–26 and read these lines aloud, creating gestures for each key word. For example, you might gesture rocking a baby for 'infant'.

c. Paraphrase lines 23–26 and write it down.

d. Romeo enters as the Friar speaks these words. What connection do you think the audience might make between the Friar's description of the flower and how Romeo is feeling?

Glossary

4 **Titan** the sun god

7 **osier cage** willow basket

8 **baleful weeds** poisonous plants

15 **mickle** great

23 **infant rind** undeveloped part

At the time

Using page 269, discuss why Friar Laurence is collecting herbs.

Friar Laurence, 2010

Enter Friar Laurence, collecting plants

Friar Laurence The grey-eyed morn smiles on the frowning night,
Checkering the eastern clouds with streaks of light,
And fleckled darkness like a drunkard reels
From forth day's path and Titan's burning wheels.
Now, ere the sun advance his burning eye,   5
The day to cheer and night's dank dew to dry,
I must upfill this osier cage of ours
With baleful weeds and precious juicèd flowers.
The earth that's nature's mother is her tomb;
What is her burying grave, that is her womb,   10
And from her womb children of divers kind
We sucking on her natural bosom find.
Many for many virtues excellent,
None but for some and yet all different.
O mickle is the powerful grace that lies   15
In plants, herbs, stones, and their true qualities.
For nought so vile that on the earth doth live
But to the earth some special good doth give.
Nor aught so good but strained from that fair use
Revolts from true birth, stumbling on abuse.   20
Virtue itself turns vice, being misapplied,
And vice sometime by action dignified.

Enter Romeo

Within the infant rind of this weak flower
Poison hath residence and medicine power.
For this, being smelt, with that part cheers each part,   25
Being tasted, slays all senses with the heart.
Two such opposèd kings encamp them still
In man as well as herbs, grace and rude will,

Romeo greets the Friar, who is surprised to see him up so early, but then guesses that Romeo is not up early but out late. The Friar is shocked to think Romeo may have been with Rosaline, but Romeo tells him he has forgotten her and instead loves Lord Capulet's daughter.

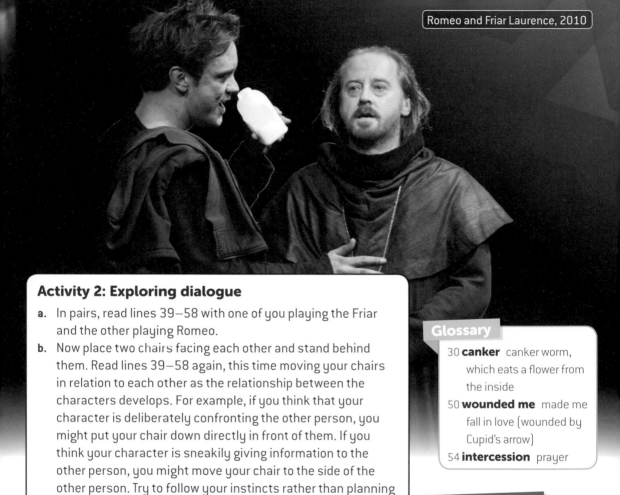

Romeo and Friar Laurence, 2010

Activity 2: Exploring dialogue

a. In pairs, read lines 39–58 with one of you playing the Friar and the other playing Romeo.

b. Now place two chairs facing each other and stand behind them. Read lines 39–58 again, this time moving your chairs in relation to each other as the relationship between the characters develops. For example, if you think that your character is deliberately confronting the other person, you might put your chair down directly in front of them. If you think your character is sneakily giving information to the other person, you might move your chair to the side of the other person. Try to follow your instincts rather than planning how you will move the chair next.

c. Discuss how the way you moved the chairs reflected how the Friar and Romeo feel as they speak and listen at this point. How would you describe the relationship between Romeo and the Friar?

d. Look at the photo on this page. How would you describe the relationship between Romeo and the Friar at this moment? How far does this agree with the relationship you discovered through Activity 2?

Glossary

30 **canker** canker worm, which eats a flower from the inside

50 **wounded me** made me fall in love (wounded by Cupid's arrow)

54 **intercession** prayer

Did you know?

To help actors feel connected to the words they speak, they sometimes use objects, such as the chairs in the activity on this page, to represent physically the feelings behind the words.

	And where the worser is predominant,	
	Full soon the canker death eats up that plant.	30
Romeo	Good morrow, father.	
Friar Laurence	Benedicite!	
	What early tongue so sweet saluteth me?	
	Young son, it argues a distempered head	
	So soon to bid good morrow to thy bed.	
	Care keeps his watch in every old man's eye,	35
	And where care lodges, sleep will never lie.	
	But where unbruisèd youth with unstuffed brain	
	Doth couch his limbs, there golden sleep doth reign.	
	Therefore thy earliness doth me assure	
	Thou art uproused with some distemperature,	40
	Or if not so, then here I hit it right,	
	Our Romeo hath not been in bed tonight.	
Romeo	That last is true, the sweeter rest was mine.	
Friar Laurence	God pardon sin! Wast thou with Rosaline?	
Romeo	With Rosaline, my ghostly father? No,	45
	I have forgot that name, and that name's woe.	
Friar Laurence	That's my good son. But where hast thou been, then?	
Romeo	I'll tell thee ere thou ask it me again.	
	I have been feasting with mine enemy,	
	Where on a sudden one hath wounded me,	50
	That's by me wounded. Both our remedies	
	Within thy help and holy physic lies.	
	I bear no hatred, blessèd man, for lo,	
	My intercession likewise steads my foe.	
Friar Laurence	Be plain, good son, rest homely in thy drift,	55
	Riddling confession finds but riddling shrift.	
Romeo	Then plainly know my heart's dear love is set	
	On the fair daughter of rich Capulet.	
	As mine on hers, so hers is set on mine,	

Romeo asks Friar Laurence to marry him to Juliet. The Friar is amazed that Romeo has so quickly forgotten Rosaline and now loves someone else but agrees to help him with his plan.

Romeo and Friar Laurence, 2006

Activity 3: Exploring the theme of love

a. In pairs, read the Friar's speech, lines 65–80, aloud together.

b. Stand facing your partner and again read the speech aloud together. This time when you read a word addressing Romeo, such as 'thou' or 'thy', point at your partner. Every time you read 'Rosaline' point behind you.

c. Discuss what the Friar might be thinking about Romeo's change of affection.

d. Now read lines 81–94 in pairs, with one of you playing the Friar and the other playing Romeo.

e. Place two chairs facing each other and stand behind them. Read lines 81–94 again, this time moving your chairs in relation to each other as the relationship between the characters develops. For example, if you think that your character is deliberately confronting the other person, you might put your chair down directly in front of them. If you think your character is sneakily giving information to the other person, you might move your chair to the side. Try to follow your instincts rather than planning how you will move the chair next.

f. At which moment do you think the Friar decides to help Romeo? Why does he decide to help him?

Glossary

69 **brine** salt water; tears

70 **sallow** pale

85 **chide** tell off

Did you know?

In Shakespeare's time, people used 'thou' as a more familiar version of 'you', for people close to them, like friends. 'Thou' was also used to address people of a lower social status. They used 'you' when they wanted to be more polite or formal. In this scene, it is useful for actors to note how Romeo and the Friar use 'thou' with each other, as it suggests they have a close relationship.

	And all combined, save what thou must combine	60
	By holy marriage. When and where and how	
	We met, we wooed and made exchange of vow,	
	I'll tell thee as we pass, but this I pray,	
	That thou consent to marry us today.	
Friar Laurence	Holy Saint Francis, what a change is here!	65
	Is Rosaline, that thou didst love so dear,	
	So soon forsaken? Young men's love then lies	
	Not truly in their hearts, but in their eyes.	
	Jesu Maria, what a deal of brine	
	Hath washed thy sallow cheeks for Rosaline.	70
	How much salt water thrown away in waste,	
	To season love, that of it doth not taste.	
	The sun not yet thy sighs from heaven clears,	
	Thy old groans yet ringing in my ancient ears.	
	Lo, here upon thy cheek the stain doth sit	75
	Of an old tear that is not washed off yet.	
	If e'er thou wast thyself and these woes thine,	
	Thou and these woes were all for Rosaline.	
	And art thou changed? Pronounce this sentence then:	
	Women may fall, when there's no strength in men.	80
Romeo	Thou chid'st me oft for loving Rosaline.	
Friar Laurence	For doting, not for loving, pupil mine.	
Romeo	And bad'st me bury love.	
Friar Laurence	Not in a grave,	
	To lay one in, another out to have.	
Romeo	I pray thee, chide me not. Her I love now	85
	Doth grace for grace and love for love allow.	
	The other did not so.	
Friar Laurence	O, she knew well	
	Thy love did read by rote and could not spell.	
	But come, young waverer, come, go with me,	
	In one respect I'll thy assistant be.	90

Activity 4: Writing a soliloquy for the Friar

a. Read the Friar's speech, lines 89–92.

b. Discuss how you think the Friar feels about Romeo marrying Juliet Capulet.

c. Imagine you are the Friar. Write down and complete the following three sentences on three separate pieces of paper:

   i. a sentence explaining how the Friar feels, beginning 'I feel…'

   ii. a sentence explaining what the Friar wants to say and who he wants to say it to, beginning 'I want to tell…'

   iii. a sentence explaining why the Friar wants to help Romeo and Juliet get married, beginning 'I will help Romeo marry Juliet because…'.

d. In pairs, compare your sentences and combine them in order to create a speech that the Friar might make.

e. How has Activity 4 developed your understanding of the character of the Friar?

Glossary

91 **alliance** a formal, legal agreement through marriage, as well as a love match

92 **rancour** hatred

Friar Laurence and Romeo, 2008

For this alliance may so happy prove,
To turn your households' rancour to pure love.

Romeo   O, let us hence! I stand on sudden haste.

Friar Laurence   Wisely and slow; they stumble that run fast.

Exeunt

Benvolio and Mercutio are wondering what happened to Romeo after the Capulet party. Benvolio says Tybalt has sent a letter to the Montague house challenging Romeo to a duel. Mercutio makes fun of Romeo for being too lovesick to fight Tybalt and describes Tybalt as an excellent sword fighter.

Activity 1: Exploring Tybalt

a. In pairs, read lines 11–14, swapping reader at each punctuation mark.

b. Write a sentence together in your own words that summarises Mercutio's description of Romeo.

c. Create a **freeze-frame** of Romeo as Mercutio describes him.

d. In pairs, read lines 16–21, swapping reader at each punctuation mark.

e. Write a sentence together in your own words that summarises Mercutio's description of Tybalt.

f. Create a freeze-frame of Tybalt as Mercutio describes him.

g. Mercutio asks whether Romeo is 'a man to encounter Tybalt'. Thinking about your two freeze-frames, how do you think Romeo will answer Tybalt's challenge?

h. Write Tybalt's letter to Romeo challenging him to a duel. Include Tybalt's reasons for the challenge (look back at pages 65–67) and what he will do if Romeo doesn't respond.

Glossary

13 **blind bow-boy's butt-shaft** Cupid's arrow

17 **prick-song** written music; Mercutio compares Tybalt's skills in sword fighting with the skill of a musician

Key term

Freeze-frame a physical, still image created by people to represent an object, place, person or feeling

At the time

Using page 268, find out about the skills of sword fighting in Shakespeare's time to help you with the activity on this page.

Benvolio and Mercutio, 2008

Act 2 | Scene 4

Enter Benvolio and Mercutio

Mercutio Where the devil should this Romeo be?
Came he not home tonight?

Benvolio Not to his father's, I spoke with his man.

Mercutio Why, that same pale hard-hearted wench, that Rosaline,
Torments him so, that he will sure run mad.   5

Benvolio Tybalt, the kinsman to old Capulet,
Hath sent a letter to his father's house.

Mercutio A challenge, on my life.

Benvolio   Romeo will answer it.

Mercutio Any man that can write may answer a letter.

Benvolio Nay, he will answer the letter's master, how he dares, being dared.   10

Mercutio Alas, poor Romeo, he is already dead, stabbed with a white
wench's black eye, run through the ear with a love-song, the very
pin of his heart cleft with the blind bow-boy's butt-shaft. And is he
a man to encounter Tybalt?

Benvolio Why, what is Tybalt?   15

Mercutio More than prince of cats. O he's the courageous captain of
compliments. He fights as you sing prick-song, keeps time,
distance and proportion. He rests his minim rests, one, two, and the
third in your bosom, the very butcher of a silk button; a duellist, a
duellist, a gentleman of the very first house, of the first and second   20
cause. Ah, the immortal passado, the punto reverso, the hay!

Benvolio The what?

Mercutio continues to make fun of Tybalt for taking himself too seriously and Romeo for being in love. When Romeo arrives, he and Mercutio joke with each other about what Romeo may have been up to the night before.

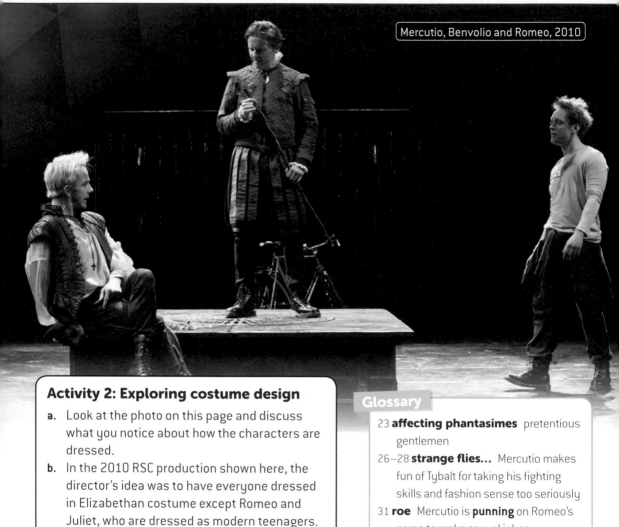

Mercutio, Benvolio and Romeo, 2010

Activity 2: Exploring costume design

a. Look at the photo on this page and discuss what you notice about how the characters are dressed.
b. In the 2010 RSC production shown here, the director's idea was to have everyone dressed in Elizabethan costume except Romeo and Juliet, who are dressed as modern teenagers. This production included **anachronisms** like Romeo riding a bike and Juliet eating a chocolate bar. How do you think the director's idea might affect what the audience thinks about Romeo in this scene?
c. Why do you think the director made this decision? What might it say about the characters of Romeo and Juliet?

Glossary

23 **affecting phantasimes** pretentious gentlemen
26–28 **strange flies...** Mercutio makes fun of Tybalt for taking his fighting skills and fashion sense too seriously
31 **roe** Mercutio is **punning** on Romeo's name to make sexual jokes
32–35 **Petrarch...** Mercutio mentions love stories that involve suicide

Key terms

Anachronism something wrongly placed in the time period represented
Pun a play on words

Mercutio	The pox of such antic, lisping, affecting phantasimes, these new tuners of accent. Jesu, a very good blade, a very tall man, a very good whore. Why, is not this a lamentable thing, grandsire, that we should be thus afflicted with these strange flies, these fashion-mongers, these 'pardon-me's', who stand so much on the new form, that they cannot sit at ease on the old bench? O their bones, their bones!

25

Enter Romeo

Benvolio	Here comes Romeo, here comes Romeo.

30

Mercutio	Without his roe, like a dried herring. O flesh, flesh, how art thou fishified! Now is he for the numbers that Petrarch flowed in, Laura to his lady was a kitchen-wench, marry, she had a better love to berhyme her. Dido a dowdy, Cleopatra a gypsy, Helen and Hero hildings and harlots. Thisbe a grey eye or so, but not to the purpose. Signior Romeo, bon jour! There's a French salutation to your French slop. You gave us the counterfeit fairly last night.

35

Romeo	Good morrow to you both. What counterfeit did I give you?
Mercutio	The slip, sir, the slip, can you not conceive?
Romeo	Pardon, good Mercutio, my business was great, and in such a case as mine a man may strain courtesy.

40

Mercutio	That's as much as to say, such a case as yours constrains a man to bow in the hams.
Romeo	Meaning, to curtsy.
Mercutio	Thou hast most kindly hit it.

45

Romeo	A most courteous exposition.
Mercutio	Nay, I am the very pink of courtesy.
Romeo	Pink for flower.
Mercutio	Right.
Romeo	Why then is my pump well flowered.

50

Mercutio and Romeo continue their friendly **banter**. Mercutio is delighted that Romeo seems more like his old self again rather than always thinking about Rosaline.

Romeo and Mercutio, 2010

Activity 3: Exploring banter

Mercutio and Romeo continue their jokey dialogue using cultural references Shakespeare's audience would have understood and found funny. It is hard now to understand all these references, just as Shakespeare would find it very hard to understand our conversations with friends, but we can still get a sense of the playfulness of their conversation.

a. In pairs, read lines 56–70 with one of you playing Mercutio and the other playing Romeo.

b. Now read the lines again, but this time the person playing Romeo holds an object as they speak the first line, such as a water bottle or pencil case. When the person playing Mercutio speaks, they snatch the object away from Romeo. Continue the lines, grabbing the object from each other each time you speak a line.

c. Discuss how you think Romeo and Mercutio feel at this point and what mood their words and actions might create.

d. Create a freeze-frame of Mercutio and Romeo for line 70.

e. Write a paragraph about the depth of friendship that exists between Mercutio and Romeo.

Glossary

56 **Switch and spurs** Romeo is enjoying the exchange of verbal wit and encouraging Mercutio to continue

57 **wild-goose** Mercutio and Romeo play around with the idea that geese are stupid and 'goose' is a name for a prostitute

72 **natural** idiot; fool

Key term

Banter playful dialogue where the speakers verbally score points off each other

Mercutio   Sure wit, follow me this jest now till thou hast worn out thy pump, that when the single sole of it is worn, the jest may remain after the wearing sole singular.

Romeo   O single-soled jest, solely singular for the singleness.

Mercutio   Come between us, good Benvolio, my wits faints.   55

Romeo   Switch and spurs, switch and spurs, or I'll cry a match.

Mercutio   Nay, if our wits run the wild-goose chase, I am done, for thou hast more of the wild-goose in one of thy wits than I am sure I have in my whole five. Was I with you there for the goose?

Romeo   Thou wast never with me for any thing when thou wast not there   60
for the goose.

Mercutio   I will bite thee by the ear for that jest.

Romeo   Nay, good goose, bite not.

Mercutio   Thy wit is a very bitter sweeting: it is a most sharp sauce.

Romeo   And is it not then well served into a sweet goose?   65

Mercutio   O here's a wit of cheverel, that stretches from an inch narrow to an ell broad.

Romeo   I stretch it out for that word 'broad', which added to the goose, proves thee far and wide a broad goose.

Mercutio   Why, is not this better now than groaning for love? Now art thou   70
sociable, now art thou Romeo, now art thou what thou art, by art
as well as by nature. For this drivelling love is like a great natural,
that runs lolling up and down to hide his bauble in a hole.

Benvolio   Stop there, stop there.

Mercutio   Thou desirest me to stop in my tale against the hair.   75

Benvolio   Thou wouldst else have made thy tale large.

Mercutio   O, thou art deceived. I would have made it short, for I was come
to the whole depth of my tale, and meant indeed to occupy the
argument no longer.

The Nurse arrives, accompanied by Peter. She is looking for Romeo but Mercutio enjoys involving her in his banter.

Mercutio and the Nurse, 2010

Activity 4: Exploring a character's thoughts and feelings

Peter says very little but was a popular character with the audience in Shakespeare's time. As you go through the following tasks, think about how best to use Peter to engage the audience.

a. In groups of four or five, decide who will play the Nurse, Peter, Romeo, Mercutio and, if you have five, Benvolio. Read aloud lines 80–101 in your groups.

b. To help you understand more about the characters, their relationships and their motives, read lines 80–101 again. This time, as you speak and listen, you should keep choosing between the following movements:

- Take a step towards another character.
- Take a step away from another character.
- Turn towards another character.
- Turn away from another character.
- Stand still.

Try to make instinctive choices rather than planning what to do.

c. Discuss as a group:
   i. your understanding of the characters in this section
   ii. which decisions worked best in task b to make the scene engaging for the audience.

d. Write a paragraph describing the events in lines 80–101 from the point of view of the character you played.

Glossary

80 **goodly gear** new material for jokes

93 **mar** spoil

103 **bawd** a hare, but also a pimp

105 **Lenten pie** a pie that should have no meat inside because Lent is a time for fasting

Did you know?

Often characters are present in scenes but do not have lines to speak. When we stage a play we realise how important these characters are as their behaviour and reactions help develop the themes and relationships of the play. It can be interesting to consider why a character might be present in a scene but not speak.

Enter Nurse and Peter

Romeo	Here's goodly gear. A sail, a sail!	80
Mercutio	Two, two: a shirt and a smock.	
Nurse	Peter?	
Peter	Anon.	
Nurse	My fan, Peter.	
Mercutio	Good Peter, to hide her face, for her fan's the fairer face.	85
Nurse	God ye good morrow, gentlemen.	
Mercutio	God ye good e'en, fair gentlewoman.	
Nurse	Is it good e'en?	
Mercutio	'Tis no less, I tell you, for the bawdy hand of the dial is now upon the prick of noon.	90
Nurse	Out upon you! What a man are you?	
Romeo	One, gentlewoman, that God hath made himself to mar.	
Nurse	By my troth, it is well said, 'for himself to mar', quoth a. Gentlemen, can any of you tell me where I may find the young Romeo?	95
Romeo	I can tell you, but young Romeo will be older when you have found him than he was when you sought him. I am the youngest of that name, for fault of a worse.	
Nurse	You say well.	
Mercutio	Yea, is the worst well? Very well took, i'faith, wisely, wisely.	100
Nurse	If you be he, sir, I desire some confidence with you.	
Benvolio	She will indite him to some supper.	
Mercutio	A bawd, a bawd, a bawd! So ho.	
Romeo	What hast thou found?	
Mercutio	No hare, sir, unless a hare, sir, in a Lenten pie, that is something stale and hoar ere it be spent.	105

Mercutio sings a rude song, continuing to make fun of the Nurse. After Mercutio and Benvolio leave, the Nurse tells Romeo she has come as a messenger from Juliet.

The Nurse and Peter, 2008

Activity 5: Exploring Peter

Look at Peter's lines 126–129 and at the photo on this page. Thinking also about the lines on page 109, how would you describe the relationship between Peter and the Nurse?

Did you know?

Often the words we don't understand in Shakespeare's text are 16th-century slang words – just as Shakespeare would not understand the slang we use today. An actor needs to research what the words used to mean. Once the actors understand the meaning of the words, they can convey that to the audience through tone and gesture.

(Singing) An old hare hoar,
    And an old hare hoar,
    Is very good meat in Lent.
    But a hare that is hoar 110
    Is too much for a score,
    When it hoars ere it be spent.

Romeo, will you come to your father's? We'll to dinner thither.

Romeo I will follow you.

Mercutio Farewell, ancient lady, farewell, lady, lady, lady. 115

Exeunt Mercutio, Benvolio

Nurse I pray you, sir, what saucy merchant was this that was so full of
his ropery?

Romeo A gentleman, nurse, that loves to hear himself talk, and will speak
more in a minute than he will stand to in a month.

Nurse And a speak anything against me, I'll take him down, and a were 120
lustier than he is, and twenty such Jacks, and if I cannot, I'll find
those that shall. Scurvy knave, I am none of his flirt-gills, I am
none of his skains-mates.

(To Peter) And thou must stand by too, and suffer every knave to
use me at his pleasure? 125

Peter I saw no man use you at his pleasure. If I had, my weapon should
quickly have been out, I warrant you. I dare draw as soon as
another man, if I see occasion in a good quarrel, and the law on
my side.

Nurse Now, afore God, I am so vexed that every part about me quivers. 130
Scurvy knave!

(To Romeo) Pray you, sir, a word, and as I told you, my young lady
bid me inquire you out. What she bid me say, I will keep to myself.
But first let me tell ye, if ye should lead her in a fool's paradise,
as they say, it were a very gross kind of behaviour, as they say, 135
for the gentlewoman is young, and therefore, if you should deal

Romeo asks the Nurse to tell Juliet to go to Friar Laurence's chapel that afternoon where he will meet her and marry her. Romeo then tells the Nurse to wait for his servant, who will bring a rope ladder for the Nurse to take home so that Romeo can climb up to Juliet's bedroom later that night.

The Nurse and Romeo, 2008

Activity 6: Exploring the theme of family

a. In pairs, read lines 130–138, swapping reader at each punctuation mark.
b. Now one of you plays the Nurse and reads the lines, while the other plays Romeo. Try two different versions of these lines.
   i. Read lines 130–138 as if the Nurse has enjoyed the banter and is continuing the jokey tone with Romeo, while Romeo listens and encourages her with smiles and nods.
   ii. Read lines 130–138 as if the Nurse was upset by the banter and is warning Romeo not to treat Juliet so badly. This time Romeo listens and shows he is sorry for the jokes and is serious about Juliet.
c. Discuss which version you think worked best in task b and why.
d. What do you think the Nurse's encounter with Romeo tells us about her relationship with the Capulet family?

Glossary

147 and 149 **shrift/ shrived** confession/ confessed

double with her, truly it were an ill thing to be offered to any
gentlewoman, and very weak dealing.

Romeo   Nurse, commend me to thy lady and mistress. I protest unto
thee—   140

Nurse   Good heart, and i'faith I will tell her as much. Lord, Lord, she will
be a joyful woman.

Romeo   What wilt thou tell her, nurse? Thou dost not mark me.

Nurse   I will tell her, sir, that you do protest, which, as I take it, is a
gentlemanlike offer.   145

Romeo   Bid her devise
Some means to come to shrift this afternoon,
And there she shall at Friar Laurence' cell
Be shrived and married. Here is for thy pains.

Nurse   No truly, sir, not a penny.   150

Romeo   Go to, I say you shall.

Nurse   This afternoon, sir? Well, she shall be there.

Romeo   And stay, good nurse, behind the abbey wall,
Within this hour, my man shall be with thee
And bring thee cords made like a tackled stair,   155
Which to the high top-gallant of my joy
Must be my convoy in the secret night.
Farewell, be trusty and I'll quit thy pains.
Farewell, commend me to thy mistress.

Nurse   Now God in heaven bless thee! Hark you, sir.   160

Romeo   What say'st thou, my dear nurse?

Nurse   Is your man secret? Did you ne'er hear say,
'Two may keep counsel, putting one away'?

Romeo   Warrant thee, my man's as true as steel.

Nurse   Well, sir, my mistress is the sweetest lady –   165
Lord, lord, lord! When 'twas a little prating thing –

The Nurse talks of how Romeo and rosemary both begin with the letter R, hinting that rosemary is a herb **symbolising** faithfulness and remembrance. Then she leaves with Peter.

The Nurse, 2010

Activity 7: Exploring the theme of love

a. In pairs, read aloud the Nurse's lines 165–175, swapping reader at each punctuation mark.

b. Imagine Juliet spoke to the Nurse after talking to Romeo in Act 2 Scene 2 and convinced the Nurse to meet him the next day. In pairs, improvise the conversation between Juliet and the Nurse. The Nurse begins with the line: 'What were you doing out on the balcony at this time of night?' At some point, the Nurse should include the question: 'And what about Paris?'

c. What ideas about love came up in your improvisation for task b? How did you develop the characters of the Nurse and Juliet?

d. How has task b developed your understanding of the relationship between Juliet and the Nurse, particularly in terms of the key themes of loyalty and love?

Did you know?

Actors sometimes find it useful to improvise an offstage scene, like the one suggested on this page. These are scenes that we assume could have taken place because a character refers to them in some way. For example, Juliet must have spoken to the Nurse about Romeo and asked her to meet him the next morning.

O, there is a nobleman in town, one Paris,
That would fain lay knife aboard, but she, good soul,
Had as lief see a toad, a very toad,
As see him. I anger her sometimes   170
And tell her that Paris is the properer man,
But, I'll warrant you, when I say so, she looks
As pale as any clout in the versal world.
Doth not rosemary and Romeo begin
Both with a letter?   175

Romeo   Ay, nurse, what of that? Both with an R.

Nurse   Ah, mocker! That's the dog's name. R is for the – no, I know
it begins with some other letter – and she hath the prettiest
sententious of it, of you and rosemary, that it would do you good
to hear it.   180

Romeo   Commend me to thy lady.

Nurse   Ay, a thousand times. Peter?

Peter   Anon.

Nurse   Before and apace.

Exeunt

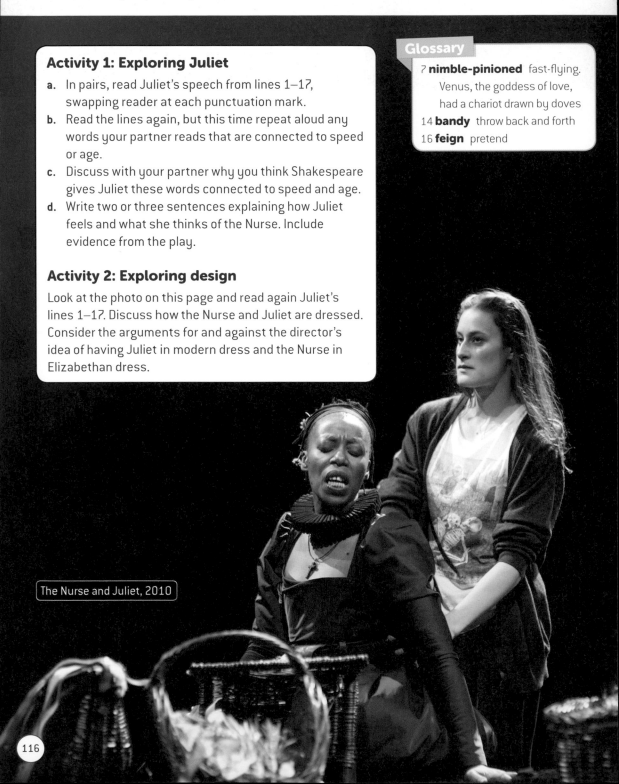

Activity 1: Exploring Juliet

a. In pairs, read Juliet's speech from lines 1–17, swapping reader at each punctuation mark.

b. Read the lines again, but this time repeat aloud any words your partner reads that are connected to speed or age.

c. Discuss with your partner why you think Shakespeare gives Juliet these words connected to speed and age.

d. Write two or three sentences explaining how Juliet feels and what she thinks of the Nurse. Include evidence from the play.

Activity 2: Exploring design

Look at the photo on this page and read again Juliet's lines 1–17. Discuss how the Nurse and Juliet are dressed. Consider the arguments for and against the director's idea of having Juliet in modern dress and the Nurse in Elizabethan dress.

Glossary

7 **nimble-pinioned** fast-flying. Venus, the goddess of love, had a chariot drawn by doves

14 **bandy** throw back and forth

16 **feign** pretend

The Nurse and Juliet, 2010

Act 2 | Scene 5

Enter Juliet

Juliet The clock struck nine when I did send the nurse.
In half an hour she promised to return.
Perchance she cannot meet him? That's not so.
O she is lame! Love's herald should be thoughts,
Which ten times faster glides than the sun's beams,　　　　5
Driving back shadows over louring hills.
Therefore do nimble-pinioned doves draw love,
And therefore hath the wind-swift Cupid wings.
Now is the sun upon the highmost hill
Of this day's journey, and from nine till twelve　　　　10
Is three long hours, yet she is not come.
Had she affections and warm youthful blood,
She would be as swift in motion as a ball.
My words would bandy her to my sweet love,
And his to me.　　　　15
But old folks, many feign as they were dead,
Unwieldy, slow, heavy and pale as lead.

Enter Nurse and Peter

O God, she comes. O honey nurse, what news?
Hast thou met with him? Send thy man away.

Nurse Peter, stay at the gate.　　　　20

Exit Peter

Juliet Now, good sweet nurse – O lord, why look'st thou sad?
Though news be sad, yet tell them merrily.
If good, thou sham'st the music of sweet news
By playing it to me with so sour a face.

The Nurse teases Juliet, complaining about having a headache, a backache and being tired after going out to find Romeo. Juliet tries to be sympathetic but is impatient to hear what Romeo said.

The Nurse and Juliet, 2006

Activity 3: Exploring tactics

a. In pairs, read lines 21–37 with one of you playing Juliet and the other playing the Nurse.

b. Read the lines again, but this time the Nurse keeps trying to get away from Juliet, while Juliet keeps trying to stop the Nurse and get the Nurse to look at her. How might this make Juliet feel?

c. Now read lines 43–53, playing the same characters.

d. Read lines 43–53 again with Juliet trying out different **tactics** to get the Nurse to tell her about Romeo. For example, she might flatter her, threaten her, or show affection towards her or ignore her.

e. Discuss which tactics you found worked best for tasks b and d, and why.

f. How does Activity 3 develop your understanding of the characters of Juliet and the Nurse?

Glossary

26 **jaunt** tiring journey
43 **warrant** guarantee
50 **Beshrew** curse

Key term

Tactics the methods a character uses to get what they want, e.g. Juliet might flatter the Nurse or threaten her

118

Nurse   I am aweary, give me leave awhile.   25
          Fie, how my bones ache. What a jaunt have I had!

Juliet   I would thou had'st my bones, and I thy news.
          Nay, come, I pray thee speak, good, good nurse, speak.

Nurse   Jesu, what haste? Can you not stay awhile?
          Do you not see that I am out of breath?   30

Juliet   How art thou out of breath, when thou hast breath
          To say to me that thou art out of breath?
          The excuse that thou dost make in this delay
          Is longer than the tale thou dost excuse.
          Is thy news good or bad? Answer to that.   35
          Say either, and I'll stay the circumstance.
          Let me be satisfied, is't good or bad?

Nurse   Well, you have made a simple choice, you know not how to
          choose a man. Romeo? No, not he – though his face be better
          than any man's, yet his leg excels all men's, and for a hand and   40
          a foot and a body, though they be not to be talked on, yet they
          are past compare. He is not the flower of courtesy, but, I'll
          warrant him, as gentle as a lamb. Go thy ways, wench, serve God.
          What, have you dined at home?

Juliet   No, no. But all this did I know before.   45
          What says he of our marriage? What of that?

Nurse   Lord, how my head aches! What a head have I!
          It beats as it would fall in twenty pieces.
          My back o't'other side. O, my back, my back!
          Beshrew your heart for sending me about,   50
          To catch my death with jaunting up and down.

Juliet   I'faith, I am sorry that thou art not well.
          Sweet, sweet, sweet nurse, tell me, what says my love?

Nurse   Your love says, like an honest gentleman, and a courteous, and
          a kind, and a handsome, and, I warrant, a virtuous – Where is   55
          your mother?

The Nurse finally tells Juliet the message from Romeo that she should meet him at Friar Laurence's chapel that afternoon to get married. Meanwhile the Nurse will go and get the rope ladder so that Romeo can climb up to Juliet's bedroom that night.

Activity 4: Writing a soliloquy for the Nurse

a. Read the Nurse's speech, lines 67–76.

b. How do you think the Nurse feels about Juliet marrying Romeo Montague?

c. Imagine you are the Nurse. Write and complete the following three sentences in modern English on three separate pieces of paper:
   i. a sentence explaining how the Nurse feels, beginning 'I feel…'
   ii. a sentence explaining what the Nurse wants to say and who she wants to say it to, beginning 'I want to tell…'
   iii. a sentence explaining why the Nurse is helping Juliet to marry Romeo, beginning 'I am helping Juliet to marry Romeo because…'.

d. In pairs, compare your sentences and combine them in order to create a speech that the Nurse would make at this point in the play.

e. How has Activity 4 developed your understanding of the character of the Nurse?

The Nurse and Juliet, 2008

Glossary

62 **poultice** a mix of herbs applied to soothe a pain

64 **coil** fuss

69 **wanton** unrestrained

76 **Hie** hurry

Juliet   Where is my mother? Why, she is within,
　　　　Where should she be? How oddly thou repliest:
　　　　'Your love says, like an honest gentleman,
　　　　"Where is your mother?"'

Nurse　　　　　　　　　O God's lady dear!　　　　　　60
　　　　Are you so hot? Marry, come up, I trow.
　　　　Is this the poultice for my aching bones?
　　　　Henceforward do your messages yourself.

Juliet   Here's such a coil! Come, what says Romeo?

Nurse   Have you got leave to go to shrift today?　　　　65

Juliet   I have.

Nurse   Then hie you hence to Friar Laurence' cell,
　　　　There stays a husband to make you a wife.
　　　　Now comes the wanton blood up in your cheeks,
　　　　They'll be in scarlet straight at any news.　　　　70
　　　　Hie you to church, I must another way,
　　　　To fetch a ladder, by the which your love
　　　　Must climb a bird's nest soon when it is dark.
　　　　I am the drudge and toil in your delight,
　　　　But you shall bear the burden soon at night.　　　　75
　　　　Go, I'll to dinner. Hie you to the cell.

Juliet   Hie to high fortune. Honest nurse, farewell.

　　　　Exeunt

Romeo is waiting with Friar Laurence for Juliet at the chapel. Juliet arrives ready to marry Romeo.

Activity 1: Exploring Romeo

a. In pairs, read Romeo's speech from lines 3–8, swapping reader at each punctuation mark.

b. Read the speech again and then, in pairs, create gestures for the key words in each line. For example, for 'cannot countervail' you might spread your hands and show you are weighing up two ideas, and then on 'joy' show how one side far outweighs the other.

c. What do you think Romeo is thinking about as he says these lines?

Glossary

2 **chide** scold

4 **countervail** counterbalance

17 **everlasting flint** hard-wearing cobbles

21 **ghostly confessor** spiritual father; priest

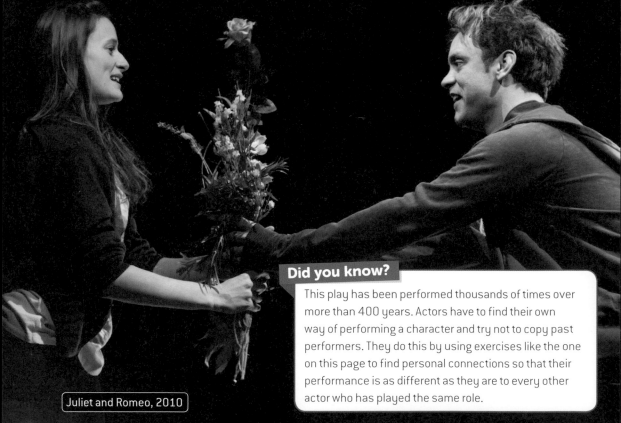

Juliet and Romeo, 2010

Did you know?

This play has been performed thousands of times over more than 400 years. Actors have to find their own way of performing a character and try not to copy past performers. They do this by using exercises like the one on this page to find personal connections so that their performance is as different as they are to every other actor who has played the same role.

Enter Friar Laurence and Romeo

Friar Laurence So smile the heavens upon this holy act,
That after-hours with sorrow chide us not.

Romeo Amen, amen. But come what sorrow can,
It cannot countervail the exchange of joy
That one short minute gives me in her sight.   5
Do thou but close our hands with holy words,
Then love-devouring Death do what he dare,
It is enough I may but call her mine.

Friar Laurence These violent delights have violent ends,
And in their triumph die, like fire and powder,   10
Which as they kiss consume. The sweetest honey
Is loathsome in his own deliciousness,
And in the taste confounds the appetite:
Therefore love moderately, long love doth so;
Too swift arrives as tardy as too slow.   15

Enter Juliet

Here comes the lady. O, so light a foot
Will ne'er wear out the everlasting flint:
A lover may bestride the gossamers
That idles in the wanton summer air,
And yet not fall, so light is vanity.   20

Juliet Good even to my ghostly confessor.

Friar Laurence Romeo shall thank thee, daughter, for us both.

Juliet As much to him, else is his thanks too much.

Romeo Ah, Juliet, if the measure of thy joy
Be heaped like mine, and that thy skill be more   25

Romeo and Juliet are both impatient to be married. The Friar leads them into the church to conduct the ceremony.

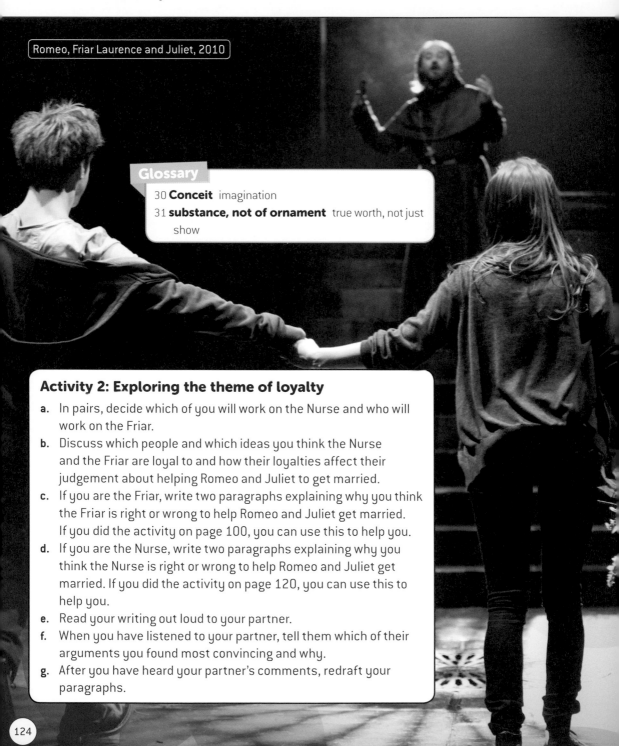

Romeo, Friar Laurence and Juliet, 2010

Glossary

30 **Conceit** imagination
31 **substance, not of ornament** true worth, not just show

Activity 2: Exploring the theme of loyalty

a. In pairs, decide which of you will work on the Nurse and who will work on the Friar.
b. Discuss which people and which ideas you think the Nurse and the Friar are loyal to and how their loyalties affect their judgement about helping Romeo and Juliet to get married.
c. If you are the Friar, write two paragraphs explaining why you think the Friar is right or wrong to help Romeo and Juliet get married. If you did the activity on page 100, you can use this to help you.
d. If you are the Nurse, write two paragraphs explaining why you think the Nurse is right or wrong to help Romeo and Juliet get married. If you did the activity on page 120, you can use this to help you.
e. Read your writing out loud to your partner.
f. When you have listened to your partner, tell them which of their arguments you found most convincing and why.
g. After you have heard your partner's comments, redraft your paragraphs.

To blazon it, then sweeten with thy breath
This neighbour air, and let rich music's tongue
Unfold the imagined happiness that both
Receive in either by this dear encounter.

Juliet   Conceit, more rich in matter than in words,   30
Brags of his substance, not of ornament.
They are but beggars that can count their worth,
But my true love is grown to such excess
I cannot sum up sum of half my wealth.

Friar Laurence   Come, come with me, and we will make short work,   35
For, by your leaves, you shall not stay alone
Till holy church incorporate two in one.

Exeunt

Activity 1: Exploring the story

a. In groups, look back through Act 2 and agree on three moments that seem the most important. Looking at the page summaries may help you.

b. Choose one or two lines of text for each of your three moments.

c. Create three freeze-frames, showing each of your moments and include a way of speaking your chosen lines of text aloud in your freeze-frames.

d. Record your freeze-frames by photographing, drawing or describing them. Give each one your chosen line as a title.

e. Explain:
   i. why you feel the three moments you chose are the most important
   ii. why you chose the lines of text for each of your three moments
   iii. how your freeze-frame shows your chosen moments and lines effectively.

Juliet, Friar Laurence and Romeo, 2006

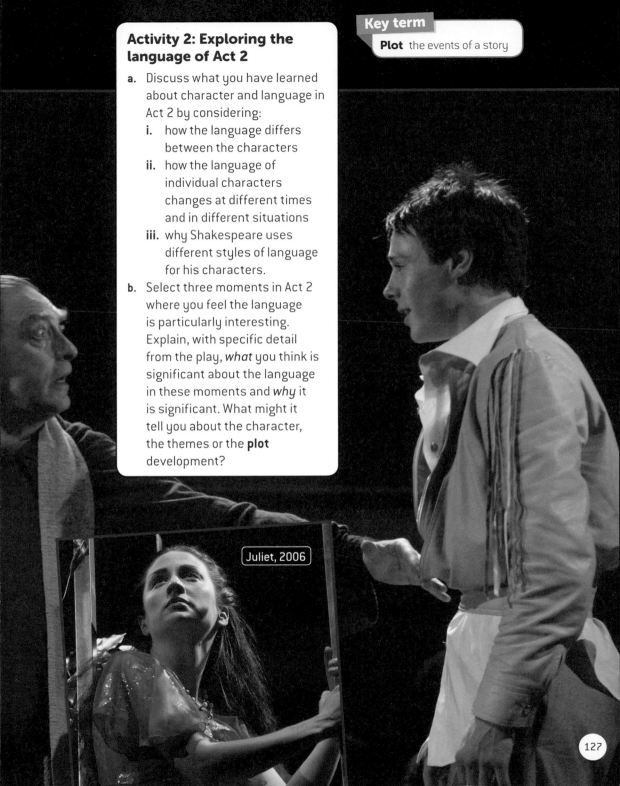

Activity 2: Exploring the language of Act 2

a. Discuss what you have learned about character and language in Act 2 by considering:
  i. how the language differs between the characters
  ii. how the language of individual characters changes at different times and in different situations
  iii. why Shakespeare uses different styles of language for his characters.

b. Select three moments in Act 2 where you feel the language is particularly interesting. Explain, with specific detail from the play, *what* you think is significant about the language in these moments and *why* it is significant. What might it tell you about the character, the themes or the **plot** development?

Juliet, 2006

Mercutio and Benvolio are out on the streets of Verona. Benvolio comments on how hot it is and how they should go home before they meet any Capulets and get into a fight. Mercutio says that Benvolio shouldn't criticise others for starting fights when he is usually the one to start them.

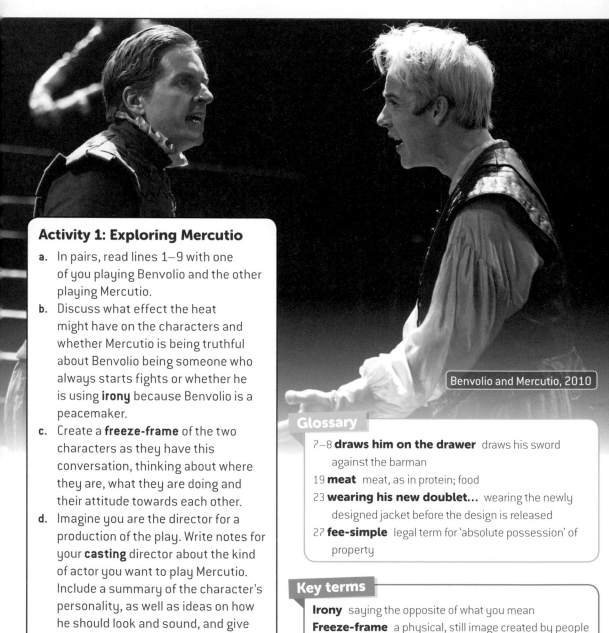

Benvolio and Mercutio, 2010

Activity 1: Exploring Mercutio

a. In pairs, read lines 1–9 with one of you playing Benvolio and the other playing Mercutio.

b. Discuss what effect the heat might have on the characters and whether Mercutio is being truthful about Benvolio being someone who always starts fights or whether he is using **irony** because Benvolio is a peacemaker.

c. Create a **freeze-frame** of the two characters as they have this conversation, thinking about where they are, what they are doing and their attitude towards each other.

d. Imagine you are the director for a production of the play. Write notes for your **casting** director about the kind of actor you want to play Mercutio. Include a summary of the character's personality, as well as ideas on how he should look and sound, and give examples of famous actors who could play your Mercutio.

Glossary

7–8 **draws him on the drawer** draws his sword against the barman

19 **meat** meat, as in protein; food

23 **wearing his new doublet...** wearing the newly designed jacket before the design is released

27 **fee-simple** legal term for 'absolute possession' of property

Key terms

Irony saying the opposite of what you mean

Freeze-frame a physical, still image created by people to represent an object, place, person or feeling

Casting deciding which actors should play which roles

Act 3 | Scene 1

Enter Mercutio, Benvolio and others

Benvolio   I pray thee, good Mercutio, let's retire.
The day is hot, the Capulets abroad,
And if we meet, we shall not scape a brawl,
For now, these hot days, is the mad blood stirring.

Mercutio   Thou art like one of these fellows that when he enters the confines   5
of a tavern, claps me his sword upon the table and says 'God send
me no need of thee.' And by the operation of the second cup draws
him on the drawer, when indeed there is no need.

Benvolio   Am I like such a fellow?

Mercutio   Come, come, thou art as hot a Jack in thy mood as any in Italy,   10
and as soon moved to be moody, and as soon moody to be moved.

Benvolio   And what to?

Mercutio   Nay, and there were two such, we should have none shortly, for
one would kill the other. Thou, why, thou wilt quarrel with a man
that hath a hair more or a hair less in his beard than thou hast.   15
Thou wilt quarrel with a man for cracking nuts, having no other
reason but because thou hast hazel eyes. What eye but such an
eye would spy out such a quarrel? Thy head is as full of quarrels
as an egg is full of meat, and yet thy head hath been beaten as
addle as an egg for quarrelling. Thou hast quarrelled with a man   20
for coughing in the street, because he hath wakened thy dog that
hath lain asleep in the sun. Didst thou not fall out with a tailor
for wearing his new doublet before Easter? With another for tying
his new shoes with old ribbon? And yet thou wilt tutor me from
quarrelling?   25

Benvolio   And I were so apt to quarrel as thou art, any man should buy the
fee-simple of my life for an hour and a quarter.

Mercutio   The fee-simple? O, simple!

Tybalt arrives, along with his followers, looking for Romeo. Mercutio gets into an argument with him and draws his sword. Benvolio tries to calm them down. Romeo arrives and Tybalt turns to him and deliberately insults him.

Tybalt, Romeo and Mercutio, 2010

Glossary

39 **minstrels** musicians
49 **livery** uniform
50 **go before to field** lead the way to the duelling ground
53 **villain** scoundrel; peasant (a serious insult)
55 **appertaining rage** appropriate anger

Activity 2: Exploring mood

a. In groups, cast yourselves as Mercutio, Benvolio, Tybalt and Tybalt's follower(s). Read aloud lines 29–47.

b. In your groups, create two freeze-frames: one for line 29 and one for line 47.

c. Working together, choose one line from lines 29–47 for Tybalt to speak, one line for Mercutio and one line for Benvolio.

d. Create a performance of lines 29–47 that begins with the first freeze-frame, comes to life with the lines spoken by each character and ends on the second freeze-frame.

e. From this last freeze-frame, each character (including Tybalt's followers) speaks aloud their thoughts about the situation.

f. With your group, discuss how you would describe the mood of this moment and which words and actions are most important in creating that mood.

g. Write a paragraph summarising your discussion about the mood.

Did you know?

Actors guide the audience emotionally through the play and use changes in **tone** and **body language** to help the audience understand shifts in mood.

Key terms

Tone as in 'tone of voice'; expressing an attitude through how you say something

Body language how we communicate feelings to each other using our bodies (including facial expressions) rather than words

Enter Tybalt with others

Benvolio By my head, here comes the Capulets.

Mercutio By my heel, I care not.   30

Tybalt Follow me close, for I will speak to them.
Gentlemen, good e'en, a word with one of you.

Mercutio And but one word with one of us? Couple it with something,
make it a word and a blow.

Tybalt You shall find me apt enough to that, sir, and you will give me   35
occasion.

Mercutio Could you not take some occasion without giving?

Tybalt Mercutio, thou consort'st with Romeo—

Mercutio Consort? What, dost thou make us minstrels? And thou make
minstrels of us, look to hear nothing but discords. Here's my   40
fiddlestick; here's that shall make you dance. Zounds, consort!

Benvolio We talk here in the public haunt of men.
Either withdraw unto some private place,
Or reason coldly of your grievances,
Or else depart. Here all eyes gaze on us.   45

Mercutio Men's eyes were made to look, and let them gaze.
I will not budge for no man's pleasure, I.

Enter Romeo

Tybalt Well, peace be with you, sir, here comes my man.

Mercutio But I'll be hanged, sir, if he wear your livery.
Marry, go before to field, he'll be your follower.   50
Your worship in that sense may call him man.

Tybalt Romeo, the love I bear thee can afford
No better term than this: thou art a villain.

Romeo Tybalt, the reason that I have to love thee
Doth much excuse the appertaining rage   55
To such a greeting. Villain am I none.
Therefore farewell, I see thou know'st me not.

Romeo tries to make peace with Tybalt, knowing that Tybalt is now his cousin through his marriage to Juliet. Mercutio is amazed at how Romeo behaves and offers to fight Tybalt himself. Tybalt accepts and they fight. Romeo tries to stop them but, because he gets in the way, Tybalt stabs Mercutio. Tybalt runs off.

Tybalt, Romeo and Mercutio, 2006

Glossary

58 **Boy** This is a serious insult

66 **Alla stoccado** 'at the thrust', a fencing term

71–72 **out of his pilcher by the ears** out of its case without ceremony

76 **passado** This is another fencing term

Activity 3: Exploring the theme of loyalty

a. In groups, decide who will be Mercutio, Tybalt, Romeo, Benvolio and Tybalt's follower(s). Read aloud lines 52–83.

b. Pick out any words, such as 'villain', that seem to be insults. Try saying these words to each other as though they are the most insulting things you can say to someone.

c. Discuss who or what you think each character is loyal to.

d. Look through the lines again and reduce the scene to just 12 words. These 12 words can come from anywhere in lines 52–83 and can be next to each other.

e. In your group, create a performance of this moment in the play using only your 12 words, accompanied by actions and **gestures**. Make sure that your words and actions tell the story of what happens clearly and that everyone in the scene responds to the words and actions of the other characters.

f. Discuss who you think is to blame for the fight. How could any of the characters have behaved differently? How do you think the characters' loyalties affect what happens in this fight?

Did you know?

An onstage fight is carefully **choreographed** by a specialist fight director, whose job is to make sure the fight looks and sounds convincing but that the actors are kept safe and no one gets hurt.

Key terms

Choreograph create a sequence of moves

Theme the main ideas explored in a piece of literature, e.g. the themes of love, loyalty, friendship, family and fate might be considered key themes of *Romeo and Juliet*

Gesture a movement, often using the hands or head, to express a feeling or idea

Tybalt   Boy, this shall not excuse the injuries
That thou hast done me. Therefore turn and draw.

Romeo   I do protest I never injured thee,   60
But love thee better than thou canst devise
Till thou shalt know the reason of my love.
And so, good Capulet, which name I tender
As dearly as my own, be satisfied.

Mercutio   O calm, dishonourable, vile submission!   65
Alla stoccado carries it away.
Tybalt, you rat-catcher, will you walk?

Tybalt   What wouldst thou have with me?

Mercutio   Good king of cats, nothing but one of your nine lives that I mean
to make bold withal, and as you shall use me hereafter, dry-beat   70
the rest of the eight. Will you pluck your sword out of his pilcher
by the ears? Make haste, lest mine be about your ears ere it
be out.

Tybalt   I am for you.

Romeo   Gentle Mercutio, put thy rapier up.   75

Mercutio   Come, sir, your passado.

Romeo   Draw, Benvolio, beat down their weapons!
Gentlemen, for shame, forbear this outrage!
Tybalt, Mercutio, the Prince expressly hath
Forbid this bandying in Verona streets!   80
Hold, Tybalt! Good Mercutio!

Tybalt stabs Mercutio under Romeo's arm. Exit Tybalt

Mercutio   I am hurt.
A plague o'both the houses I am sped.
Is he gone and hath nothing?

Benvolio   What, art thou hurt?

Mercutio is dying from the stab wound Tybalt gave him. Benvolio helps him away to find a doctor but soon returns with the news that Mercutio is dead. Romeo is horrified that his friend is dead because of him. Tybalt returns.

Activity 4: Exploring Mercutio's death

a. In pairs, read lines 87–93, swapping reader at each punctuation mark.

b. Now one of you reads the lines aloud as the other acts out Mercutio's dying moments. The person reading pauses at each punctuation mark, while the person playing Mercutio repeats the words, adding tone and gesture to what he says.

c. Which line does Mercutio repeat from earlier in the scene in lines 87–93? Who or what do you think he blames and why?

d. Now read Romeo's speech, lines 99–105, swapping reader at each punctuation mark.

e. Who or what do you think Romeo blames for Mercutio's death and why?

f. Mercutio is always a popular character in the play, but he is the first to die. Why do you think Shakespeare kills him off at this point? What effect might his death have on the other characters? What effect might all this have on the audience?

g. How are the play's themes of love, loyalty, family, friendship and fate reflected in Mercutio's death?

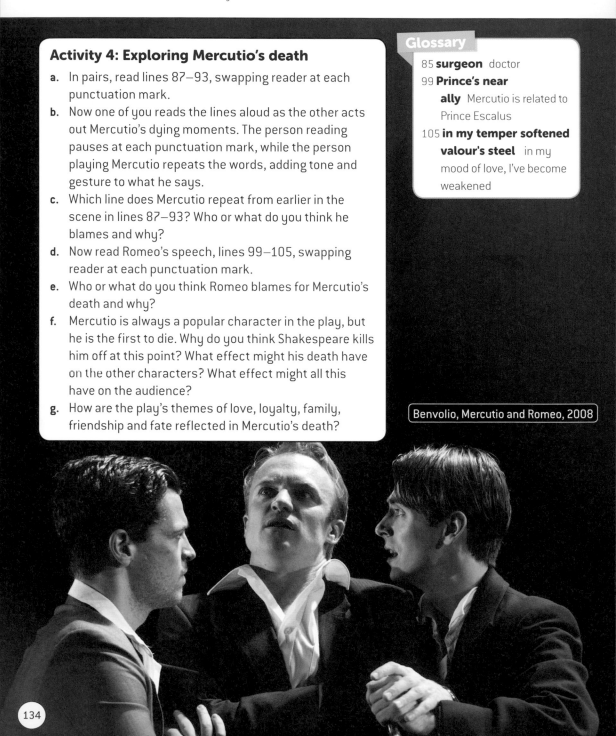

Benvolio, Mercutio and Romeo, 2008

Mercutio   Ay, ay, a scratch, a scratch, marry, 'tis enough.
Where is my page? Go, villain, fetch a surgeon.   85

Romeo   Courage, man, the hurt cannot be much.

Mercutio   No, 'tis not so deep as a well, nor so wide as a church door, but 'tis
enough, 'twill serve. Ask for me tomorrow, and you shall find me
a grave man. I am peppered, I warrant, for this world. A plague
o'both your houses! What, a dog, a rat, a mouse, a cat, to scratch   90
a man to death? A braggart, a rogue, a villain, that fights by the
book of arithmetic! Why the devil came you between us? I was
hurt under your arm.

Romeo   I thought all for the best.

Mercutio   Help me into some house, Benvolio,   95
Or I shall faint. A plague o'both your houses!
They have made worms' meat of me. I have it,
And soundly too. Your houses!

Exeunt Benvolio helping Mercutio

Romeo   This gentleman, the Prince's near ally,
My very friend, hath got his mortal hurt   100
In my behalf. My reputation stained
With Tybalt's slander, Tybalt, that an hour
Hath been my cousin. O sweet Juliet,
Thy beauty hath made me effeminate,
And in my temper softened valour's steel.   105

Enter Benvolio

Benvolio   O Romeo, Romeo, brave Mercutio is dead.
That gallant spirit hath aspired the clouds,
Which too untimely here did scorn the earth.

Romeo   This day's black fate on more days doth depend,
This but begins the woe others must end.   110

Enter Tybalt

Benvolio   Here comes the furious Tybalt back again.

Romeo turns on Tybalt. They fight and Romeo kills Tybalt. Benvolio tells Romeo to run away before anyone comes to arrest him. The citizens of Verona arrive and hold Benvolio so that he can explain what has happened to the Prince and to the Montague and Capulet families.

Activity 5: Exploring the theme of fate

a. Look at Romeo's lines 114 and 126. How do you think Romeo feels as he speaks each line?

b. In pairs, create two freeze-frames that include both Romeo and Tybalt: the first showing line 114 and the second showing line 126.

c. How much do you blame Romeo for responding as he does? Discuss why you think Romeo kills Tybalt and what the consequences might be.

Activity 6: Exploring the themes of friendship and loyalty

a. Act 3 Scene 1 brings together the young men of the play with tragic consequences. Discuss how their different personalities contribute to the outcome.

b. How is the theme of loyalty reflected in how the young men behave towards each other?

c. Write a paragraph or two summarising your discussion in Activity 6.

Glossary

113 **respective lenity** considerations of mercy; Romeo pushes away any feelings for Tybalt except revenge

123 **The citizens are up** people are coming to see what's going on

133 **unlucky manage** unfortunate conduct

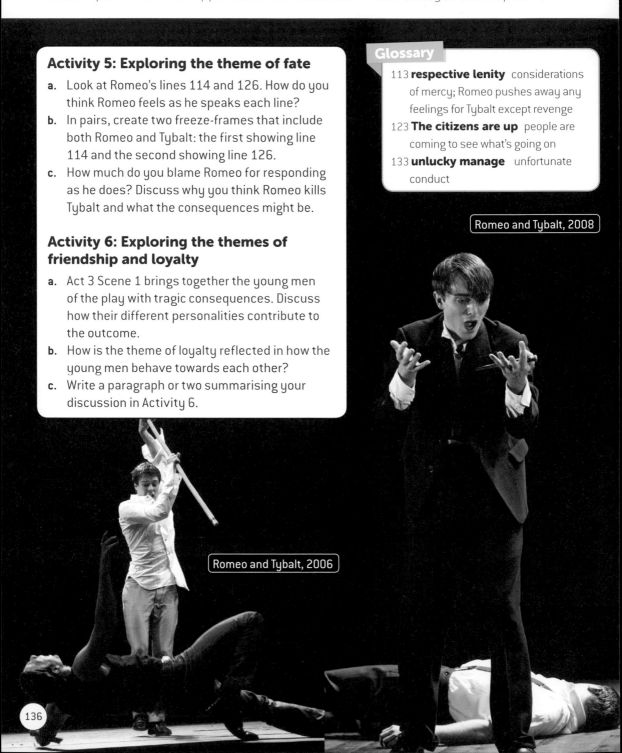

Romeo and Tybalt, 2008

Romeo and Tybalt, 2006

Romeo   He gone in triumph and Mercutio slain?
Away to heaven, respective lenity,
And fire and fury be my conduct now.
Now, Tybalt, take the 'villain' back again   115
That late thou gav'st me. For Mercutio's soul
Is but a little way above our heads,
Staying for thine to keep him company.
Either thou or I, or both, must go with him.

Tybalt   Thou, wretched boy, that didst consort him here,   120
Shalt with him hence.

Romeo   This shall determine that.

They fight. Tybalt falls

Benvolio   Romeo, away, be gone!
The citizens are up, and Tybalt slain.
Stand not amazed, the Prince will doom thee death
If thou art taken. Hence, be gone, away!   125

Romeo   O, I am fortune's fool!

Benvolio   Why dost thou stay?

Exit Romeo. Enter Citizens

Citizen   Which way ran he that killed Mercutio?
Tybalt, that murderer, which way ran he?

Benvolio   There lies that Tybalt.

Citizen   Up, sir, go with me.
I charge thee in the Prince's name, obey.   130

Enter Prince, Lord and Lady Montague, Lord and Lady Capulet,
and Citizens

Prince   Where are the vile beginners of this fray?

Benvolio   O, noble Prince, I can discover all
The unlucky manage of this fatal brawl.

Lady Capulet is horrified at Tybalt's death and demands revenge. Benvolio explains what happened, including how Tybalt started it. Lady Capulet doubts his word and demands that Romeo die.

Tybalt, Lord and Lady Capulet, 200[

Activity 7: Exploring narrative

a. In groups, read lines 142–165, swapping reader for each line.

b. Cast three people in your group as Mercutio, Tybalt and Romeo. The others read the lines aloud, swapping reader for each line. The people playing Mercutio, Romeo and Tybalt should act out what is described as the speech is read.

c. With your group, discuss how truthful you think Benvolio's account is.

d. As a group, pick out five **adjectives** from lines 142–165 and discuss what effect they have on how we understand the action.

e. Now look at how many sentences there are in this speech. Why do you think Benvolio speaks in such long sentences?

f. Why do you think Shakespeare has Benvolio retell us what we have just seen?

g. Imagine you are Benvolio. Write an account of the fight as though you are describing it later to your mother or father when you get home. Write the account in your own words, but choose some of the words and phrases from the original text to include in your writing. Include how you think Benvolio feels about the idea of revenge.

Key term

Adjective a word that describes a noun, e.g. *blue, happy, big*

Glossary

143 **spoke him fair** spoke politely to him
144 **nice** trivial
147 **unruly spleen** fiery temper
148 **tilts** thrusts
151 **martial scorn** military efficiency
159 **stout** brave

	There lies the man, slain by young Romeo,	
	That slew thy kinsman, brave Mercutio.	135

Lady Capulet   Tybalt, my cousin? O my brother's child!
O Prince! O husband! O, the blood is spilled
Of my dear kinsman! Prince, as thou art true,
For blood of ours, shed blood of Montague.
O cousin, cousin!   140

Prince   Benvolio, who began this bloody fray?

Benvolio   Tybalt, here slain, whom Romeo's hand did slay.
Romeo that spoke him fair, bid him bethink
How nice the quarrel was, and urged withal
Your high displeasèd. All this utterèd   145
With gentle breath, calm look, knees humbly bowed,
Could not take truce with the unruly spleen
Of Tybalt, deaf to peace, but that he tilts
With piercing steel at bold Mercutio's breast,
Who, all as hot, turns deadly point to point,   150
And with a martial scorn, with one hand beats
Cold death aside, and with the other sends
It back to Tybalt, whose dexterity
Retorts it. Romeo he cries aloud,
'Hold, friends! Friends, part!' and swifter than his tongue,   155
His agile arm beats down their fatal points,
And 'twixt them rushes, underneath whose arm
An envious thrust from Tybalt hit the life
Of stout Mercutio, and then Tybalt fled.
But by and by comes back to Romeo,   160
Who had but newly entertained revenge,
And to't they go like lightning, for, ere I
Could draw to part them, was stout Tybalt slain.
And as he fell, did Romeo turn and fly.
This is the truth, or let Benvolio die.   165

Lady Capulet   He is a kinsman to the Montague,
Affection makes him false, he speaks not true.
Some twenty of them fought in this black strife,

Lord Montague argues that Romeo carried out justice by killing Tybalt because he killed Mercutio. The Prince announces that Romeo is exiled from Verona and will be killed if he is found in the city.

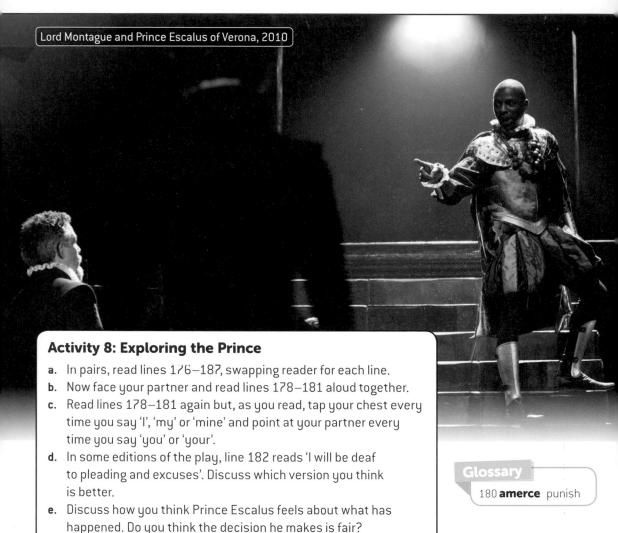

Lord Montague and Prince Escalus of Verona, 2010

Activity 8: Exploring the Prince

a. In pairs, read lines 176–187, swapping reader for each line.

b. Now face your partner and read lines 178–181 aloud together.

c. Read lines 178–181 again but, as you read, tap your chest every time you say 'I', 'my' or 'mine' and point at your partner every time you say 'you' or 'your'.

d. In some editions of the play, line 182 reads 'I will be deaf to pleading and excuses'. Discuss which version you think is better.

e. Discuss how you think Prince Escalus feels about what has happened. Do you think the decision he makes is fair?

f. Which of the play's themes of love, loyalty, family, friendship and fate do you think are reflected in this speech (lines 176–187)?

Activity 9: Exploring the theme of loyalty

Look back through Act 3 Scene 1 to remind yourself of what happens from Romeo's entrance on page 131 to his exit on page 137. How does Romeo feel when he first enters the scene and how does he feel by the time he leaves? How do his loyalties affect this journey?

Glossary

180 **amerce** punish

	And all those twenty could but kill one life.	
	I beg for justice, which thou, Prince, must give:	170
	Romeo slew Tybalt, Romeo must not live.	
Prince	Romeo slew him, he slew Mercutio.	
	Who now the price of his dear blood doth owe?	
Lord Montague	Not Romeo, Prince, he was Mercutio's friend.	
	His fault concludes but what the law should end:	175
	The life of Tybalt.	
Prince	And for that offence	
	Immediately we do exile him hence.	
	I have an interest in your hearts' proceeding,	
	My blood for your rude brawls doth lie a-bleeding.	
	But I'll amerce you with so strong a fine	180
	That you shall all repent the loss of mine.	
	It will be deaf to pleading and excuses,	
	Nor tears nor prayers shall purchase out abuses.	
	Therefore use none. Let Romeo hence in haste,	
	Else, when he is found, that hour is his last.	185
	Bear hence this body and attend our will.	
	Mercy but murders, pardoning those that kill.	

Exeunt

Juliet is waiting in her bedroom, eager for Romeo to arrive so that they can spend their first night together.

Juliet, 2008

Activity 1: Exploring Juliet's soliloquy

a. In pairs, read lines 1–7 aloud together.

b. Next, one of you reads aloud lines 8–13, while the other closes their eyes, listens and repeats any words connected to dark and light, for example, 'see', 'blind'.

c. Now swap roles so that the person who was listening last time reads aloud lines 14–19. The person who was reading last time should now listen with their eyes closed, again repeating any words connected to light and dark.

d. Together, read aloud lines 20–31, creating gestures for the key words in each line.

e. Discuss how Juliet feels as she speaks this **soliloquy**. Which lines best tell you how she feels? How did tasks a–d help you to understand how she feels? How do you think Shakespeare wants his audience to feel as they listen to Juliet?

Glossary

3 **Phaethon** In Greek legend, his father drew the sun across the sky in a chariot, but when Phaethon tried to drive the chariot, he lost control

6 **runaway's eyes** Phaethon's eyes, and anyone else running away in the night

8 **amorous rites** rituals of love-making

12 **lose a winning match** Juliet will lose her virginity but win a husband

14 **unmanned** untrained, another falconry term; without a man

Key term

Soliloquy a speech in which a character is alone on stage and expresses their thoughts and feelings aloud to the audience

Act 3 | Scene 2

Enter Juliet

Juliet   Gallop apace, you fiery-footed steeds,
Towards Phoebus' lodging. Such a wagoner
As Phaethon would whip you to the west,
And bring in cloudy night immediately.
Spread thy close curtain, love-performing night,   5
That runaway's eyes may wink and Romeo
Leap to these arms, untalked of and unseen.
Lovers can see to do their amorous rites
By their own beauties, or if love be blind,
It best agrees with night. Come, civil night,   10
Thou sober-suited matron all in black,
And learn me how to lose a winning match,
Played for a pair of stainless maidenhoods.
Hood my unmanned blood, bating in my cheeks,
With thy black mantle, till strange love grow bold,   15
Think true love acted simple modesty.
Come night, come Romeo, come thou day in night,
For thou wilt lie upon the wings of night
Whiter than new snow upon a raven's back.
Come, gentle night, come, loving, black-browed night,   20
Give me my Romeo, and when I shall die,
Take him and cut him out in little stars,
And he will make the face of heaven so fine
That all the world will be in love with night
And pay no worship to the garish sun.   25
O I have bought the mansion of a love,
But not possessed it, and though I am sold,
Not yet enjoyed. So tedious is this day
As is the night before some festival
To an impatient child that hath new robes   30

The Nurse arrives having found out that Tybalt has been killed by Romeo. The Nurse is so upset she is not speaking clearly and Juliet believes it is Romeo who has died.

Activity 2: Exploring emotion

a. In pairs, read aloud lines 34–47 with one of you playing Juliet and the other playing the Nurse.

b. Read the lines again, this time overemphasising the words to bring out the sounds of the **vowels**.

c. What do you think these vowel sounds might tell us about how the characters feel?

d. Read lines 34–47 again, speaking normally, but this time with the Nurse standing still and Juliet moving around her. As you read the lines, think about when it feels right for your character to make eye contact with the other character and when it feels best to look somewhere else.

e. Read the lines again with Juliet standing still and the Nurse moving around. Again think about eye contact.

f. What did you discover about how the characters feel from tasks a–e?

Key term

Vowels the letters a, e, i, o, u

Did you know?

If lines contain a lot of vowel sounds, it can indicate stronger emotions. For example, think about the sounds you make when you're watching a fireworks display or are in pain or shouting for help. We rely heavily on vowel sounds to convey emotion and feeling. As an exercise in the rehearsal room, actors sometimes speak aloud just the vowel sounds to help them connect to the emotion the character feels.

The Nurse and Juliet, 2006

And may not wear them. O here comes my nurse,

Enter Nurse, with ropes

And she brings news, and every tongue that speaks
But Romeo's name speaks heavenly eloquence.
Now, nurse, what news? What hast thou there? The cords
That Romeo bid thee fetch?

Nurse   Ay, ay, the cords.   35

Juliet Ay me, what news? Why dost thou wring thy hands?

Nurse Ah, weladay! He's dead, he's dead, he's dead!
We are undone, lady, we are undone.
Alack the day, he's gone, he's killed, he's dead.

Juliet Can heaven be so envious?

Nurse   Romeo can,   40
Though heaven cannot. O Romeo, Romeo!
Whoever would have thought it? Romeo!

Juliet What devil art thou that dost torment me thus?
This torture should be roared in dismal hell.
Hath Romeo slain himself? Say thou but 'Ay',   45
And that bare vowel 'Ay' shall poison more
Than the death-darting eye of cockatrice.
I am not I, if there be such an 'Ay',
Or those eyes shut, that makes thee answer 'Ay'.
If he be slain, say 'Ay', or if not, 'No'.   50
Brief sounds determine of my weal or woe.

Nurse I saw the wound, I saw it with mine eyes!
God save the mark! Here on his manly breast.
A piteous corpse, a bloody piteous corpse.
Pale, pale as ashes, all bedaubed in blood,   55
All in gore-blood. I swoonèd at the sight.

Juliet O, break, my heart, poor bankrupt, break at once.
To prison, eyes, ne'er look on liberty.
Vile earth, to earth resign, end motion here,
And thou and Romeo press one heavy bier.   60

The Nurse finally explains that Romeo killed Tybalt. Juliet is shocked and confused that the man she loves could do such a terrible thing.

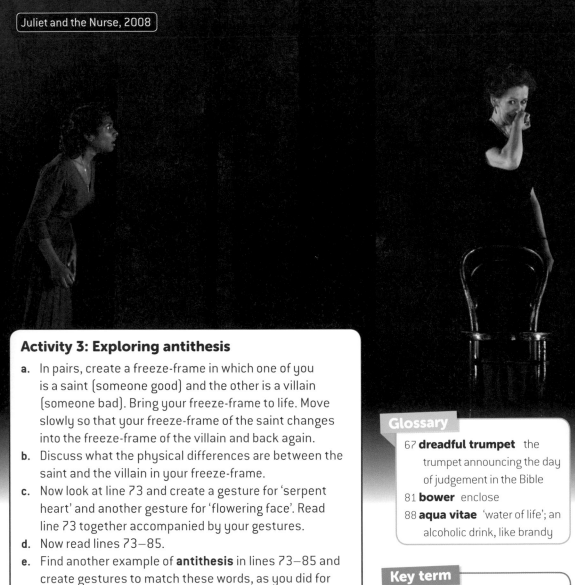

Juliet and the Nurse, 2008

Activity 3: Exploring antithesis

a. In pairs, create a freeze-frame in which one of you is a saint (someone good) and the other is a villain (someone bad). Bring your freeze-frame to life. Move slowly so that your freeze-frame of the saint changes into the freeze-frame of the villain and back again.

b. Discuss what the physical differences are between the saint and the villain in your freeze-frame.

c. Now look at line 73 and create a gesture for 'serpent heart' and another gesture for 'flowering face'. Read line 73 together accompanied by your gestures.

d. Now read lines 73–85.

e. Find another example of **antithesis** in lines 73–85 and create gestures to match these words, as you did for task c.

f. Discuss how it feels moving between the physical images and gestures you created in tasks a, c and e. What do the contrasting words from your chosen lines suggest about how Juliet is feeling at this moment?

Glossary

67 **dreadful trumpet** the trumpet announcing the day of judgement in the Bible

81 **bower** enclose

88 **aqua vitae** 'water of life'; an alcoholic drink, like brandy

Key term

Antithesis bringing two opposing concepts or ideas together, e.g. hot and cold, love and hate, loud and quiet

Nurse   O Tybalt, Tybalt, the best friend I had!
             O courteous Tybalt, honest gentleman,
             That ever I should live to see thee dead.

Juliet   What storm is this that blows so contrary?
             Is Romeo slaughtered? And is Tybalt dead?   65
             My dearest cousin, and my dearer lord.
             Then, dreadful trumpet, sound the general doom,
             For who is living, if those two are gone?

Nurse   Tybalt is gone, and Romeo banishèd,
             Romeo that killed him, he is banishèd.   70

Juliet   O, God! Did Romeo's hand shed Tybalt's blood?

Nurse   It did, it did, alas the day, it did!

Juliet   O serpent heart, hid with a flowering face.
             Did ever dragon keep so fair a cave?
             Beautiful tyrant, fiend angelical,   75
             Dove-feathered raven, wolvish-ravening lamb,
             Despisèd substance of divinest show.
             Just opposite to what thou justly seem'st,
             A damnèd saint, an honourable villain.
             O nature, what had'st thou to do in hell,   80
             When thou didst bower the spirit of a fiend
             In mortal paradise of such sweet flesh?
             Was ever book containing such vile matter
             So fairly bound? O that deceit should dwell
             In such a gorgeous palace.

Nurse   There's no trust,   85
             No faith, no honesty in men, all perjured,
             All forsworn, all naught, all dissemblers.
             Ah, where's my man? Give me some aqua vitae.
             These griefs, these woes, these sorrows make me old.
             Shame come to Romeo!

Juliet   Blistered be thy tongue   90
             For such a wish! He was not born to shame.

Juliet tells off the Nurse for speaking badly of Romeo and guesses that Tybalt provoked him into the fight. She then becomes distraught at the idea of Romeo being banished.

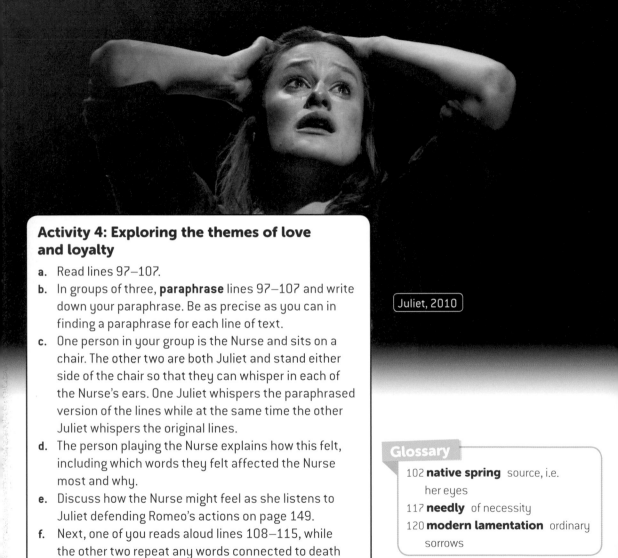

Juliet, 2010

Activity 4: Exploring the themes of love and loyalty

a. Read lines 97–107.

b. In groups of three, **paraphrase** lines 97–107 and write down your paraphrase. Be as precise as you can in finding a paraphrase for each line of text.

c. One person in your group is the Nurse and sits on a chair. The other two are both Juliet and stand either side of the chair so that they can whisper in each of the Nurse's ears. One Juliet whispers the paraphrased version of the lines while at the same time the other Juliet whispers the original lines.

d. The person playing the Nurse explains how this felt, including which words they felt affected the Nurse most and why.

e. Discuss how the Nurse might feel as she listens to Juliet defending Romeo's actions on page 149.

f. Next, one of you reads aloud lines 108–115, while the other two repeat any words connected to death or banishment.

g. Focus on line 113 and read this line aloud together to the rhythm. Notice how you have to pronounce 'banishèd' as three **syllables** rather than two.

h. Bearing in mind what you have found out from tasks a–g, discuss how Juliet feels about Romeo being banished.

Glossary

102 **native spring** source, i.e. her eyes

117 **needly** of necessity

120 **modern lamentation** ordinary sorrows

Key terms

Paraphrase put a line or section of text into your own words

Syllable part of a word that is one sound, e.g. 'dignity' has three syllables — 'dig','ni','ty'

Upon his brow shame is ashamed to sit.
For 'tis a throne where honour may be crowned
Sole monarch of the universal earth.
O, what a beast was I to chide at him.   95

Nurse   Will you speak well of him that killed your cousin?

Juliet   Shall I speak ill of him that is my husband?
Ah, poor my lord, what tongue shall smooth thy name,
When I, thy three-hours wife, have mangled it?
But wherefore, villain, didst thou kill my cousin?   100
That villain cousin would have killed my husband.
Back, foolish tears, back to your native spring,
Your tributary drops belong to woe,
Which you mistaking offer up to joy.
My husband lives that Tybalt would have slain,   105
And Tybalt's dead that would have slain my husband.
All this is comfort, wherefore weep I then?
Some word there was, worser than Tybalt's death,
That murdered me. I would forget it fain,
But, O, it presses to my memory,   110
Like damnèd guilty deeds to sinners' minds.
'Tybalt is dead, and Romeo banishèd'.
That 'banishèd', that one word 'banishèd',
Hath slain ten thousand Tybalts. Tybalt's death
Was woe enough if it had ended there.   115
Or if sour woe delights in fellowship
And needly will be ranked with other griefs,
Why followed not, when she said 'Tybalt's dead',
Thy father, or thy mother, nay, or both,
Which modern lamentation might have moved?   120
But with a rearward following Tybalt's death,
'Romeo is banishèd'. To speak that word,
Is father, mother, Tybalt, Romeo, Juliet,
All slain, all dead. 'Romeo is banishèd' –
There is no end, no limit, measure, bound,   125
In that word's death: no words can that woe sound.
Where is my father and my mother, nurse?

Juliet laments that she will die and never see Romeo again. The Nurse confesses that she knows Romeo is hiding with Friar Laurence and promises to get him to come to say goodbye.

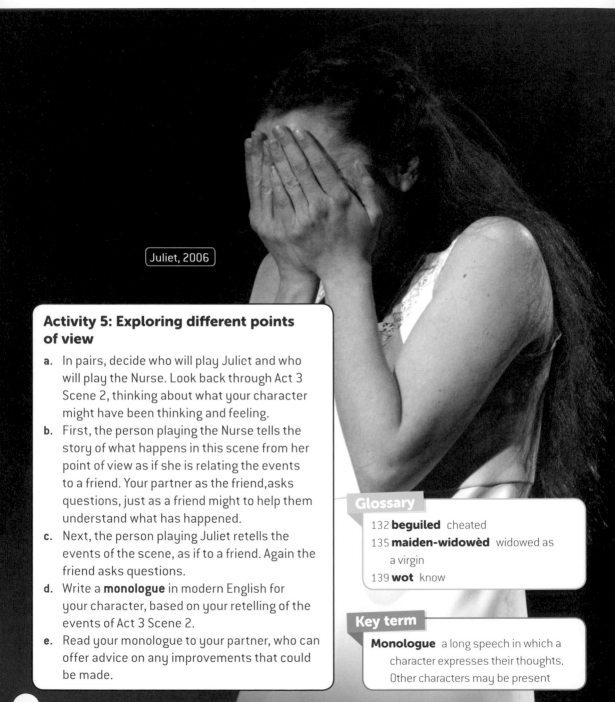

Juliet, 2006

Activity 5: Exploring different points of view

a. In pairs, decide who will play Juliet and who will play the Nurse. Look back through Act 3 Scene 2, thinking about what your character might have been thinking and feeling.

b. First, the person playing the Nurse tells the story of what happens in this scene from her point of view as if she is relating the events to a friend. Your partner as the friend, asks questions, just as a friend might to help them understand what has happened.

c. Next, the person playing Juliet retells the events of the scene, as if to a friend. Again the friend asks questions.

d. Write a **monologue** in modern English for your character, based on your retelling of the events of Act 3 Scene 2.

e. Read your monologue to your partner, who can offer advice on any improvements that could be made.

Glossary

132 **beguiled** cheated
135 **maiden-widowèd** widowed as a virgin
139 **wot** know

Key term

Monologue a long speech in which a character expresses their thoughts. Other characters may be present

Nurse   Weeping and wailing over Tybalt's corpse.
Will you go to them? I will bring you thither.

Juliet   Wash they his wounds with tears. Mine shall be spent,   130
When theirs are dry, for Romeo's banishment.
Take up those cords. Poor ropes, you are beguiled,
Both you and I, for Romeo is exiled.
He made you for a highway to my bed,
But I, a maid, die maiden-widowèd.   135
Come cord, come nurse, I'll to my wedding-bed,
And Death, not Romeo, take my maidenhead.

Nurse   Hie to your chamber, I'll find Romeo
To comfort you. I wot well where he is.
Hark ye, your Romeo will be here at night.   140
I'll to him, he is hid at Laurence' cell.

Juliet   O, find him! Give this ring to my true knight,
And bid him come to take his last farewell.

Exeunt

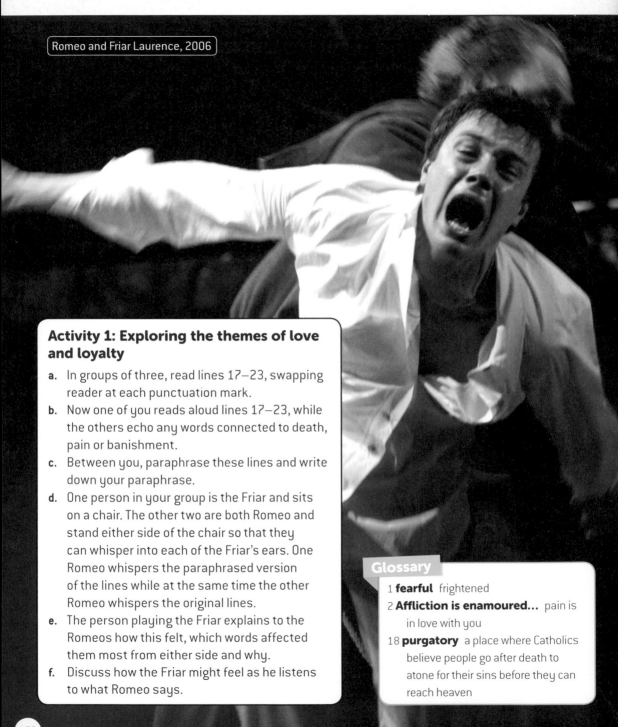

Friar Laurence brings the news to Romeo that the Prince has announced Romeo is allowed to live, but not in Verona.

Romeo and Friar Laurence, 2006

Activity 1: Exploring the themes of love and loyalty

a. In groups of three, read lines 17–23, swapping reader at each punctuation mark.

b. Now one of you reads aloud lines 17–23, while the others echo any words connected to death, pain or banishment.

c. Between you, paraphrase these lines and write down your paraphrase.

d. One person in your group is the Friar and sits on a chair. The other two are both Romeo and stand either side of the chair so that they can whisper into each of the Friar's ears. One Romeo whispers the paraphrased version of the lines while at the same time the other Romeo whispers the original lines.

e. The person playing the Friar explains to the Romeos how this felt, which words affected them most from either side and why.

f. Discuss how the Friar might feel as he listens to what Romeo says.

Glossary

1 **fearful** frightened
2 **Affliction is enamoured...** pain is in love with you
18 **purgatory** a place where Catholics believe people go after death to atone for their sins before they can reach heaven

Act 3 | Scene 3

Enter Friar Laurence and Romeo

Friar Laurence   Romeo, come forth, come forth, thou fearful man.
Affliction is enamoured of thy parts,
And thou art wedded to calamity.

Romeo   Father, what news? What is the Prince's doom?
What sorrow craves acquaintance at my hand,   5
That I yet know not?

Friar Laurence   Too familiar
Is my dear son with such sour company.
I bring thee tidings of the Prince's doom.

Romeo   What less than doomsday is the Prince's doom?

Friar Laurence   A gentler judgement vanished from his lips.   10
Not body's death, but body's banishment.

Romeo   Ha, banishment? Be merciful, say 'death',
For exile hath more terror in his look,
Much more than death. Do not say 'banishment'.

Friar Laurence   Here from Verona art thou banishèd.   15
Be patient, for the world is broad and wide.

Romeo   There is no world without Verona walls,
But purgatory, torture, hell itself.
Hence banishèd is banished from the world,
And world's exile is death: then banishèd,   20
Is death mistermed. Calling death banishèd,
Thou cutt'st my head off with a golden axe,
And smilest upon the stroke that murders me.

Friar Laurence   O deadly sin. O rude unthankfulness!
Thy fault our law calls death, but the kind Prince,   25

Activity 2: Exploring the themes of love and family

a. Read aloud lines 29–47. As you read:
- Point upwards whenever you say 'heaven' and point downwards for 'hell'.
- Whenever you say 'here' or 'her' or 'Juliet' point beside you.
- Whenever you say 'exile' or 'banishèd' indicate behind you.
- Whenever you say 'I', 'me' or 'Romeo' tap your chest.
- Whenever you talk of any other creatures indicate where they might be.

b. How are the play's themes of love, loyalty, family, friendship and fate reflected in these lines?

c. In your own words, write a description of what banishment means to Romeo.

Glossary

33 **More validity** more value

52 **fond mad man** foolish idiot

55 **Adversity's sweet milk** soothing comfort for hardship

59 **Displant** uproot and put somewhere else

Did you know?

Actors often find it useful when working with a long speech to indicate where the people and places they are talking about might be, as in the activity on this page.

Romeo and Friar Laurence, 2006

Taking thy part, hath rushed aside the law,
And turned that black word 'death' to 'banishment'.
This is dear mercy, and thou seest it not.

Romeo   'Tis torture and not mercy. Heaven is here,
Where Juliet lives, and every cat and dog   30
And little mouse, every unworthy thing,
Live here in heaven and may look on her,
But Romeo may not. More validity,
More honourable state, more courtship lives
In carrion-flies than Romeo. They may seize   35
On the white wonder of dear Juliet's hand
And steal immortal blessing from her lips,
Who even in pure and vestal modesty,
Still blush, as thinking their own kisses sin.
But Romeo may not. He is banishèd.   40
Flies may do this, but when I from this must fly.
They are free men, but I am banishèd:
And say'st thou yet that exile is not death?
Had'st thou no poison mixed, no sharp-ground knife,
No sudden mean of death, though ne'er so mean,   45
But 'banishèd' to kill me? 'Banishèd'?
O friar, the damnèd use that word in hell,
Howling attends it. How hast thou the heart,
Being a divine, a ghostly confessor,
A sin-absolver, and my friend professed,   50
To mangle me with that word 'banishèd'?

Friar Laurence   Thou fond mad man, hear me a little speak.

Romeo   O, thou wilt speak again of banishment.

Friar Laurence   I'll give thee armour to keep off that word.
Adversity's sweet milk, philosophy,   55
To comfort thee, though thou art banishèd.

Romeo   Yet 'banishèd'? Hang up philosophy.
Unless philosophy can make a Juliet,
Displant a town, reverse a prince's doom,
It helps not, it prevails not; talk no more.   60

Romeo tells the Friar he can't possibly understand how he feels. There is a knocking on the door, but Romeo refuses to move to hide himself. The Nurse enters and tells the Friar that Juliet is behaving just like Romeo.

Activity 3: Exploring costume decisions

a. Read lines 64–70.

b. Now look at the photo of Romeo on this page and answer these questions:
   i. What do you think is going on in this photo?
   ii. How does Romeo's costume help him express his emotion?
   iii. How well do you think this photo of Romeo matches the speech you have just looked at?

Glossary

63 **dispute with thee…** discuss your present situation

70 **Taking the measure…** ready to die and lie in a grave

84 **in my mistress' case** in just the same state as Juliet

Did you know?

Wearing the right shoes, hat or jacket in rehearsals can help an actor inhabit their character. For example, in the 2010 RSC production of the play, Romeo rehearsed while wearing a hooded jacket.

Romeo, 2010

Friar Laurence	O then I see that madmen have no ears.
Romeo	How should they, when wise men have no eyes?
Friar Laurence	Let me dispute with thee of thy estate.
Romeo	Thou canst not speak of that thou dost not feel.

Romeo Thou canst not speak of that thou dost not feel.
Wert thou as young as I, Juliet thy love,   65
An hour but married, Tybalt murderèd,
Doting like me and like me banishèd,
Then might'st thou speak, then might'st thou tear thy hair,
And fall upon the ground as I do now,
Taking the measure of an unmade grave.   70

Nurse knocks

Friar Laurence Arise, one knocks. Good Romeo, hide thyself.

Romeo Not I, unless the breath of heartsick groans,
Mist-like, enfold me from the search of eyes.

Nurse knocks again

Friar Laurence Hark, how they knock. Who's there? Romeo, arise,
Thou wilt be taken, stay awhile, stand up.   75
Run to my study. By and by! God's will,
What simpleness is this? I come, I come!

Nurse knocks again

Who knocks so hard? Whence come you? What's your will?

Enter Nurse

Nurse Let me come in, and you shall know my errand.
I come from Lady Juliet.

Friar Laurence   Welcome, then.   80

Nurse O holy friar, O, tell me, holy friar,
Where's my lady's lord? Where's Romeo?

Friar Laurence There on the ground, with his own tears made drunk.

Nurse O, he is even in my mistress' case,

Romeo asks the Nurse what Juliet thinks of him now and the Nurse replies that Juliet says nothing but weeps instead. Romeo threatens to kill himself, but the Friar stops him and tells him to pull himself together.

Activity 4: Discovering character through movement

a. In small groups, read lines 88–110 with one of you playing Romeo, one playing the Nurse and the other playing the Friar.

b. To help you understand more about the characters, their relationships and their motives, read the lines again. This time, as you speak and listen, you should keep choosing between the following movements:
   - Take a step towards another character.
   - Take a step away from another character.
   - Turn towards another character.
   - Turn away from another character.
   - Stand still.

   Try to make instinctive choices rather than planning what to do.

c. In your groups, read lines 88–110 again, but this time try making different choices about how you move.

d. Discuss as a group:
   i. your understanding of the characters in this section
   ii. which decisions worked best to make the scene engaging for the audience.

e. Now create one freeze-frame to illustrate this moment in the play. When you are in your frozen position, each character speaks aloud their thoughts about the other characters in the scene.

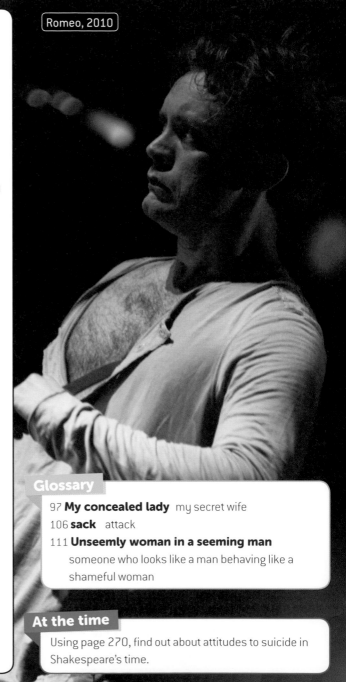

Romeo, 2010

Glossary
97 **My concealed lady** my secret wife

106 **sack** attack

111 **Unseemly woman in a seeming man** someone who looks like a man behaving like a shameful woman

At the time
Using page 270, find out about attitudes to suicide in Shakespeare's time.

Just in her case. O woeful sympathy! 85
Piteous predicament! Even so lies she,
Blubbering and weeping, weeping and blubbering.
Stand up, stand up, stand and you be a man.
For Juliet's sake, for her sake, rise and stand.
Why should you fall into so deep an O? 90

Romeo   Nurse.

Nurse   Ah sir, ah sir, death's the end of all.

Romeo   Speak'st thou of Juliet? How is it with her?
Doth not she think me an old murderer,
Now I have stained the childhood of our joy
With blood removed but little from her own? 95
Where is she? And how doth she? And what says
My concealed lady to our cancelled love?

Nurse   O she says nothing, sir, but weeps and weeps,
And now falls on her bed, and then starts up,
And Tybalt calls, and then on Romeo cries, 100
And then down falls again.

Romeo   As if that name,
Shot from the deadly level of a gun,
Did murder her, as that name's cursèd hand
Murdered her kinsman. O, tell me, friar, tell me,
In what vile part of this anatomy 105
Doth my name lodge? Tell me, that I may sack
The hateful mansion.

Friar Laurence   Hold thy desperate hand.
Art thou a man? Thy form cries out thou art.
Thy tears are womanish, thy wild acts denote
The unreasonable fury of a beast. 110
Unseemly woman in a seeming man,
And ill-beseeming beast in seeming both,
Thou hast amazed me. By my holy order,
I thought thy disposition better tempered.
Hast thou slain Tybalt? Wilt thou slay thyself? 115

The Friar tells Romeo why he should be grateful that the Prince has declared his punishment to be banishment rather than death. He then tells Romeo to go and spend the night with Juliet and say goodbye. He promises they will find a way to make everything right.

Friar Laurence, 2010

Activity 5: Exploring the Friar's advice

a. Read lines 134–144.

b. Identify the three reasons in these lines the Friar gives Romeo to be happy.

c. In small groups, create two freeze-frames for each of these three reasons (six freeze-frames in total). The first freeze-frame for each reason should show the reason not to be happy and the second should show the reason to be happy. For example, for the first reason, the first freeze-frame would show Juliet dead and Romeo miserable, and the second freeze-frame would show Juliet alive and Romeo happy.

d. Find a way to show all six freeze-frames and speak lines 134–144 in your groups. Discuss whether you think the Friar gives Romeo good advice.

Glossary

122 **usurer** moneylender

125 **a form of wax** made of wax; not real

131–132 **Like powder...** like gunpowder carried by an unskilled soldier, who accidentally causes an explosion

141 **her best array** her best appearance

150 **blaze** proclaim to the world

And slay thy lady too that in thy life lives,
By doing damnèd hate upon thyself?
Why rail'st thou on thy birth? The heaven and earth?
Since birth, and heaven, and earth, all three do meet
In thee at once, which thou at once wouldst lose.   120
Fie, fie, thou sham'st thy shape, thy love, thy wit,
Which like a usurer abound'st in all,
And usest none in that true use indeed
Which should bedeck thy shape, thy love, thy wit.
Thy noble shape is but a form of wax,   125
Digressing from the valour of a man.
Thy dear love sworn but hollow perjury,
Killing that love which thou hast vowed to cherish.
Thy wit, that ornament to shape and love,
Misshapen in the conduct of them both,   130
Like powder in a skilless soldier's flask,
Is set afire by thine own ignorance,
And thou dismembered with thine own defence.
What, rouse thee, man! Thy Juliet is alive,
For whose dear sake thou wast but lately dead.   135
There art thou happy. Tybalt would kill thee,
But thou slew'st Tybalt; there art thou happy.
The law that threatened death became thy friend
And turned it to exile; there art thou happy.
A pack of blessings light upon thy back,   140
Happiness courts thee in her best array,
But like a mishapèd and sullen wench,
Thou pouts upon thy fortune and thy love.
Take heed, take heed, for such die miserable.
Go, get thee to thy love as was decreed,   145
Ascend her chamber, hence and comfort her.
But look thou stay not till the watch be set,
For then thou canst not pass to Mantua,
Where thou shalt live till we can find a time
To blaze your marriage, reconcile your friends,   150
Beg pardon of the Prince, and call thee back
With twenty hundred thousand times more joy

The Nurse is impressed by the Friar's words and heads off to tell Juliet that Romeo is on his way. The Friar advises Romeo to leave for Mantua at dawn in disguise and promises to keep in touch through Romeo's servant.

Romeo and Friar Laurence, 2010

Activity 6: Exploring point of view

a. In pairs, decide who will play Romeo and who will play the Friar. Then look back through Act 3 Scene 3, thinking about what your character might be thinking and feeling.

b. First, the person playing the Friar tells the story of what happens in this scene from his point of view as if he is relating the events to a friend. Your partner, as the friend, asks questions, just as a friend might, to help them understand what has happened.

c. Next, the person playing Romeo retells the events of the scene, as if to a friend. Again the friend asks questions.

d. Write a monologue for your character in modern English, based on your retelling of the events of Act 3 Scene 3.

e. Read your monologue to your partner, who can offer advice on any improvements that could be made.

Glossary

153 **lamentation** sorrowful complaining

166 **before the watch be set** before the night guards come on duty

168 **Sojourn** stay

170 **Every good hap** every piece of good fortune

Than thou went'st forth in lamentation.
Go before, nurse, commend me to thy lady,
And bid her hasten all the house to bed,   155
Which heavy sorrow makes them apt unto.
Romeo is coming.

Nurse   O lord, I could have stayed here all night
To hear good counsel. O, what learning is!
My lord, I'll tell my lady you will come.   160

Romeo   Do so, and bid my sweet prepare to chide.

Nurse   Here, sir, a ring she bid me give you, sir.
Hie you, make haste, for it grows very late.

Exit Nurse

Romeo   How well my comfort is revived by this.

Friar Laurence   Go hence, good night, and here stands all your state.   165
Either be gone before the watch be set,
Or by the break of day disguised from hence.
Sojourn in Mantua. I'll find out your man,
And he shall signify from time to time
Every good hap to you that chances here.   170
Give me thy hand, 'tis late, farewell, good night.

Romeo   But that a joy past joy calls out on me,
It were a grief, so brief to part with thee.
Farewell.

Exeunt

Lord Capulet explains to Paris that he has not had time to talk to Juliet about marriage because of Tybalt's death. Paris is prepared to wait but then Lord Capulet changes his mind. Believing Juliet will do as he says, he arranges with Paris that the wedding will be in three days' time.

Activity 1: Exploring the theme of family

a. In pairs, read lines 12–21, swapping reader at each punctuation mark.

b. Discuss what you think Lord Capulet's reasons are for wanting Juliet to marry Paris. Why do you think he changes his mind to decide the wedding should happen in three days' time?

c. Look at the photo on this page. What do you think Lord Capulet is thinking at this moment? Give reasons for your suggestion.

d. Why do you think Shakespeare decided the wedding should happen so quickly? What effect might he hope this would have on his audience?

Lord and Lady Capulet, 2010

Act 3 | Scene 4

Enter Lord Capulet, Lady Capulet and Paris

Lord Capulet Things have fallen out, sir, so unluckily
That we have had no time to move our daughter.
Look you, she loved her kinsman Tybalt dearly,
And so did I. Well, we were born to die.
'Tis very late, she'll not come down tonight.   5
I promise you, but for your company,
I would have been abed an hour ago.

Paris These times of woe afford no times to woo.
Madam, goodnight, commend me to your daughter.

Lady Capulet I will, and know her mind early tomorrow.   10
Tonight she is mewed up to her heaviness.

Lord Capulet Sir Paris, I will make a desperate tender
Of my child's love. I think she will be ruled
In all respects by me, nay, more, I doubt it not.
Wife, go you to her ere you go to bed,   15
Acquaint her here of my son Paris' love,
And bid her, mark you me, on Wednesday next—
But, soft, what day is this?

Paris   Monday, my lord.

Lord Capulet Monday? Ha, ha! Well, Wednesday is too soon,
O' Thursday let it be. O' Thursday, tell her,   20
She shall be married to this noble earl.
Will you be ready? Do you like this haste?
We'll keep no great ado, a friend or two,
For hark you, Tybalt being slain so late,
It may be thought we held him carelessly,   25
Being our kinsman, if we revel much.
Therefore we'll have some half a dozen friends,
And there an end. But what say you to Thursday?

Paris is delighted to marry Juliet on Thursday. Lord Capulet sends his wife to break the news to Juliet.

Activity 2: Writing a letter from Lord Capulet

Lord Capulet hopes the wedding will make everything better. Imagine you are Lord Capulet at the end of this scene and you decide to write a letter to Prince Escalus, inviting him to the wedding. Write the letter in modern English and include:

- your response to all the recent fighting on the streets of Verona
- your response to the Prince's decision to banish Romeo
- why you feel it is a good idea for Juliet to marry Paris
- why the wedding will happen this Thursday.

Remember, the Prince is your social superior so the tone of your letter should be formal and polite.

Glossary

32 **Prepare her** make sure she is ready (to marry Paris)

33 **Light to my chamber** make sure there are torches in my room

Lord Capulet, 2010

Paris   My lord, I would that Thursday were tomorrow.

Lord Capulet   Well get you gone. O'Thursday be it, then.   30
Go you to Juliet ere you go to bed,
Prepare her, wife, against this wedding-day.
Farewell, my lord. Light to my chamber, ho!
Afore me, it is so late, that we
May call it early by and by. Goodnight.   35

Exeunt

Romeo and Juliet have spent the night together. Juliet tries to pretend it is still night so they can spend more time together but realises the dawn is breaking and they must say goodbye.

Activity 1: Exploring the theme of fate

a. In pairs, read aloud lines 6–16 with one of you playing Romeo and the other playing Juliet.

b. Read lines 6–16 again, but this time listen carefully to your partner and repeat any words you hear connected to light and dark. For example, Juliet might repeat 'lark' and 'morn' in Romeo's first line. Romeo would echo 'light' and 'daylight' in Juliet's first line.

c. Discuss why these words are so important to Romeo and Juliet. How much do you think these characters can make their own decisions at this moment in the play and how much is down to fate?

d. Now read lines 16–26.

e. As a pair, read these lines again. Stand facing each other with Romeo whispering the lines as Juliet listens carefully. When Juliet changes her mind and realises Romeo has to leave, she sits down.

f. Read lines 16–26 with Romeo saying the lines loudly as though declaring his love to the world. Does this difference in tone change the moment when Juliet sits down? Give reasons for your answer.

g. Discuss what makes Juliet change her mind and tell Romeo to go in line 26.

Romeo and Juliet, 2010

Act 3 | Scene 5

Enter Romeo and Juliet

Juliet   Wilt thou be gone? It is not yet near day.
It was the nightingale, and not the lark,
That pierced the fearful hollow of thine ear.
Nightly she sings on yon pomegranate tree.
Believe me, love, it was the nightingale.   5

Romeo   It was the lark, the herald of the morn,
No nightingale. Look, love, what envious streaks
Do lace the severing clouds in yonder east.
Night's candles are burnt out, and jocund day
Stands tiptoe on the misty mountain tops.   10
I must be gone and live, or stay and die.

Juliet   Yond light is not daylight, I know it, I.
It is some meteor that the sun exhales,
To be to thee this night a torch-bearer,
And light thee on thy way to Mantua.   15
Therefore stay yet, thou need'st not to be gone.

Romeo   Let me be ta'en, let me be put to death,
I am content, so thou wilt have it so.
I'll say yon grey is not the morning's eye,
'Tis but the pale reflex of Cynthia's brow,   20
Nor that is not the lark, whose notes do beat
The vaulty heaven so high above our heads.
I have more care to stay than will to go.
Come, death, and welcome. Juliet wills it so.
How is't, my soul? Let's talk, it is not day.   25

Juliet   It is, it is, hie hence, be gone away.
It is the lark that sings so out of tune,
Straining harsh discords and unpleasing sharps.

The Nurse tells Juliet that Lady Capulet is on her way. Romeo and Juliet reluctantly say a final goodbye to each other.

Activity 2: Exploring the theme of love

a. In pairs, read lines 41–59 with one of you playing Romeo and the other playing Juliet. Stand back to back as you read, leaning against each other.

b. Join with another pair. One pair plays Romeo and Juliet. Romeo and Juliet should stand facing each other ten steps apart and read lines 41–59 again while trying to grab each other's hand. Meanwhile the other pair should stand between Romeo and Juliet, trying to stop them from reaching each other. There should be no physical contact between Romeo and Juliet and the two people getting in their way.

c. Swap over and repeat task b so that the other pair gets a chance to play Romeo and Juliet.

d. Discuss how you felt during tasks a–c. How might these feelings be connected with how Romeo and Juliet feel?

e. The two Juliets should choose one line from lines 41–59 that they feel best summarises how Juliet feels. The two Romeos should choose a line to summarise his feelings. Explain your choices to each other.

f. Based on this discussion, write a paragraph for Romeo and another for Juliet, describing how they feel. Include the lines your group chose and explain why you felt each line was important.

Juliet and Romeo, 2006

Glossary

29 **division** This is a musical term for a rapid series of short, clear notes

31 **change eyes** The toad and lark have similar beady eyes

33 **Since arm from arm...** since that voice scares us away from each other

45 **For in a minute...** each minute without you seems like many days

53 **sweet discourses** sweet conversation

54 **ill-divining soul** foreboding, bad feeling

Did you know?

Actors often find it useful to speak their lines while trying to get past a physical barrier. This can connect them to the **obstacles** that lie in the way of their characters getting what they want.

Key term

Obstacle what is in the way of a character getting what they want

Some say the lark makes sweet division;
This doth not so, for she divideth us. 30
Some say the lark and loathèd toad change eyes,
O now I would they had changed voices too,
Since arm from arm that voice doth us affray,
Hunting thee hence with hunt's-up to the day.
O now be gone, more light and light it grows. 35

Romeo More light and light, more dark and dark our woes.

Enter Nurse

Nurse Madam.

Juliet Nurse.

Nurse Your lady mother is coming to your chamber.
The day is broke, be wary, look about. 40

Exit Nurse

Juliet Then, window, let day in, and let life out.

Romeo Farewell, farewell. One kiss, and I'll descend.

Juliet Art thou gone so? Love, lord, ay husband, friend,
I must hear from thee every day in the hour,
For in a minute there are many days. 45
O by this count I shall be much in years
Ere I again behold my Romeo.

Romeo Farewell.
I will omit no opportunity
That may convey my greetings, love, to thee. 50

Juliet O think'st thou we shall ever meet again?

Romeo I doubt it not, and all these woes shall serve
For sweet discourses in our time to come.

Juliet O God, I have an ill-divining soul.
Methinks I see thee, now thou art so low, 55
As one dead in the bottom of a tomb.
Either my eyesight fails or thou look'st pale.

Romeo leaves. Lady Capulet enters and assumes that Juliet is crying because she is upset over Tybalt's death. She tells Juliet to stop weeping for him.

Activity 3: Exploring the theme of family

a. In pairs, look back at page 139 and read lines 136–140 aloud together.

b. Now create two **statues** of Lady Capulet: one of you should create a statue of her at the moment she speaks lines 136–140 (page 139) and the other should create a second statue of her at Tybalt's funeral. Help each other to create these statues so that they show how you think Lady Capulet feels at each moment.

c. Read lines 68–73 on page 173 with one of you playing Lady Capulet and the other playing Juliet.

d. In your pairs, create a freeze-frame of this moment between Juliet and her mother.

e. From creating these freeze-frames, discuss how Lady Capulet might be feeling about her husband's decision that Juliet should marry Paris on Thursday.

f. What do your ideas about Lady Capulet suggest about the Capulet family?

Romeo and Juliet, 2010

Glossary

67 **unaccustomed cause** unusual event

72–73 **Some grief shows…** moderate grief shows love, but excessive grief shows a lack of sense

75–76 **So shall you feel…** you will feel bad, but it won't bring back Tybalt

Key term

Statue like a freeze-frame but usually of a single character

Romeo	And trust me, love, in my eye so do you.
	Dry sorrow drinks our blood. Adieu, adieu.

Exit Romeo

Juliet	O fortune, fortune, all men call thee fickle.	60
	If thou art fickle, what dost thou with him.	
	That is renowned for faith? Be fickle, fortune,	
	For then I hope thou wilt not keep him long,	
	But send him back.	

Enter Lady Capulet

Lady Capulet	Ho, daughter, are you up?

Juliet	Who is't that calls? It is my lady mother.	65
	Is she not down so late, or up so early?	
	What unaccustomed cause procures her hither?	

Lady Capulet	Why, how now, Juliet.

Juliet	Madam, I am not well.

Lady Capulet	Evermore weeping for your cousin's death?	
	What, wilt thou wash him from his grave with tears?	70
	And if thou couldst, thou couldst not make him live.	
	Therefore, have done. Some grief shows much of love,	
	But much of grief shows still some want of wit.	

Juliet	Yet let me weep for such a feeling loss.

Lady Capulet	So shall you feel the loss, but not the friend	75
	Which you weep for.	

Juliet	Feeling so the loss,
	I cannot choose but ever weep the friend.

Lady Capulet	Well, girl, thou weep'st not so much for his death,
	As that the villain lives which slaughtered him.

Juliet	What villain, madam?

Lady Capulet	That same villain, Romeo.	80

Lady Capulet and Juliet discuss Romeo. Lady Capulet believes that Juliet thinks like her and wants to poison Romeo in revenge for Tybalt's death. However Juliet's words tell us how much she misses Romeo.

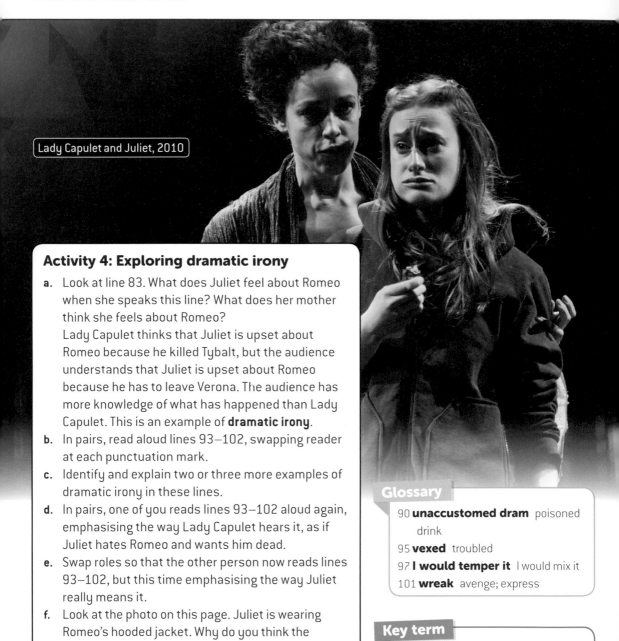

Lady Capulet and Juliet, 2010

Activity 4: Exploring dramatic irony

a. Look at line 83. What does Juliet feel about Romeo when she speaks this line? What does her mother think she feels about Romeo?

Lady Capulet thinks that Juliet is upset about Romeo because he killed Tybalt, but the audience understands that Juliet is upset about Romeo because he has to leave Verona. The audience has more knowledge of what has happened than Lady Capulet. This is an example of **dramatic irony**.

b. In pairs, read aloud lines 93–102, swapping reader at each punctuation mark.

c. Identify and explain two or three more examples of dramatic irony in these lines.

d. In pairs, one of you reads lines 93–102 aloud again, emphasising the way Lady Capulet hears it, as if Juliet hates Romeo and wants him dead.

e. Swap roles so that the other person now reads lines 93–102, but this time emphasising the way Juliet really means it.

f. Look at the photo on this page. Juliet is wearing Romeo's hooded jacket. Why do you think the director made this decision? This is an example of visual dramatic irony because the audience recognises the jacket, while Juliet's family does not.

Glossary

90 **unaccustomed dram** poisoned drink

95 **vexed** troubled

97 **I would temper it** I would mix it

101 **wreak** avenge; express

Key term

Dramatic irony when the audience knows something that some characters in the play do not

Juliet   Villain and he be many miles asunder.
God pardon him. I do with all my heart.
And yet no man like he doth grieve my heart.

Lady Capulet   That is because the traitor murderer lives.

Juliet   Ay, madam, from the reach of these my hands.   85
Would none but I might venge my cousin's death.

Lady Capulet   We will have vengeance for it, fear thou not.
Then weep no more. I'll send to one in Mantua,
Where that same banished runagate doth live,
Shall give him such an unaccustomed dram,   90
That he shall soon keep Tybalt company,
And then I hope, thou wilt be satisfied.

Juliet   Indeed, I never shall be satisfied
With Romeo, till I behold him – dead –
Is my poor heart so for a kinsman vexed.   95
Madam, if you could find out but a man
To bear a poison, I would temper it,
That Romeo should upon receipt thereof,
Soon sleep in quiet. O how my heart abhors
To hear him named and cannot come to him,   100
To wreak the love I bore my cousin
Upon his body that hath slaughtered him.

Lady Capulet   Find thou the means, and I'll find such a man.
But now I'll tell thee joyful tidings, girl.

Juliet   And joy comes well in such a needy time.   105
What are they, beseech your ladyship?

Lady Capulet   Well, well, thou hast a careful father, child,
One who, to put thee from thy heaviness,
Hath sorted out a sudden day of joy,
That thou expects not, nor I looked not for.   110

Juliet   Madam, in happy time, what day is that?

Lady Capulet announces that Juliet is to marry Paris on Thursday. Juliet says she won't. Lord Capulet and the Nurse arrive. Lady Capulet tells her husband of her daughter's refusal to marry Paris.

The Nurse, Lord Capulet and Juliet, 2010

Activity 5: Exploring the theme of family

a. In pairs, look at Lady Capulet's lines 112–115 and 124–125.

b. Create two freeze-frames of these two moments between Lady Capulet and her daughter, showing their relationship and Lady Capulet's attitude towards her daughter.

c. Now join with another pair and create a third freeze-frame for Lady Capulet's lines 139–140 that includes Juliet, the Nurse and Lord Capulet.

Activity 6: Exploring language and character

a. Read lines 129–138.

b. Read the lines again, but this time tap your book each time you say a word connected to a boat in a storm.

c. Why do you think Shakespeare gives this **extended metaphor** to Lord Capulet? What might it suggest about Lord Capulet's relationship with his daughter?

Glossary

119 **Ere he that should be husband...** Juliet and Paris have not had time to get to know each other

129 **a conduit** a fountain

131 **a bark** a boat

136 **overset** capsize

Key term

Extended metaphor describing something by comparing it to something else over several lines, e.g. Lord Capulet compares Juliet to a boat in a storm in lines 131–137?

Lady Capulet	Marry, my child, early next Thursday morn,
	The gallant, young and noble gentleman,
	The County Paris, at Saint Peter's Church,
	Shall happily make thee there a joyful bride. 115
Juliet	Now, by Saint Peter's Church and Peter too,
	He shall not make me there a joyful bride.
	I wonder at this haste, that I must wed
	Ere he that should be husband comes to woo.
	I pray you tell my lord and father, madam, 120
	I will not marry yet, and when I do, I swear
	It shall be Romeo, whom you know I hate,
	Rather than Paris. These are news indeed.
Lady Capulet	Here comes your father: tell him so yourself,
	And see how he will take it at your hands. 125

Enter Lord Capulet and Nurse

Lord Capulet	When the sun sets, the earth doth drizzle dew,
	But for the sunset of my brother's son
	It rains downright.
	How now, a conduit, girl? What, still in tears?
	Evermore showering. In one little body. 130
	Thou counterfeits a bark, a sea, a wind,
	For still thy eyes, which I may call the sea,
	Do ebb and flow with tears. The bark thy body is,
	Sailing in this salt flood; the winds, thy sighs,
	Who, raging with thy tears and they with them, 135
	Without a sudden calm, will overset
	Thy tempest-tossèd body. How now, wife?
	Have you delivered to her our decree?
Lady Capulet	Ay, sir, but she will none, she gives you thanks.
	I would the fool were married to her grave. 140
Lord Capulet	Soft, take me with you, take me with you, wife.
	How, will she none? Doth she not give us thanks?
	Is she not proud? Doth she not count her blest,
	Unworthy as she is, that we have wrought
	So worthy a gentleman to be her bridegroom? 145

Lord Capulet is angry with Juliet for refusing to marry Paris and threatens to disown her if she does not do as he says.

Juliet, Lord and Lady Capulet, 2010

Activity 7: Exploring the themes of family and loyalty

a. In groups, cast yourselves as Juliet, Lord Capulet, Lady Capulet and the Nurse. Then read lines 158–176.

b. Face each other in a small circle and read the lines again, whispering as if you don't want others in the household to hear you.

c. Now take a few steps apart and read the lines loudly.

d. Discuss whether some lines felt better spoken in a whisper or loudly.

e. Look at the **shared lines** on page 179 and discuss what effect you think these have in this scene.

f. Look through lines 149–176 and list all the insults you can find that Lord Capulet uses against Juliet, such as 'mistress minion' and 'green-sickness carrion'.

g. How might Juliet feel hearing her father describe her in this way?

h. How are the play's themes of family and loyalty reflected in lines 149–176?

i. Now read lines 149–176 in your groups, adding movement.

j. Write a paragraph or two describing the events in lines 149–176 from the point of view of the character you played.

Glossary

149 **Chop-logic** twisting language

153 **fettle your fine joints** get yourself ready

155 **hurdle** wooden frame on which traitors were dragged through the streets

156 **green-sickness** illness affecting adolescent girls

157 **tallow-face** pale like candle wax

168 **hilding** worthless creature

Key term

Shared lines lines of iambic pentameter shared between characters. This implies a closeness between them in some way

Juliet   Not proud you have, but thankful that you have.
Proud can I never be of what I hate,
But thankful even for hate, that is meant love.

Lord Capulet   How now? How now? Chop-logic? What is this?
'Proud' and 'I thank you' and 'I thank you not',   150
And yet 'not proud'? Mistress minion you,
Thank me no thankings, nor proud me no prouds,
But fettle your fine joints 'gainst Thursday next,
To go with Paris to Saint Peter's Church,
Or I will drag thee on a hurdle thither.   155
Out you green-sickness carrion, out you baggage,
You tallow-face!

Lady Capulet   Fie, fie, what, are you mad?

Juliet   Good father, I beseech you on my knees,
Hear me with patience but to speak a word.

Lord Capulet   Hang thee, young baggage, disobedient wretch.   160
I tell thee what, get thee to church o' Thursday,
Or never after look me in the face.
Speak not, reply not, do not answer me.
My fingers itch. Wife, we scarce thought us blest
That God had lent us but this only child,   165
But now I see this one is one too much,
And that we have a curse in having her.
Out on her, hilding.

Nurse   God in heaven bless her.
You are to blame, my lord, to rate her so.

Lord Capulet   And why, my lady wisdom? Hold your tongue,   170
Good prudence, smatter with your gossips, go.

Nurse   I speak no treason.

Lord Capulet   O, God gi' good e'en.

Nurse   May not one speak?

Lord Capulet continues to rage at his daughter and threatens to throw her out on the streets if she disobeys him. He leaves. Juliet turns to her mother for help to delay the wedding, but her mother refuses to help and leaves.

Juliet and Lady Capulet, 2010

Activity 8: Exploring the language and rhythm

a. Read aloud lines 176–196.

b. Read the lines aloud again, this time emphasising the **iambic pentameter** rhythm.

c. At which points does the rhythm break down? If breaks in the rhythm suggest a character is feeling disturbed, what words could you use to describe how Lord Capulet is feeling here?

d. Form small groups. Look at lines 189–196. One person in the group volunteers to be Juliet and stands in the middle of the others. The others in the group read the lines, swapping reader at each punctuation mark and directing their lines at Juliet.

e. Discuss how it felt to be Juliet hearing these lines and how it felt to be Lord Capulet saying them.

Glossary

174 **Utter your gravity...** speak your wisdom when drinking with your friends

181 **demesnes** lands

184 **wretched puling fool** silly whimpering child

Key term

Iambic pentameter the rhythm Shakespeare uses to write his plays. Each line in this rhythm contains approximately ten syllables. 'Iambic' means putting the stress on the second syllable of each beat. 'Pentameter' means five beats with two syllables in each beat

Lord Capulet	Peace, you mumbling fool.
	Utter your gravity o'er a gossip's bowl,
	For here we need it not.

Lady Capulet   You are too hot.   175

Lord Capulet God's bread, it makes me mad.
Day, night, hour, tide, time, work, play,
Alone, in company, still my care hath been
To have her matched, and having now provided
A gentleman of noble parentage,   180
Of fair demesnes, youthful, and nobly allied,
Stuffed, as they say, with honourable parts,
Proportioned as one's thought would wish a man,
And then to have a wretched puling fool,
A whining mammet, in her fortune's tender,   185
To answer 'I'll not wed, I cannot love,
I am too young, I pray you pardon me.'
But, and you will not wed, I'll pardon you.
Graze where you will you shall not house with me.
Look to't, think on't, I do not use to jest.   190
Thursday is near, lay hand on heart, advise.
And you be mine, I'll give you to my friend,
And you be not, hang, beg, starve, die in the streets,
For, by my soul, I'll ne'er acknowledge thee,
Nor what is mine shall never do thee good.   195
Trust to't, bethink you, I'll not be forsworn.

Exit Lord Capulet

Juliet Is there no pity sitting in the clouds,
That sees into the bottom of my grief?
O, sweet my mother, cast me not away.
Delay this marriage for a month, a week,   200
Or if you do not, make the bridal bed
In that dim monument where Tybalt lies.

Lady Capulet Talk not to me, for I'll not speak a word.
Do as thou wilt, for I have done with thee.

Juliet turns to her Nurse for help and advice. The Nurse tells her to forget about Romeo and marry Paris instead.

Activity 9: Exploring the Nurse's advice

a. In pairs, read the Nurse's speech, lines 213–226, swapping reader at each punctuation mark.
b. One of you stands still and reads the Nurse's lines aloud, while the other listens as Juliet. Every time the person playing Juliet feels the Nurse is giving good advice they take a step closer to her. Every time they feel the Nurse is giving the wrong advice they take a step away.
c. Discuss how you think Juliet might feel listening to the Nurse's advice. What might the audience think about the Nurse's advice in our own time and in Shakespeare's time? For information about marriage in Elizabethan England, see pages 267–268.

Glossary

210 **practise stratagems** play cruel tricks
215 **challenge you** claim you as his wife
220 **dishclout** a rag to wash dishes
222 **Beshrew my very heart** curse my heart

The Nurse and Juliet, 2010

Exit Lady Capulet

Juliet	O God! O nurse, how shall this be prevented?	205
	My husband is on earth, my faith in heaven.	
	How shall that faith return again to earth,	
	Unless that husband send it me from heaven	
	By leaving earth? Comfort me, counsel me.	
	Alack, alack, that heaven should practise stratagems	210
	Upon so soft a subject as myself.	
	What say'st thou? Hast thou not a word of joy?	
	Some comfort, nurse.	
Nurse	Faith, here it is.	
	Romeo is banished, and all the world to nothing,	
	That he dares ne'er come back to challenge you,	215
	Or if he do, it needs must be by stealth.	
	Then, since the case so stands as now it doth,	
	I think it best you married with the County.	
	O, he's a lovely gentleman.	
	Romeo's a dishclout to him. An eagle, madam,	220
	Hath not so green, so quick, so fair an eye	
	As Paris hath. Beshrew my very heart,	
	I think you are happy in this second match,	
	For it excels your first. Or if it did not,	
	Your first is dead, or 'twere as good he were,	225
	As living here and you no use of him.	
Juliet	Speakest thou from thy heart?	
Nurse	And from my soul too, else beshrew them both.	
Juliet	Amen.	
Nurse	What?	230
Juliet	Well, thou hast comforted me marvellous much.	
	Go in and tell my lady I am gone,	
	Having displeased my father, to Laurence' cell,	
	To make confession and to be absolved.	

The Nurse leaves and, left alone, Juliet tells us she will never confide in the Nurse again after hearing the 'sinful' advice the Nurse gave her. She decides to ask the Friar for help and to kill herself if he can't help her.

Activity 10: Exploring Juliet's response

a. Read lines 236–243.
b. How does Juliet feel about the Nurse's advice?
c. A **rhyming couplet** at the end of a speech often shows a character has reached a decision. What decision has Juliet reached here?
d. Write a paragraph or two explaining how the themes of love and loyalty are shown in this speech through Juliet's feelings towards the Nurse and Romeo.

Glossary

236 **Ancient damnation** damned old woman
237 **forsworn** a promise-breaker to God
241 **henceforth shall be twain** from now on will be separated; I won't confide in her

Key term

Rhyming couplet two lines of verse where the last words of each line rhyme

Did you know?

The way we speak can say a lot about us. Actors sometimes use an accent different from their own to suggest something about their character, but often in an RSC rehearsal room they are encouraged to use their own accent to help them connect more personally with the text. We don't know exactly how Shakespeare spoke, but it was probably more like the accent used in the Black Country today (an area of the West Midlands in England) so that 'remedy' would rhyme with 'die' in lines 242–243.

Nurse   Marry, I will, and this is wisely done.   235

Exit Nurse

Juliet   Ancient damnation, O most wicked fiend!
Is it more sin to wish me thus forsworn,
Or to dispraise my lord with that same tongue
Which she hath praised him with above compare
So many thousand times? Go, counsellor,   240
Thou and my bosom henceforth shall be twain.
I'll to the friar, to know his remedy.
If all else fail, myself have power to die.

Exit Juliet

Exploring Act 3

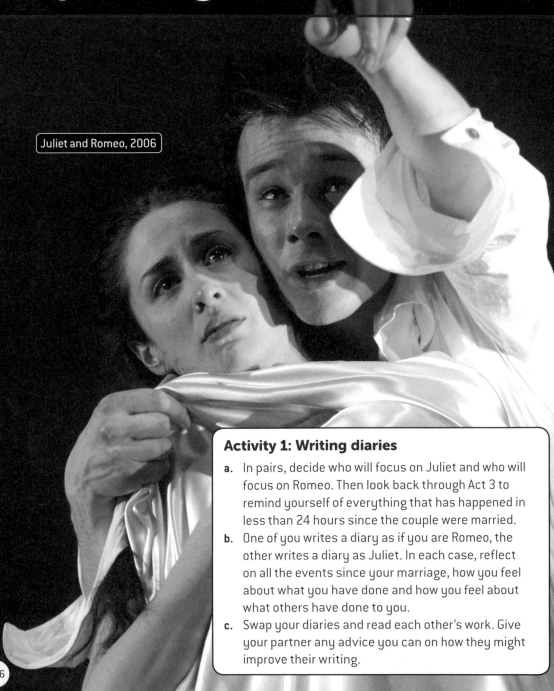

Juliet and Romeo, 2006

Activity 1: Writing diaries

a. In pairs, decide who will focus on Juliet and who will focus on Romeo. Then look back through Act 3 to remind yourself of everything that has happened in less than 24 hours since the couple were married.

b. One of you writes a diary as if you are Romeo, the other writes a diary as Juliet. In each case, reflect on all the events since your marriage, how you feel about what you have done and how you feel about what others have done to you.

c. Swap your diaries and read each other's work. Give your partner any advice you can on how they might improve their writing.

Activity 2: *The Verona Times*

a. In groups, discuss what the citizens of Verona might be thinking about recent events. How might they feel about the deaths of Mercutio and Tybalt, and the Prince's decision to banish Romeo?

b. One of you takes on the role of editor of the local Verona newspaper, while the others are journalists on your team. Together create the centre spread of the paper, which focuses exclusively on the latest news on the Capulet–Montague feud. The editor is responsible for how the page looks, for ensuring there is a good balance of facts, opinions, interviews and images, and for writing the newspaper's editorial comments on the story. Included on the pages, alongside a factual piece about what happened, might be a piece looking back at how the feud started, speculation about Juliet marrying Paris, what people say about Tybalt, etc.

Tybalt and Romeo, 2008

Paris tells the Friar that his wedding to Juliet is to take place on Thursday. Juliet arrives and Paris is happy to see the woman he believes will soon be his wife.

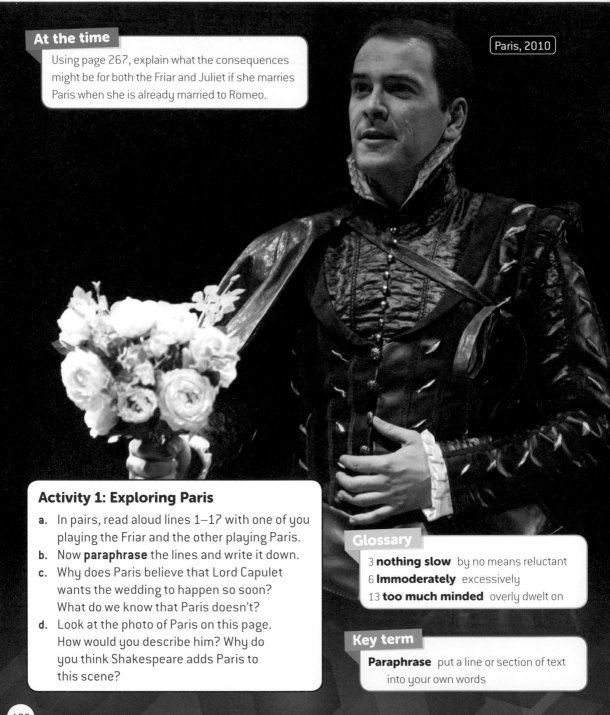

Paris, 2010

At the time

Using page 267, explain what the consequences might be for both the Friar and Juliet if she marries Paris when she is already married to Romeo.

Activity 1: Exploring Paris

a. In pairs, read aloud lines 1–17 with one of you playing the Friar and the other playing Paris.

b. Now **paraphrase** the lines and write it down.

c. Why does Paris believe that Lord Capulet wants the wedding to happen so soon? What do we know that Paris doesn't?

d. Look at the photo of Paris on this page. How would you describe him? Why do you think Shakespeare adds Paris to this scene?

Glossary

3 **nothing slow** by no means reluctant

6 **Immoderately** excessively

13 **too much minded** overly dwelt on

Key term

Paraphrase put a line or section of text into your own words

188

Enter Friar Laurence and Paris

Friar Laurence On Thursday, sir? The time is very short.

Paris My father Capulet will have it so,
And I am nothing slow to slack his haste.

Friar Laurence You say you do not know the lady's mind?
Uneven is the course; I like it not.   5

Paris Immoderately she weeps for Tybalt's death,
And therefore have I little talk of love,
For Venus smiles not in a house of tears.
Now, sir, her father counts it dangerous
That she doth give her sorrow so much sway,   10
And in his wisdom hastes our marriage,
To stop the inundation of her tears,
Which, too much minded by herself alone,
May be put from her by society.
Now do you know the reason of this haste.   15

Friar Laurence I would I knew not why it should be slowed.
Look, sir, here comes the lady towards my cell.

Enter Juliet

Paris Happily met, my lady and my wife.

Juliet That may be, sir, when I may be a wife.

Paris That 'may be' must be, love, on Thursday next.   20

Juliet What must be shall be.

Friar Laurence   That's a certain text.

Paris Come you to make confession to this father?

Despite her distress, Juliet talks wittily with Paris. When Paris leaves and she is alone with the Friar, she breaks down in tears.

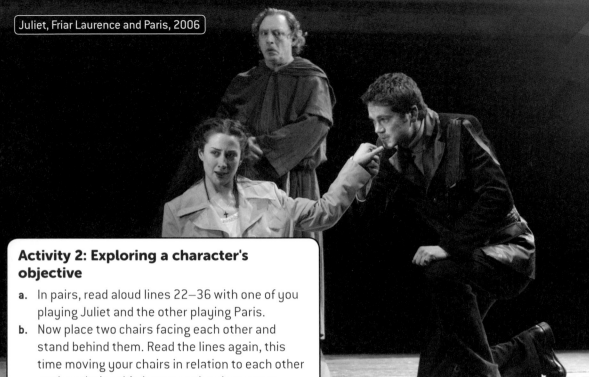

Juliet, Friar Laurence and Paris, 2006

Activity 2: Exploring a character's objective

a. In pairs, read aloud lines 22–36 with one of you playing Juliet and the other playing Paris.

b. Now place two chairs facing each other and stand behind them. Read the lines again, this time moving your chairs in relation to each other as the relationship between the characters develops. For example, if you think that your character wants a clear answer from the other person, you might put your chair down directly in front of them. If you think your character wants the other person to like you, you might move your chair gently to the side of them. Try to follow your instincts rather than planning how you will move the chair next.

c. What do you think Paris wants in this scene (his **objective**) and how might he try to get it (his **tactics**)?

d. What tactics do you think Juliet might use to get away from Paris?

e. Discuss how the way you moved the chairs reflected how Juliet and Paris feel as they speak and listen at this point. How would you describe the relationship between Juliet and Paris?

Glossary

27 **more price** greater worth

43 **holy kiss** Paris gently kisses her forehead, hand or cheek

47 **compass of my wits** limits of my mind

48 **prorogue** delay

Key terms

Objective what a character wants to get or achieve in a scene, e.g. Juliet wants to get away from Paris in this scene

Tactics the methods a character uses to get what they want, e.g. Juliet might pretend to be shy or speak faster to end the conversation

Juliet	To answer that, I should confess to you.	
Paris	Do not deny to him that you love me.	
Juliet	I will confess to you that I love him.	25
Paris	So will ye, I am sure, that you love me.	
Juliet	If I do so, it will be of more price, Being spoke behind your back, than to your face.	
Paris	Poor soul, thy face is much abused with tears.	
Juliet	The tears have got small victory by that, For it was bad enough before their spite.	30
Paris	Thou wrong'st it more than tears with that report.	
Juliet	That is no slander, sir, which is a truth, And what I spake, I spake it to my face.	
Paris	Thy face is mine, and thou hast slandered it.	35
Juliet	It may be so, for it is not mine own. Are you at leisure, holy father, now, Or shall I come to you at evening mass?	
Friar Laurence	My leisure serves me, pensive daughter, now. My lord, we must entreat the time alone.	40
Paris	God shield I should disturb devotion. Juliet, on Thursday early will I rouse ye. Till then, adieu, and keep this holy kiss.	
	Exit Paris	
Juliet	O, shut the door, and when thou hast done so, Come weep with me, past hope, past care, past help.	45
Friar Laurence	O, Juliet, I already know thy grief, It strains me past the compass of my wits. I hear thou must, and nothing may prorogue it, On Thursday next be married to this County.	

Juliet feels her situation is desperate. She is determined to kill herself with a dagger she is carrying rather than marry Paris, unless the Friar can suggest another course of action. The Friar is impressed by her bravery and says he has an idea.

Activity 3: Exploring Juliet's fears

a. In pairs, read lines 52–59 aloud together.
b. Create **gestures** for the key words in each line. For example, in line 52 you might tap your head for 'wisdom' and hold out your arms for 'help'.
c. Read the lines aloud again, adding the gestures.
d. Discuss why you think Juliet is so determined to die rather than marry Paris.
e. Now read lines 77–88 in your pairs, swapping reader at each punctuation mark.
f. In pairs, one person reads lines 77–88 again, while the other listens with eyes closed, repeating aloud any words that help them to imagine what Juliet is describing. For example, you might repeat 'leap', 'battlements' and 'tower' in the first two lines as you imagine Juliet jumping from a tall tower.
g. Discuss which of the things Juliet describes you would find the most frightening. Why does Shakespeare have Juliet describe all these frightening things?
h. Write a paragraph or two with the title: 'How Juliet feels about marrying Paris'. In your writing, include examples of some of the **imagery** Juliet uses.

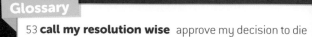

Glossary

53 **call my resolution wise** approve my decision to die
62 **my extremes** my desperation
64 **commission** authority
74 **chide away this shame** drive away this potential sin
81 **charnel-house** chapel where bones are kept
83 **reeky shanks** bones with rotting flesh

Juliet, 2010

Key terms

Gesture a movement, often using the hands or head, to express a feeling or idea
Imagery visually descriptive language

Juliet Tell me not, friar, that thou hearest of this, 50
  Unless thou tell me how I may prevent it.
  If in thy wisdom thou canst give no help,
  Do thou but call my resolution wise,
  And with this knife I'll help it presently.
  God joined my heart and Romeo's, thou our hands, 55
  And ere this hand, by thee to Romeo sealed,
  Shall be the label to another deed,
  Or my true heart with treacherous revolt
  Turn to another, this shall slay them both.
  Therefore, out of thy long-experienced time, 60
  Give me some present counsel, or behold
  'Twixt my extremes and me this bloody knife
  Shall play the umpire, arbitrating that
  Which the commission of thy years and art
  Could to no issue of true honour bring. 65
  Be not so long to speak, I long to die,
  If what thou speak'st speak not of remedy.

Friar Laurence Hold, daughter. I do spy a kind of hope,
  Which craves as desperate an execution
  As that is desperate which we would prevent. 70
  If, rather than to marry County Paris,
  Thou hast the strength of will to slay thyself,
  Then is it likely thou wilt undertake
  A thing like death to chide away this shame,
  That cop'st with death himself to 'scape from it. 75
  And if thou dar'st, I'll give thee remedy.

Juliet O bid me leap, rather than marry Paris,
  From off the battlements of any tower,
  Or walk in thievish ways, or bid me lurk
  Where serpents are. Chain me with roaring bears, 80
  Or hide me nightly in a charnel-house,
  O'er-covered quite with dead men's rattling bones,
  With reeky shanks and yellow chapless skulls.
  Or bid me go into a new-made grave
  And hide me with a dead man in his tomb – 85
  Things that to hear them told have made me tremble –

The Friar explains his plan that Juliet should agree to marry Paris but, on the night before her wedding, she should drink a potion, which will send her into a sleep so deep that, for 42 hours, everyone will think she is dead. Romeo will meet her when she wakes up in the Capulet tomb and they will run away together.

Friar Laurence and Juliet, 2010

Activity 4: Exploring the Friar's plan

a. In groups, read the Friar's speech, lines 89–120, swapping reader at each punctuation mark.
b. Create three to five **freeze-frames** showing the Friar's plan.
c. Choose a line or phrase from the Friar's speech as a title for each of your freeze-frames.
d. Rehearse a performance of your freeze-frames, finding a way to move smoothly from one image to the next. Agree who will speak aloud the line or phrase giving the title for each image.
e. Discuss whether you think the Friar's plan is a good idea. What might go wrong?

Glossary

88 **an unstained wife** faithful to my wedding vows
93 **vial** small bottle
94 **distilling liquor** liquid that will infuse the whole body
97 **surcease** stop
100 **wanny ashes** pale as ashes
119 **inconstant toy** change of mind
120 **Abate thy valour** weaken your strength

Key term

Freeze-frame a physical, still image created by people to represent an object, place, person or feeling

And I will do it without fear or doubt,
To live an unstained wife to my sweet love.

Friar Laurence   Hold, then. Go home, be merry, give consent
To marry Paris. Wednesday is tomorrow.   90
Tomorrow night look that thou lie alone,
Let not thy nurse lie with thee in thy chamber.
Take thou this vial, being then in bed,
And this distilling liquor drink thou off;
When presently through all thy veins shall run   95
A cold and drowsy humour; for no pulse
Shall keep his native progress, but surcease.
No warmth, no breath shall testify thou liv'st.
The roses in thy lips and cheeks shall fade
To wanny ashes; thy eyes' windows fall,   100
Like death when he shuts up the day of life.
Each part, deprived of supple government,
Shall stiff and stark and cold appear like death.
And in this borrowed likeness of shrunk death
Thou shalt continue two-and-forty hours,   105
And then awake as from a pleasant sleep.
Now when the bridegroom in the morning comes
To rouse thee from thy bed, there art thou dead.
Then as the manner of our country is,
In thy best robes, uncovered on the bier,   110
Thou shalt be borne to that same ancient vault
Where all the kindred of the Capulets lie.
In the mean time, against thou shalt awake,
Shall Romeo by my letters know our drift,
And hither shall he come, and he and I   115
Will watch thy waking, and that very night
Shall Romeo bear thee hence to Mantua.
And this shall free thee from this present shame,
If no inconstant toy, nor womanish fear,
Abate thy valour in the acting it.   120

Juliet   Give me, give me, O, tell not me of fear.

The Friar tells Juliet to go home and he will send the letters to Romeo in Mantua. Juliet goes home with some hope.

Friar Laurence, 2010

Activity 5: Writing the Friar's letter

Imagine you are the Friar. Write the letter to Romeo in Mantua in modern English. Include:

- what has happened since Romeo left Verona
- your impression of how Juliet is coping with it all
- what your plan is and what you need Romeo to do
- your hopes for the future.

Glossary

123 **In this resolve** in this determination
125 **help afford** give help

Friar Laurence   Hold, get you gone, be strong and prosperous
In this resolve. I'll send a friar with speed
To Mantua, with my letters to thy lord.

Juliet   Love give me strength, and strength shall help afford.   125
Farewell, dear father.

Exeunt

Lord Capulet gives orders to the servants in preparation for the wedding. Juliet arrives back from seeing Friar Laurence and apologises to her father, promising to obey him from now on.

Activity 1: Exploring the theme of family

a. In pairs, read lines 15–28 with one of you playing Lord Capulet and the other playing Juliet.

b. Read lines 15–28 aloud again, as if Lord Capulet loves his daughter and wants her to forgive him for being angry, while Juliet also wants her father to love and forgive her.

c. Read lines 15–28 aloud again, but this time read the lines as if Lord Capulet wants Juliet to admit she was wrong and give him the respect he deserves, while Juliet wants to get away from her father as quickly as she can and is pretending to respect him.

d. Discuss which of these versions from tasks b or c you think worked best. Try to think of other 'as ifs' you could apply to lines 15–28 and try them out with your partner.

e. Write a short account of what happens in these lines from the point of view of the character you played.

Glossary

9 **unfurnished** unprepared

11 **forsooth** in truth

13 **peevish self-willed harlotry** foolish, headstrong wretch

Key term

Theme the main ideas explored in a piece of literature, e.g. the themes of love, loyalty, friendship, family and fate might be considered key themes of *Romeo and Juliet*

Lord Capulet and his servants, 2010

Act 4 | Scene 2

Enter Lord Capulet, Lady Capulet, Nurse and a Servant

Lord Capulet   So many guests invite as here are writ.
                   Sirrah, go hire me twenty cunning cooks.

Servant   You shall have none ill, sir, for I'll try if they
              can lick their fingers.

Lord Capulet   How canst thou try them so?   5

Servant   Marry, sir, 'tis an ill cook that cannot lick his own fingers.
              Therefore he that cannot lick his fingers goes not with me.

Lord Capulet   Go, be gone.

Exit Servant

                   We shall be much unfurnished for this time.
                   What, is my daughter gone to Friar Laurence?   10

Nurse   Ay, forsooth.

Lord Capulet   Well, he may chance to do some good on her.
                   A peevish self-willed harlotry it is.

Enter Juliet

Nurse   See where she comes from shrift with merry look.

Lord Capulet   How now, my headstrong, where have you been gadding?   15

Juliet   Where I have learned me to repent the sin
             Of disobedient opposition
             To you and your behests, and am enjoined
             By holy Laurence to fall prostrate here,
             To beg your pardon. *(Juliet kneels)* Pardon, I beseech you. 20
             Henceforward I am ever ruled by you.

Lord Capulet   Send for the County, go tell him of this.
                   I'll have this knot knit up tomorrow morning.

Lord Capulet is delighted that Juliet has changed her mind. Juliet asks the Nurse to help her prepare for the wedding and Lord Capulet decides the wedding should be the following day, Wednesday, instead of Thursday.

Activity 2: Exploring Lord Capulet's actions

a. Read lines 32–39. Then discuss your responses to the following questions:
   i. Why do you think Juliet says the wedding is tomorrow in line 34? Is it just a mistake?
   ii. Why does Lady Capulet say it should be on Thursday?
   iii. Why does Lord Capulet decide to bring the wedding forward to Wednesday?

b. Paris first asked Lord Capulet about marrying Juliet just two days ago on Sunday. Why do you think Lord Capulet is pleased to see his daughter married to Paris so quickly?

c. Imagine you are Lord Capulet. Write a paragraph that begins 'As the head of the Capulet household, I feel my responsibilities to my family are…'.

Glossary

25 **becomèd** appropriate

33 **needful ornaments** necessary clothes and accessories

39 **warrant** guarantee

Did you know?

Playwrights often raise the stakes in situations, making something seem more important or more pressing by creating time restrictions. For example, because the wedding to Paris is to happen so quickly, Juliet is forced into action.

Lord Capulet and Juliet, 2006

Juliet   I met the youthful lord at Laurence' cell,
And gave him what becomèd love I might,   25
Not stepping o'er the bounds of modesty.

Lord Capulet Why, I am glad on't, this is well, stand up.

Juliet rises

This is as't should be. Let me see the County.
Ay, marry, go, I say, and fetch him hither.
Now, afore God, this reverend holy friar,   30
All our whole city is much bound to him.

Juliet   Nurse, will you go with me into my closet,
To help me sort such needful ornaments
As you think fit to furnish me tomorrow?

Lady Capulet No, not till Thursday, there's time enough.   35

Lord Capulet Go, nurse, go with her. We'll to church tomorrow.

Exeunt Juliet and Nurse

Lady Capulet We shall be short in our provision,
'Tis now near night.

Lord Capulet   Tush, I will stir about,
And all things shall be well, I warrant thee, wife.
Go thou to Juliet, help to deck up her.   40
I'll not to bed tonight, let me alone.
I'll play the housewife for this once. What, ho?
They are all forth. Well, I will walk myself
To County Paris, to prepare him up
Against tomorrow. My heart is wondrous light,   45
Since this same wayward girl is so reclaimed.

Exeunt

Juliet is with her Nurse, organising what to wear for her wedding the next day. Lady Capulet offers help, but Juliet says goodnight and sends both the Nurse and her mother away. After they are gone she considers calling them back, believing she will never see them again.

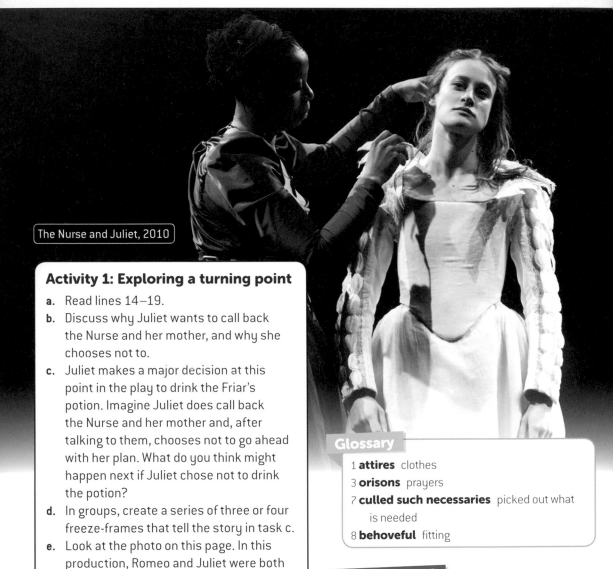

The Nurse and Juliet, 2010

Activity 1: Exploring a turning point

a. Read lines 14–19.

b. Discuss why Juliet wants to call back the Nurse and her mother, and why she chooses not to.

c. Juliet makes a major decision at this point in the play to drink the Friar's potion. Imagine Juliet does call back the Nurse and her mother and, after talking to them, chooses not to go ahead with her plan. What do you think might happen next if Juliet chose not to drink the potion?

d. In groups, create a series of three or four freeze-frames that tell the story in task c.

e. Look at the photo on this page. In this production, Romeo and Juliet were both dressed in modern clothing, with the rest of the cast in Elizabethan dress, up until this point. Discuss why you think this is the moment the director of this production chose to put Juliet in Elizabethan costume.

Glossary

1 **attires** clothes

3 **orisons** prayers

7 **culled such necessaries** picked out what is needed

8 **behoveful** fitting

Did you know?

Imagining what else could have happened at a turning point in a play helps an actor to consider the consequences of the choice their character makes and the importance of how and why they make that choice.

Enter Juliet and Nurse

Juliet   Ay, those attires are best, but, gentle nurse,
I pray thee leave me to myself tonight,
For I have need of many orisons
To move the heavens to smile upon my state,
Which, well thou know'st, is cross and full of sin.   5

Enter Lady Capulet

Lady Capulet   What, are you busy, ho? Need you my help?

Juliet   No, madam, we have culled such necessaries
As are behoveful for our state tomorrow.
So please you, let me now be left alone,
And let the nurse this night sit up with you,   10
For I am sure you have your hands full all,
In this so sudden business.

Lady Capulet   Goodnight.
Get thee to bed, and rest, for thou hast need.

Exeunt Lady Capulet and Nurse

Juliet   Farewell. God knows when we shall meet again.
I have a faint cold fear thrills through my veins,   15
That almost freezes up the heat of life.
I'll call them back again to comfort me.
Nurse! What should she do here?
My dismal scene I needs must act alone.
Come, vial.   20
What if this mixture do not work at all?
Shall I be married then tomorrow morning?
No, no, this shall forbid it. Lie thou there.

She lays down a dagger

Juliet thinks carefully before drinking the potion and considers everything that might happen to her if she does.

Activity 2: Exploring the Capulet vault

a. In pairs, read lines 24–58, swapping reader at each punctuation mark.

b. Identify all the things that Juliet is scared might happen if she drinks the potion.

c. Make a list of words and phrases from Juliet's speech that help you imagine the place she is describing.

d. Add any words of your own to the list that you think would describe the Capulet vault. Include words that describe how it might smell, feel and sound, as well as what it looks like.

e. In pairs, one of you should close your eyes and listen as the other uses the list of words from tasks c and d to describe the vault as though you are both inside it.

f. Swap over and repeat task e so that both of you have an opportunity to listen and imagine being in the vault.

g. Now write a description of being in the vault in your own words.

h. Look at the photo on this page. Why do you think the director of this production chose to have Tybalt's ghost appear behind Juliet at this moment?

Tybalt and Juliet, 2010

What if it be a poison, which the friar
Subtly hath ministered to have me dead,   25
Lest in this marriage he should be dishonoured,
Because he married me before to Romeo?
I fear it is, and yet methinks it should not,
For he hath still been tried a holy man.
How if, when I am laid into the tomb,   30
I wake before the time that Romeo
Come to redeem me? There's a fearful point.
Shall I not then be stifled in the vault,
To whose foul mouth no healthsome air breathes in,
And there die strangled ere my Romeo comes?   35
Or if I live, is it not very like,
The horrible conceit of death and night,
Together with the terror of the place,
As in a vault, an ancient receptacle:
Where for these many hundred years the bones   40
Of all my buried ancestors are packed;
Where bloody Tybalt, yet but green in earth,
Lies festering in his shroud; where, as they say,
At some hours in the night spirits resort.
Alack, alack, is it not like that I,   45
So early waking what with loathsome smells,
And shrieks like mandrakes' torn out of the earth,
That living mortals, hearing them, run mad –
O if I wake, shall I not be distraught,
Environèd with all these hideous fears,   50
And madly play with my forefathers' joints?
And pluck the mangled Tybalt from his shroud?
And in this rage, with some great kinsman's bone,
As with a club, dash out my desperate brains?
O look, methinks I see my cousin's ghost   55
Seeking out Romeo that did spit his body
Upon a rapier's point. Stay, Tybalt, stay.
Romeo, Romeo, Romeo! Here's drink. I drink to thee.

She drinks and falls on the bed

205

Lord and Lady Capulet, the Nurse and the Capulet servants rush around making preparations for the wedding.

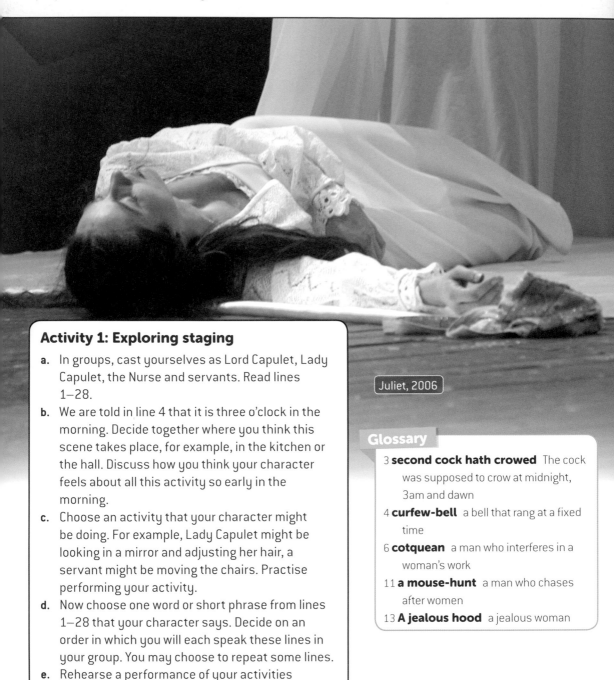

Juliet, 2006

Activity 1: Exploring staging

a. In groups, cast yourselves as Lord Capulet, Lady Capulet, the Nurse and servants. Read lines 1–28.

b. We are told in line 4 that it is three o'clock in the morning. Decide together where you think this scene takes place, for example, in the kitchen or the hall. Discuss how you think your character feels about all this activity so early in the morning.

c. Choose an activity that your character might be doing. For example, Lady Capulet might be looking in a mirror and adjusting her hair, a servant might be moving the chairs. Practise performing your activity.

d. Now choose one word or short phrase from lines 1–28 that your character says. Decide on an order in which you will each speak these lines in your group. You may choose to repeat some lines.

e. Rehearse a performance of your activities and lines in your group.

Glossary

3 **second cock hath crowed** The cock was supposed to crow at midnight, 3am and dawn

4 **curfew-bell** a bell that rang at a fixed time

6 **cotquean** a man who interferes in a woman's work

11 **a mouse-hunt** a man who chases after women

13 **A jealous hood** a jealous woman

Act 4 | Scene 4

Enter Lady Capulet and Nurse

Lady Capulet Hold, take these keys, and fetch more spices, nurse.

Nurse They call for dates and quinces in the pastry.

Enter Lord Capulet

Lord Capulet Come, stir, stir, stir! The second cock hath crowed,
The curfew-bell hath rung, 'tis three o'clock.
Look to the baked meats, good Angelica.   5
Spare not for cost.

Nurse   Go, you cotquean, go,
Get you to bed. Faith, you'll be sick tomorrow
For this night's watching.

Lord Capulet No, not a whit. What, I have watched ere now
All night for less cause, and ne'er been sick.   10

Lady Capulet Ay, you have been a mouse-hunt in your time,
But I will watch you from such watching now.

Exeunt Lady Capulet and Nurse

Lord Capulet A jealous hood, a jealous hood!

Enter Servants carrying various items
                  Now fellow,

What is there?

Servant 1 Things for the cook, sir, but I know not what.   15

Lord Capulet Make haste, make haste!

Exit Servant 1

               Sirrah, fetch drier logs.
Call Peter, he will show thee where they are.

Activity 2: Exploring the theme of fate

a. Juliet ended Act 4 Scene 3 by falling down, drugged into a deep sleep. In a stage production of the play where might she be lying during Act 4 Scene 4? Discuss whether you would have her visible to the audience or hidden in some way and why.

b. How far do you consider fate to be a reason for Juliet's decision to drink the potion? How far are she and other characters responsible for her decision?

c. Write a paragraph or two considering the theme of fate at this moment in the play.

Glossary

21 **logger-head** in charge of fetching logs; also a term for an idiot

25 **trim her up** get her dressed

The Nurse, 2010

Servant 2 I have a head, sir, that will find out logs,
And never trouble Peter for the matter.

Lord Capulet Mass, and well said, a merry whoreson, ha!   20
Thou shalt be logger-head.

Exit Servant 2. Music plays

Good faith, 'tis day.

The County will be here with music straight,
For so he said he would. I hear him near.
Nurse, Wife, what, ho! What, Nurse, I say!

Enter Nurse

Go waken Juliet, go and trim her up,   25
I'll go and chat with Paris. Hie, make haste,
Make haste, the bridegroom he is come already.
Make haste, I say!

Exit Lord Capulet. Nurse goes to wake Juliet

Activity 1: Exploring the Nurse

a. Read lines 1–7.

b. On your feet, read the lines again, but every time you reach a full stop, question mark or exclamation mark stand up or sit down. Every time you reach a comma, shift your position a little to face a different direction.

c. What do you think task b tells you about the Nurse's state of mind at this point?

d. Bearing in mind the advice she gave Juliet about marrying Paris on page 183, what do you think the Nurse might be thinking at this moment? Does she feel responsible for Juliet's death?

e. Imagine the Nurse speaks aloud her thoughts at this moment, addressing the audience in a short **soliloquy**. Write her speech in modern English. Include whether or not she blames herself for Juliet's death and what she thinks will happen to her next.

Glossary

16 **aqua vitae** 'water of life'; an alcoholic drink, like brandy

Key term

Soliloquy a speech in which a character is alone on stage and expresses their thoughts and feelings aloud to the audience

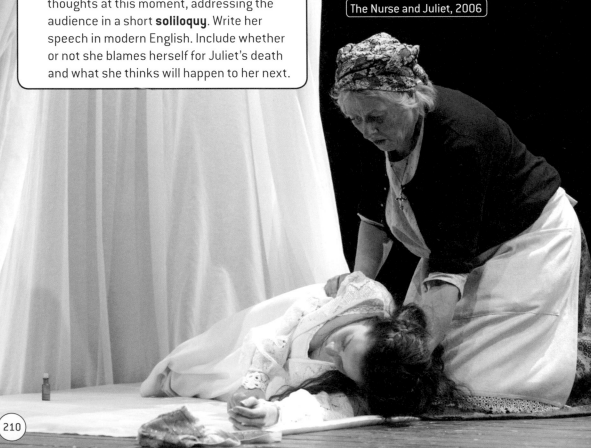

The Nurse and Juliet, 2006

Nurse	Mistress, what, mistress? Juliet? Fast, I warrant her, she.
	Why, lamb, why, lady! Fie, you slug-a-bed.
	Why, love, I say? Madam, sweetheart! Why, bride?
	What, not a word? You take your pennyworths now.
	Sleep for a week, for the next night, I warrant,
	The County Paris hath set up his rest,
	That you shall rest but little. God forgive me,
	Marry and amen. How sound is she asleep?
	I must needs wake her. Madam, madam, madam!
	Ay, let the County take you in your bed,
	He'll fright you up, i'faith. Will it not be?
	What, dressed, and in your clothes, and down again?
	I must needs wake you! Lady, lady, lady?
	Alas, alas! Help, help! My lady's dead!
	O, weladay, that ever I was born.
	Some aqua vitae, ho! My lord! My lady!

Enter Lady Capulet

Lady Capulet	What noise is here?
Nurse	O lamentable day!
Lady Capulet	What is the matter?
Nurse	Look, look! O heavy day!
Lady Capulet	O me, O me! My child, my only life!
	Revive, look up, or I will die with thee.
	Help, help! Call help.

Enter Lord Capulet

Lord Capulet	For shame, bring Juliet forth. Her lord is come.
Nurse	She's dead, deceased, she's dead, alack the day!

5

10

15

20

Juliet's parents rush into her bedroom, horrified that she is dead. Friar Laurence, Paris and the musicians arrive. Everyone is distraught at the discovery.

Activity 2: What does Juliet's death mean for the Capulets?

a. In groups, read lines 38–40 aloud together.

b. In lines 38–40, death is **personified**. Create a freeze-frame of Juliet's wedding with Death as the groom.

c. Juliet is an only child. Discuss what her death means for the Capulet family.

d. Imagine Lord Capulet speaks aloud his private thoughts at this moment in a short soliloquy. What do you think he might say? Write his speech in modern English. Include whether or not he feels he is to blame for Juliet's death and what he thinks will happen to his fortune and to the Capulet name.

Key term

Personification giving an object or concept human qualities

At the time

Using page 270, explain how death was personified in Shakespeare's time.

Lady and Lord Capulet with Juliet, 2006

Lady Capulet	Alack the day, she's dead, she's dead, she's dead!
Lord Capulet	Ha? Let me see her. Out, alas, she's cold. 25
	Her blood is settled, and her joints are stiff.
	Life and these lips have long been separated.
	Death lies on her like an untimely frost
	Upon the sweetest flower of all the field.
Nurse	O lamentable day!
Lady Capulet	O woeful time. 30
Lord Capulet	Death, that hath ta'en her hence to make me wail,
	Ties up my tongue, and will not let me speak.

Enter Friar Laurence, Paris and Musicians

Friar Laurence	Come, is the bride ready to go to church?
Lord Capulet	Ready to go, but never to return.
	O son, the night before thy wedding-day 35
	Hath Death lain with thy wife. There she lies,
	Flower as she was, deflowered by him.
	Death is my son-in-law; Death is my heir.
	My daughter he hath wedded. I will die,
	And leave him all, life, living, all is Death's. 40
Paris	Have I thought long to see this morning's face,
	And doth it give me such a sight as this?
Lady Capulet	Accursed, unhappy, wretched, hateful day!
	Most miserable hour that e'er time saw
	In lasting labour of his pilgrimage. 45
	But one, poor one, one poor and loving child,
	But one thing to rejoice and solace in,
	And cruel death hath catched it from my sight.
Nurse	O woe, O woeful, woeful, woeful day!
	Most lamentable day, most woeful day, 50
	That ever, ever, I did yet behold.
	O day, O day, O day, O hateful day!
	Never was seen so black a day as this.
	O woeful day, O woeful day!

The Capulet family and Paris continue to weep and wail about Juliet's death. The Friar calls for peace and says they should be pleased that Juliet is now in heaven, which is the best place to be.

Lord Capulet and Juliet, 2010

Glossary

55 **Beguiled** cheated

61 **murder our solemnity** destroy our celebrations

70 **heaven keeps his part...** her soul lives on in heaven

71 **her promotion** her social advancement in marrying Paris, now her spiritual advancement to heaven

79 **rosemary** a herb **symbolising** remembrance, which also helped mask the smell of death

83 **Yet nature's tears...** although we feel we want to cry, we should be happy that Juliet is now in heaven

90 **And all things change them...** everything takes on a different meaning

Activity 3: Exploring reactions to Juliet's death

a. Read aloud the Nurse's speech, lines 49–54 (page 213).

b. Read the lines again, overemphasising the words to bring out the **vowel** sounds.

c. What is the effect of so many vowel sounds so close together and of so much **repetition** in these lines?

d. In groups, cast yourselves as Lord Capulet, Lady Capulet, Paris, the Nurse and Friar Laurence. Create a freeze-frame of your reactions to Juliet's death, based on lines 1–83.

e. Choose three words each to speak and add these to your freeze-frame.

f. Imagine the Friar speaks aloud his thoughts at this moment. He walks downstage and addresses the audience in a short soliloquy. Write his speech in modern English. Include how he feels about the reactions from the family and what he thinks will happen next.

Key terms

Vowels the letters a, e, i, o, u

Repetition saying the same thing again

Symbol a thing that represents or stands for something else

Paris   Beguiled, divorced, wronged, spited, slain!   55
        Most detestable death, by thee beguiled,
        By cruel, cruel thee, quite overthrown.
        O love! O life! Not life, but love in death!

Lord Capulet   Despised, distressèd, hated, martyred, killed!
        Uncomfortable time, why cam'st thou now   60
        To murder, murder our solemnity?
        O child, O child! My soul, and not my child.
        Dead art thou, alack, my child is dead,
        And with my child my joys are burièd.

Friar Laurence   Peace, ho, for shame! Confusion's care lives not   65
        In these confusions. Heaven and yourself
        Had part in this fair maid, now heaven hath all,
        And all the better is it for the maid.
        Your part in her you could not keep from death,
        But heaven keeps his part in eternal life.   70
        The most you sought was her promotion,
        For 'twas your heaven she should be advanced.
        And weep ye now, seeing she is advanced
        Above the clouds, as high as heaven itself?
        O in this love, you love your child so ill   75
        That you run mad, seeing that she is well.
        She's not well married that lives married long,
        But she's best married that dies married young.
        Dry up your tears, and stick your rosemary
        On this fair corpse, and as the custom is,   80
        And in her best array, bear her to church.
        For though some nature bids us all lament,
        Yet nature's tears are reason's merriment.

Lord Capulet   All things that we ordainèd festival,
        Turn from their office to black funeral.   85
        Our instruments to melancholy bells,
        Our wedding cheer to a sad burial feast,
        Our solemn hymns to sullen dirges change,
        Our bridal flowers serve for a buried corpse,
        And all things change them to the contrary.   90

The Friar instructs the Capulet family to prepare for Juliet's funeral rather than her wedding. Peter enters and asks the musicians to play a happy song.

Activity 4: Exploring antithesis

a. Read aloud lines 84–90 (page 215).

b. In groups, list the various people, such as cooks and florists, who may have been employed by the Capulets to make the wedding happen.

c. Each person in the group chooses an activity to represent one of their jobs. Act this out and experiment with how that activity might change when the event becomes a funeral rather than a wedding.

d. Share Lord Capulet's speech (lines 84–90) between you and create a group performance where you speak these lines and perform your activities, changing their focus from a wedding to a funeral.

Key term

Antithesis bringing two opposing concepts or ideas together, e.g. hot and cold, love and hate, loud and quiet

Friar Laurence, Paris, Juliet and Lord Capulet, 2010

Friar Laurence   Sir, go you in, and madam, go with him,
And go, Sir Paris. Everyone prepare
To follow this fair corpse unto her grave.
The heavens do lour upon you for some ill,
Move them no more by crossing their high will.   95

Exeunt except Nurse and Musicians

Musician 1   Faith, we may put up our pipes, and be gone.

Nurse   Honest goodfellows. Ah, put up, put up,
For well you know this is a pitiful case.

Musician 1   Ay, by my troth, the case may be amended.

Enter Peter

Peter   Musicians, O, musicians, 'Heart's ease', 'Heart's ease'. O, and   100
you will have me live, play 'Heart's ease'.

Musician 1   Why 'Heart's ease'?

Peter   O, musicians, because my heart itself plays 'My heart is full of
woe'. O play me some merry dump to comfort me.

Musician 1   Not a dump we, 'tis no time to play now.   105

Peter   You will not, then?

Musician 1   No.

Peter   I will then give it you soundly.

Musician 1   What will you give us?

Peter   No money, on my faith, but the gleek. I will give you the minstrel.   110

Musician 1   Then will I give you the serving-creature.

Peter   Then will I lay the serving-creature's dagger on your pate. I will
carry no crotchets. I'll re you, I'll fa you. Do you note me?

Musician 1   An you re us and fa us, you note us.

Musician 2   Pray you put up your dagger, and put out your wit.   115

Activity 5: Exploring Shakespeare's clowns

a. In small groups, read lines 100–117 with one of you playing Peter and the others playing the musicians.

b. Read the lines again. This time the speaker holds an object such as a pencil case or a bottle of water and the next speaker must grab the object before speaking their own line. The person holding the object can make it easy or difficult for the next speaker to take it. This exercise can help us understand how Peter and the musicians try to score points off each other in this witty exchange.

c. Discuss what you think the musicians might be thinking about all that they have witnessed after entering with Paris at line 32.

d. This scene is often cut at line 95. Try to make an argument for keeping the exchange between Peter and the musicians at the end of this scene. Why do you think Shakespeare included it?

Friar Laurence and Lord Capulet, 2010

Glossary

116 **dry-beat** beat without drawing blood

124 **Prates** nonsense

Did you know?

Before rehearsals begin, a director edits the play, cutting lines and sometimes even scenes.

Key term

Clown an actor skilled in comedy and improvisation who could often sing and dance as well

Peter   Then have at you with my wit. I will dry-beat you with an iron
              wit, and put up my iron dagger. Answer me like men:
              (Sings) When griping griefs the heart doth wound,
                        And doleful dumps the mind oppress,
                        Then music with her silver sound—   120
              Why 'silver sound'? Why 'music with her silver sound'? What say
              you, Simon Catling?

Musician 1 Marry, sir, because silver hath a sweet sound.

Peter   Prates. What say you, Hugh Rebeck?

Musician 2 I say 'silver sound', because musicians sound for silver.   125

Peter   Prates too. What say you, James Soundpost?

Musician 3 Faith, I know not what to say.

Peter   O I cry you mercy, you are the singer. I will say for you. It is
              'music with her silver sound' because musicians have no gold
              for sounding.   130
              (Sings) Then music with her silver sound
                        With speedy help doth lend redress.

              Exit Peter

Musician 1 What a pestilent knave is this same!

Musician 2 Hang him, Jack! Come, we'll in here, tarry for the mourners,
              and stay dinner.   135

              Exeunt

219

Exploring Act 4

Activity 1: Looking at tension and plot development

a. Look back through Act 4 and list the main events. You could look back at the page summaries to help you.

b. Why do you think the scenes in Act 4 are relatively short?

c. What do you think the **dramatic climax** of this play might be? How do the events of Acts 3 and 4 suggest what might happen at the end of the play?

Key terms

Plot the events of a story

Dramatic climax the most intense or important point in the action of a play

Falling action the part of a play, before the very end, in which the consequences of the dramatic climax become clear

The Nurse and Juliet, 2006

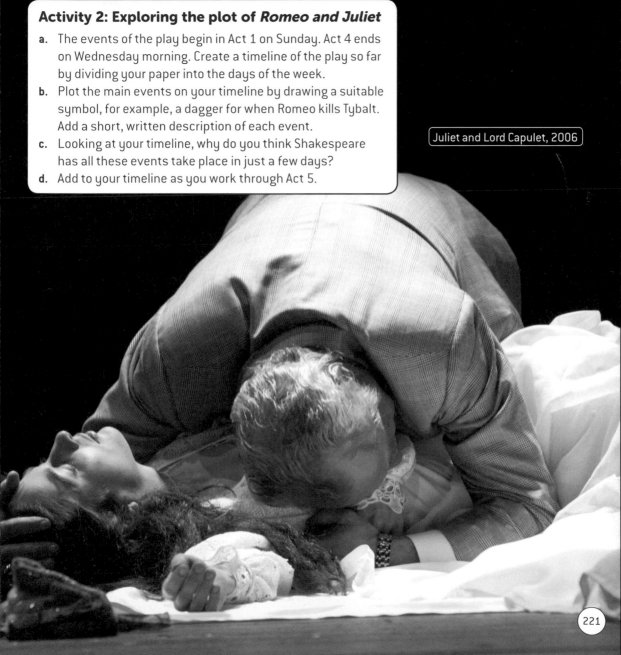

Activity 2: Exploring the plot of *Romeo and Juliet*

a. The events of the play begin in Act 1 on Sunday. Act 4 ends on Wednesday morning. Create a timeline of the play so far by dividing your paper into the days of the week.

b. Plot the main events on your timeline by drawing a suitable symbol, for example, a dagger for when Romeo kills Tybalt. Add a short, written description of each event.

c. Looking at your timeline, why do you think Shakespeare has all these events take place in just a few days?

d. Add to your timeline as you work through Act 5.

Juliet and Lord Capulet, 2006

Romeo is dreaming about how wonderful it would be to be with Juliet again. His servant Balthasar arrives with the news that Juliet is dead and lying in the Capulet tomb. Romeo immediately determines to go back to Verona to see her.

Activity 1: Exploring Romeo

a. In small groups, read lines 1–11, swapping reader at each punctuation mark.

b. One person in the group now reads aloud lines 6–9, while the others enact Romeo's dream. This should be your best over-the-top 'cartoon' acting.

c. How do you think Romeo feels as he speaks lines 1–11?

d. Read line 24 and discuss how you think Romeo feels now. What do you think he means by 'I defy you, stars!'?

Romeo, 2010

Did you know?

In rehearsals, actors sometimes act a scene in a fast, over-the-top way to bring out all of the emotions, like a 'cartoon' version of the scene. This disturbs the way the actors normally act the scene and stops them getting into set ways of performing.

Enter Romeo

Romeo   If I may trust the flattering truth of sleep,
My dreams presage some joyful news at hand.
My bosom's lord sits lightly in his throne,
And all this day an unaccustomed spirit
Lifts me above the ground with cheerful thoughts.   5
I dreamt my lady came and found me dead –
Strange dream, that gives a dead man leave to think –
And breathed such life with kisses in my lips,
That I revived, and was an emperor.
Ah me, how sweet is love itself possessed,   10
When but love's shadows are so rich in joy.

Enter Balthasar

News from Verona! How now, Balthasar?
Dost thou not bring me letters from the friar?
How doth my lady? Is my father well?
How doth my lady Juliet? That I ask again,   15
For nothing can be ill, if she be well.

Balthasar   Then she is well, and nothing can be ill.
Her body sleeps in Capel's monument,
And her immortal part with angels lives.
I saw her laid low in her kindred's vault,   20
And presently took post to tell it you.
O pardon me for bringing these ill news,
Since you did leave it for my office, sir.

Romeo   Is it even so? Then I defy you, stars!
Thou know'st my lodging, get me ink and paper,   25
And hire post-horses. I will hence tonight.

Balthasar says he has heard nothing from the Friar and leaves to arrange horses for Romeo. Meanwhile Romeo visits a poor apothecary, who he hopes will sell him some poison.

At the time

Using page 269, discuss the work of an apothecary in Shakespeare's time.

Romeo, 2010

Activity 2: Exploring the Apothecary's shop

a. Read lines 37–48.

b. Imagine you are in the Apothecary's shop. Discuss all the things that you can see and smell. What might you hear? How would you feel and what could you reach out and touch?

c. Form groups. Each person in the group writes three sentences on three separate pieces of paper. Each sentence should describe some aspect of what you can see, hear, smell or touch in the Apothecary's shop. Use **adjectives** to make your sentences more descriptive.

d. Spread all of your group's sentences out on the floor or desk. Pair up with someone else in your group. One of each pair should close their eyes as the other 'guides' them around the shop, describing what it is like using the group's sentences and adding any further descriptions they can think of. Swap over so you both get a chance to describe and listen.

e. Write your own description of the Apothecary's shop based on the group's sentences, your experience listening and your experience describing.

Glossary

37 **apothecary** a person who made and sold medicine

39 **tattered weeds** ragged clothes

39 **overwhelming brows** unkempt, bushy eyebrows

40 **Culling of simples** gathering herbs

47 **Remnants of packthread** bits of string

47 **cakes of roses** rose petals compressed for perfume

49 **penury** poverty

52 **caitiff** miserable

Key term

Adjective a word that describes a noun, e.g. blue, happy, big

Balthasar	I do beseech you, sir, have patience.
	Your looks are pale and wild, and do import
	Some misadventure.
Romeo	Tush, thou art deceived.
	Leave me, and do the thing I bid thee do.
	Hast thou no letters to me from the friar?
Balthasar	No, my good lord.
Romeo	No matter. Get thee gone,
	And hire those horses, I'll be with thee straight.

Exit Balthasar

Well, Juliet, I will lie with thee tonight.
Let's see for means. O mischief, thou art swift
To enter in the thoughts of desperate men.
I do remember an apothecary,
And hereabouts a dwells, which late I noted
In tattered weeds, with overwhelming brows,
Culling of simples. Meagre were his looks,
Sharp misery had worn him to the bones,
And in his needy shop a tortoise hung,
An alligator stuffed, and other skins
Of ill-shaped fishes; and about his shelves
A beggarly account of empty boxes,
Green earthen pots, bladders and musty seeds,
Remnants of packthread and old cakes of roses,
Were thinly scattered, to make up a show.
Noting this penury, to myself I said,
'And if a man did need a poison now,
Whose sale is present death in Mantua,
Here lives a caitiff wretch would sell it him.'
O this same thought did but forerun my need,
And this same needy man must sell it me.
As I remember, this should be the house.
Being holy-day, the beggar's shop is shut.
What, ho, apothecary!

Enter Apothecary

The Apothecary is reluctant to sell poison to Romeo as it is against the law, but Romeo tells him he is too poor to worry about obeying the world's laws when the world does not help him. Romeo takes the poison and heads back to Verona.

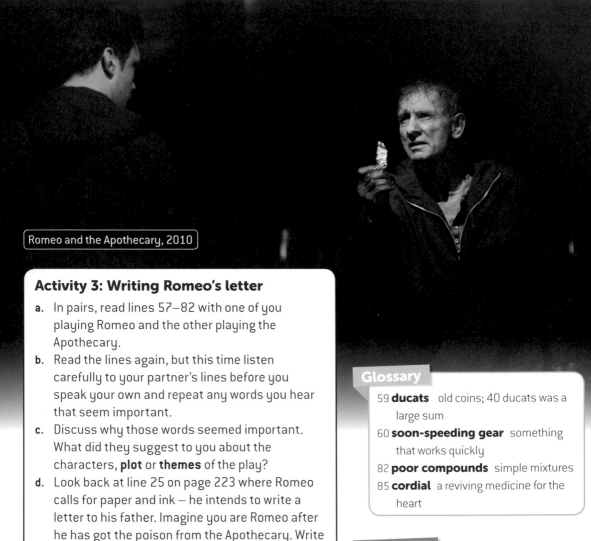

Romeo and the Apothecary, 2010

Activity 3: Writing Romeo's letter

a. In pairs, read lines 57–82 with one of you playing Romeo and the other playing the Apothecary.

b. Read the lines again, but this time listen carefully to your partner's lines before you speak your own and repeat any words you hear that seem important.

c. Discuss why those words seemed important. What did they suggest to you about the characters, **plot** or **themes** of the play?

d. Look back at line 25 on page 223 where Romeo calls for paper and ink – he intends to write a letter to his father. Imagine you are Romeo after he has got the poison from the Apothecary. Write the letter to Lord Montague in modern English, including:
- an account of how you met and married Juliet
- why you didn't tell your father until now
- why you feel you must return to Verona
- what you intend to do
- what you want your father to think about you.

Glossary

59 **ducats** old coins; 40 ducats was a large sum
60 **soon-speeding gear** something that works quickly
82 **poor compounds** simple mixtures
85 **cordial** a reviving medicine for the heart

Key terms

Plot the events of a story
Theme the main ideas explored in a piece of literature, e.g. the themes of love, loyalty, friendship, family and fate might be considered key themes of *Romeo and Juliet*

Apothecary	Who calls so loud?	
Romeo	Come hither, man. I see that thou art poor.	
	Hold, there is forty ducats. Let me have	
	A dram of poison, such soon-speeding gear	60
	As will disperse itself through all the veins	
	That the life-weary taker may fall dead	
	And that the trunk may be discharged of breath	
	As violently as hasty powder fired	
	Doth hurry from the fatal cannon's womb.	65
Apothecary	Such mortal drugs I have, but Mantua's law	
	Is death to any he that utters them.	
Romeo	Art thou so bare and full of wretchedness,	
	And fear'st to die? Famine is in thy cheeks,	
	Need and oppression starveth in thy eyes,	70
	Contempt and beggary hangs upon thy back.	
	The world is not thy friend, nor the world's law.	
	The world affords no law to make thee rich,	
	Then be not poor, but break it and take this.	
Apothecary	My poverty, but not my will, consents.	75
Romeo	I pay thy poverty, and not thy will.	
Apothecary	Put this in any liquid thing you will	
	And drink it off, and if you had the strength	
	Of twenty men, it would dispatch you straight.	
Romeo	There's thy gold, worse poison to men's souls,	80
	Doing more murder in this loathsome world,	
	Than these poor compounds that thou may'st not sell.	
	I sell thee poison, thou hast sold me none.	
	Farewell, buy food, and get thyself in flesh.	

Exit Apothecary

Come, cordial and not poison, go with me — 85
To Juliet's grave, for there must I use thee.

Exit Romeo

Friar Laurence hears from Friar John that he was unable to deliver to Romeo the letter that explains Friar Laurence's plan. Friar John was suspected of having the plague and locked in a house.

Activity 1: Exploring plot

a. In pairs, read lines 1–22 with one of you playing Friar John and the other playing Friar Laurence.
b. Edit lines 1–22 to just 12 words. These can be single words or phrases from the text.
c. Create **gestures** to go with the 12 words you have chosen. For example, if you chose 'Romeo?' in line 3, you might use your hands to gesture that this is a question. If you chose 'pestilence' in line 10, you might gesture that this is something horrible.
d. In your pairs, perform the scene using only your 12 chosen words and accompanying gestures.
e. Discuss why you chose the words you did. What emotions did your choices bring out? Did you need to make any changes to your words or gestures to make your performance better?
f. Discuss who or what is to blame for the truth about Juliet's death not getting to Romeo.
g. Why do you think Shakespeare includes this short scene?

Key term

Gesture a movement, often using the hands or head, to express a feeling or idea

At the time

Using pages 269–270, discuss how plague affected people's lives in Shakespeare's time.

Friar John and Friar Laurence, 2010

Act 5 | Scene 2

Enter Friar John

Friar John   Holy Franciscan friar, brother, ho?

Enter Friar Laurence

Friar Laurence   This same should be the voice of Friar John.
Welcome from Mantua. What says Romeo?
Or if his mind be writ, give me his letter.

Friar John   Going to find a barefoot brother out,   5
One of our order, to associate me,
Here in this city visiting the sick,
And finding him, the searchers of the town,
Suspecting that we both were in a house
Where the infectious pestilence did reign,   10
Sealed up the doors, and would not let us forth,
So that my speed to Mantua there was stayed.

Friar Laurence   Who bare my letter then to Romeo?

Friar John   I could not send it – here it is again –
Nor get a messenger to bring it thee,   15
So fearful were they of infection.

Friar Laurence   Unhappy fortune. By my brotherhood,
The letter was not nice but full of charge,
Of dear import, and the neglecting it
May do much danger. Friar John, go hence,   20
Get me an iron crow, and bring it straight
Unto my cell.

Friar John   Brother, I'll go and bring it thee.

Exit Friar John

Friar Laurence is very worried, knowing Juliet will soon wake up. He decides to fetch her and hide her in his home until Romeo arrives.

Activity 2: Exploring the Friar

a. Look at the photo on this page and try to copy the Friar's position and facial expression.

b. Discuss how you think the Friar feels at this moment.

c. Read lines 23–29. **Paraphrase** these lines and write it down.

Glossary

25 **beshrew** curse

Key term

Paraphrase put a line or section of text into your own words

Friar Laurence, 2010

Friar Laurence   Now must I to the monument alone,
Within this three hours will fair Juliet wake.
She will beshrew me much that Romeo   25
Hath had no notice of these accidents,
But I will write again to Mantua,
And keep her at my cell till Romeo come.
Poor living corpse, closed in a dead man's tomb.

Exit Friar Laurence

It is night-time in the graveyard and Paris is mourning the death of Juliet by laying flowers and perfumed water on her tomb. His servant warns him that someone else is coming and he hides. Romeo arrives with Balthasar.

Activity 1: Exploring the theme of loyalty

a. In pairs, read lines 12–17 aloud together.

b. Read the lines again, swapping reader at each punctuation mark and addressing each other as 'Juliet' when you speak.

c. Read lines 12–17 again. This time read the lines as if you are doing your duty as Juliet's fiancé, but you are already interested in someone else.

d. Read lines 12–17 again, but this time read the lines as if you really loved Juliet and feel you will never find anyone else.

e. How did your reading of the lines differ in tasks c and d? Discuss which version you think works best and why.

f. What do you think about Paris? Is he arrogant for believing Juliet would want to marry him or misled and unlucky to be caught up in this tragedy? How do you think the theme of loyalty is reflected in the character of Paris?

g. Imagine you are the director for a production of the play. Write notes for your **casting** director about the kind of actor you want to play Paris. Include a summary of the character's personality, as well as ideas on how he should look and sound, and give examples of famous actors who could play your Paris.

Paris and Juliet, 2010

Glossary

1 **aloof** at a distance

12 **Sweet flower** Paris is addressing Juliet

14 **dew** sprinkle

16 **obsequies** funeral rites

22 **mattock and the wrenching iron** pickaxe and crowbar

Key term

Casting deciding which actors should play which roles

Act 5 | Scene 3

Enter Paris and his Page

Paris   Give me thy torch, boy. Hence, and stand aloof.
Yet put it out, for I would not be seen.
Under yon yew trees lay thee all along,
Holding thy ear close to the hollow ground,
So shall no foot upon the churchyard tread,   5
Being loose, unfirm with digging up of graves,
But thou shalt hear it. Whistle then to me
As signal that thou hear'st something approach.
Give me those flowers. Do as I bid thee, go.

Page   I am almost afraid to stand alone   10
Here in the churchyard, yet I will adventure.

Paris   Sweet flower, with flowers thy bridal bed I strew
O woe, thy canopy is dust and stones,
Which with sweet water nightly I will dew,
Or wanting that, with tears distilled by moans.   15
The obsequies that I for thee will keep
Nightly shall be to strew thy grave and weep.

Page whistles

The boy gives warning something doth approach.
What cursèd foot wanders this way tonight,
To cross my obsequies and true love's rite?   20
What, with a torch? Muffle me, night, awhile.

Enter Romeo and Balthasar

Romeo   Give me that mattock and the wrenching iron.
Hold, take this letter. Early in the morning
See thou deliver it to my lord and father.
Give me the light. Upon thy life, I charge thee,   25
Whate'er thou hear'st or see'st, stand all aloof,

Romeo has come prepared to break into the tomb. He sends Balthasar away after giving him money, but Balthasar is worried about what Romeo intends to do and hides close by. Paris recognises Romeo and challenges him.

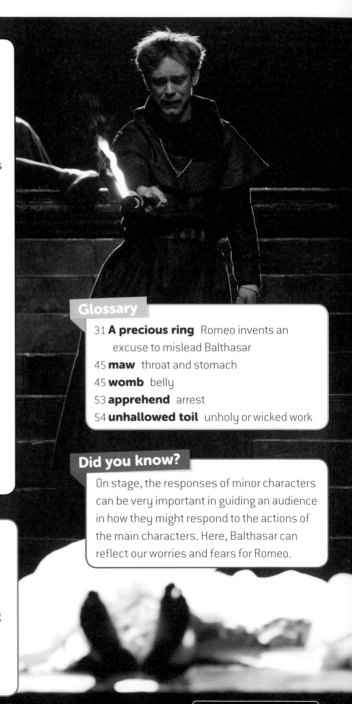

Activity 2: Exploring the theme of love

a. Read lines 45–48.

b. Create gestures for the key words in each line. For example, for 'detestable maw' you could open your mouth wide and use your hands to indicate a huge mouth.

c. Create a performance of lines 45–48, thinking about **tone** of voice and **emphasis**, and adding your gestures.

d. Discuss how Romeo feels as he speaks lines 45–48. What does he want? How effective is the **extended metaphor** he uses here?

e. How do you think a positive feeling like love has brought Romeo to this moment?

f. Imagine you are Balthasar, listening to Romeo as he speaks lines 45–48. Write a paragraph in modern English explaining how you feel at this point and what you think Romeo will do next.

Glossary

31 **A precious ring** Romeo invents an excuse to mislead Balthasar
45 **maw** throat and stomach
45 **womb** belly
53 **apprehend** arrest
54 **unhallowed toil** unholy or wicked work

Did you know?

On stage, the responses of minor characters can be very important in guiding an audience in how they might respond to the actions of the main characters. Here, Balthasar can reflect our worries and fears for Romeo.

Key terms

Tone as in 'tone of voice'; expressing an attitude through how you say something

Emphasis stress given to words when speaking

Extended metaphor describing something by comparing it to something else over several lines, e.g. Romeo compares the Capulet tomb to a mouth and stomach in lines 45–48

Romeo and Juliet, 2010

And do not interrupt me in my course.
Why I descend into this bed of death
Is partly to behold my lady's face,
But chiefly to take thence from her dead finger 30
A precious ring, a ring that I must use
In dear employment. Therefore hence, be gone.
But if thou, jealous, dost return to pry
In what I further shall intend to do,
By heaven, I will tear thee joint by joint 35
And strew this hungry churchyard with thy limbs.
The time and my intents are savage-wild,
More fierce and more inexorable far
Than empty tigers or the roaring sea.

Balthasar I will be gone, sir, and not trouble you. 40

Romeo So shalt thou show me friendship. Take thou that.

Gives him money

Live and be prosperous, and farewell, good fellow.

Balthasar [Aside] For all this same, I'll hide me hereabout.
His looks I fear, and his intents I doubt.

Romeo Thou detestable maw, thou womb of death, 45
Gorged with the dearest morsel of the earth.
Thus I enforce thy rotten jaws to open,
And in despite I'll cram thee with more food.

Paris This is that banished haughty Montague,
That murdered my love's cousin, with which grief 50
It is supposèd the fair creature died,
And here is come to do some villainous shame
To the dead bodies. I will apprehend him.
Stop thy unhallowed toil, vile Montague!
Can vengeance be pursued further than death? 55
Condemnèd villain, I do apprehend thee.
Obey and go with me, for thou must die.

Romeo tells Paris to leave, but Paris refuses and they fight. Romeo kills Paris and then remembers that Balthasar told him Paris was to marry Juliet. Romeo drags Paris into the tomb and then he sees Juliet.

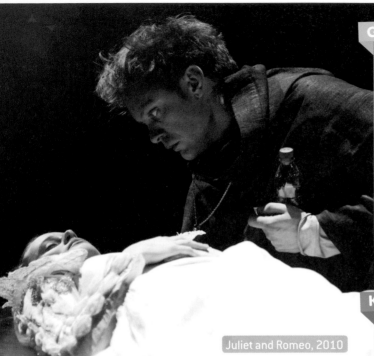

Juliet and Romeo, 2010

Activity 3: Exploring rhythm

a. On your feet, read aloud lines 74–87.

b. Read the lines aloud again, but this time stand or sit each time you reach a full stop or question mark.

c. How does task b help you to understand how Romeo feels?

d. Read the lines aloud again, emphasising the **iambic pentameter** rhythm.

e. When lines don't fit the rhythm, as in line 78, what might this suggest about how Romeo feels?

f. Make a list of all the words you can think of to describe how Romeo feels as he speaks lines 74–87.

g. How do you think the way Shakespeare uses rhythm in lines 74–87 might help an actor understand how Romeo feels?

Key terms

Iambic pentameter the rhythm Shakespeare uses to write his plays. Each line in this rhythm contains approximately ten **syllables**. 'Iambic' means putting the stress on the second syllable of each beat. 'Pentameter' means five beats with two syllables in each beat

Syllable part of a word that is one sound, e.g. 'dignity' has three syllables – 'dig', 'ni', 'ty'

Did you know?

The way Shakespeare plays with the rhythm helps actors to understand how a character feels. The short questions in line 79, for example, give a sense of how distracted Romeo is.

Romeo   I must indeed, and therefore came I hither.
Good gentle youth, tempt not a desperate man,
Fly hence, and leave me. Think upon these gone,   60
Let them affright thee. I beseech thee, youth,
Put not another sin upon my head,
By urging me to fury. O, be gone!
By heaven, I love thee better than myself,
For I come hither armed against myself.   65
Stay not, be gone, live, and hereafter say,
A madman's mercy bid thee run away.

Paris   I do defy thy commiseration,
And apprehend thee for a felon here.

Romeo   Wilt thou provoke me? Then have at thee, boy!   70

Page   O lord, they fight! I will go call the watch.

Exit Page

Paris   O, I am slain. If thou be merciful,
Open the tomb, lay me with Juliet.

Paris dies

Romeo   In faith, I will. Let me peruse this face.
Mercutio's kinsman, noble County Paris.   75
What said my man, when my betossèd soul
Did not attend him as we rode? I think
He told me Paris should have married Juliet.
Said he not so? Or did I dream it so?
Or am I mad, hearing him talk of Juliet,   80
To think it was so? O, give me thy hand,
One writ with me in sour misfortune's book.
I'll bury thee in a triumphant grave.
A grave? O no, a lantern, slaughtered youth,
For here lies Juliet, and her beauty makes   85
This vault a feasting presence full of light.
Death, lie thou there, by a dead man interred.
How oft when men are at the point of death
Have they been merry? Which their keepers call

Romeo admires Juliet's beauty once more before he says goodbye and drinks the poison. He dies quickly by her side.

Activity 4: Exploring the theme of fate

a. Read lines 92–96.

b. Read the lines again in a whisper, emphasising the sounds in every word. How does this change your understanding of the lines?

c. Which words are repeated in lines 92–96? Why do you think these words are important to Romeo?

d. What does Romeo's description of Juliet tell the audience?

e. In groups, read lines 101–120. One of you plays Romeo, one is Juliet and the others are directors. One director **feeds the lines** to the person playing Romeo. The directors should also advise on what Romeo might be doing and how he might be speaking. Try to build tension for the audience as we wonder if Juliet will wake up in time.

f. Decide in your group at what point Juliet will wake up. Will it be during or after Romeo's speech? How might this decision affect the audience as they watch the scene?

g. Write a paragraph or two about the role fate has to play in Romeo's death.

Romeo and Juliet, 2006

Did you know?

In some productions, Juliet begins to wake up during Romeo's speech, but he does not notice until it is too late.

A lightning before death? O, how may I   90
Call this a lightning? O my love, my wife!
Death that hath sucked the honey of thy breath,
Hath had no power yet upon thy beauty.
Thou art not conquered; beauty's ensign yet
Is crimson in thy lips and in thy cheeks,   95
And Death's pale flag is not advancèd there.
Tybalt, liest thou there in thy bloody sheet?
O what more favour can I do to thee
Than with that hand that cut thy youth in twain
To sunder his that was thy enemy?   100
Forgive me, cousin. Ah, dear Juliet,
Why art thou yet so fair? Shall I believe
That unsubstantial Death is amorous,
And that the lean abhorrèd monster keeps
Thee here in dark to be his paramour?   105
For fear of that, I still will stay with thee,
And never from this palace of dim night
Depart again. Here, here will I remain
With worms that are thy chambermaids. O, here
Will I set up my everlasting rest,   110
And shake the yoke of inauspicious stars
From this world-wearied flesh. Eyes, look your last.
Arms, take your last embrace. And, lips, O you
The doors of breath, seal with a righteous kiss
A dateless bargain to engrossing Death.   115
Come, bitter conduct, come, unsavoury guide!
Thou desperate pilot, now at once run on
The dashing rocks thy sea-sick weary bark!
Here's to my love.

Romeo drinks the poison

                O true apothecary,
Thy drugs are quick. Thus with a kiss I die.   120

Enter Friar Laurence

Friar Laurence   Saint Francis be my speed! How oft tonight
Have my old feet stumbled at graves. Who's there?

Balthasar   Here's one, a friend, and one that knows you well.

Friar Laurence reaches the tomb and hears from Balthasar that Romeo is inside. He finds the bodies of both Romeo and Paris. Juliet wakes up.

Activity 5: Exploring character through movement

a. In pairs, read lines 124–136 with one of you playing the Friar and the other playing Balthasar.

b. To help you understand more about the characters, their relationships and their motives, read the lines again. This time, as you speak and listen, you should keep choosing between the following movements:

- Take a step towards the other character.
- Take a step away from the other character.
- Turn towards the other character.
- Turn away from the other character.
- Stand still.

Try to make instinctive choices rather than planning what to do.

c. In your pairs, read lines 124–136 again, but this time try making different choices about how you move.

d. Discuss:

  i. your understanding of the characters in this section

  ii. which decisions worked best in tasks b and c to make the scene engaging for the audience.

e. Now create a **freeze-frame** in your pairs to illustrate this moment in the play. From their frozen position, each character speaks aloud their thoughts about the other characters in the scene.

f. Explain what you now understand about the Friar and Balthasar that you didn't understand before.

Juliet and Romeo, 2010

Glossary

125 **yon** over there

126 **discern** think; work out

143 **discoloured** stained (with blood)

Key term

Freeze-frame a physical, still image created by people to represent an object, place, person or feeling

Friar Laurence   Bliss be upon you. Tell me, good my friend,
What torch is yon that vainly lends his light   125
To grubs and eyeless skulls? As I discern,
It burneth in the Capels' monument.

Balthasar   It doth so, holy sir, and there's my master,
One that you love.

Friar Laurence   Who is it?

Balthasar   Romeo.

Friar Laurence   How long hath he been there?

Balthasar   Full half an hour.   130

Friar Laurence   Go with me to the vault.

Balthasar   I dare not, sir.
My master knows not but I am gone hence,
And fearfully did menace me with death
If I did stay to look on his intents.

Friar Laurence   Stay then, I'll go alone. Fear comes upon me.   135
O, much I fear some ill unlucky thing.

Balthasar   As I did sleep under this yew tree here,
I dreamt my master and another fought,
And that my master slew him.

Friar Laurence   Romeo!
Alack, alack, what blood is this which stains   140
The stony entrance of this sepulchre?
What mean these masterless and gory swords
To lie discoloured by this place of peace?
Romeo, O, pale! Who else? What, Paris too?
And steeped in blood? Ah, what an unkind hour   145
Is guilty of this lamentable chance?
The lady stirs.

Juliet   O, comfortable friar, where's my lord?
I do remember well where I should be,
And there I am. Where is my Romeo?   150

Friar Laurence tries to persuade Juliet to go with him and become a nun, but she refuses to leave Romeo. Paris's page has alerted the Watch. The Friar hears them approach and is scared of being caught, so runs away. Juliet refuses to go with him; instead she stabs herself. The Constable arrives to find three newly dead bodies.

Juliet and Romeo, 2010

Activity 6: Exploring the theme of love

a. Read lines 161–169 (ignoring the Constable's line).

b. Read the lines again in a whisper, emphasising the sounds in every word. How does this change your understanding of the lines?

c. In groups, read lines 161–169. One of you plays Juliet, one is Romeo and the others are directors. One director feeds the lines to the person playing Juliet. The directors should also advise on what Juliet might be doing and how she might be speaking. Try to build tension for the audience as we wonder if Juliet will really kill herself.

d. Why do you think Juliet's death happens more quickly than Romeo's?

e. Write a paragraph or two explaining how you think the themes of love and fate come together in Juliet's death.

At the time

Using page 263, discuss what you discover about the role of the Watch in Shakespeare's time.

Glossary

153 **A greater power** Friar Laurence could mean fate, luck or God

162 **timeless** untimely or eternal

166 **restorative** Juliet means the kiss that should have woken her up

Friar Laurence	I hear some noise. Lady, come from that nest	
	Of death, contagion, and unnatural sleep.	
	A greater power than we can contradict	
	Hath thwarted our intents. Come, come away.	
	Thy husband in thy bosom there lies dead,	155
	And Paris too. Come, I'll dispose of thee	
	Among a sisterhood of holy nuns.	
	Stay not to question, for the watch is coming.	
	Come, go, good Juliet, I dare no longer stay.	

Exit Friar Laurence

Juliet	Go, get thee hence, for I will not away.	160
	What's here? A cup closed in my true love's hand?	
	Poison I see hath been his timeless end.	
	O churl, drink all and left no friendly drop	
	To help me after? I will kiss thy lips,	
	Haply some poison yet doth hang on them,	165
	To make me die with a restorative.	
	Thy lips are warm.	

Enter Page and Constable with The Watch

Constable	Lead, boy, which way?	

Juliet	Yea, noise? Then I'll be brief. O happy dagger,	
	This is thy sheath. There rust, and let me die.	

Juliet kills herself

Page	This is the place, there where the torch doth burn.	170

Constable	The ground is bloody. Search about the churchyard.	
	Go, some of you, whoe'er you find, attach.	
	Pitiful sight! Here lies the County slain,	
	And Juliet bleeding, warm, and newly dead,	
	Who here hath lain these two days burièd.	175
	Go, tell the Prince, run to the Capulets,	
	Raise up the Montagues, some others search.	

The Watch bring in Balthasar and the Friar. The Prince arrives, shortly followed by Lord and Lady Capulet. There is lots of commotion on the streets of Verona as people hear rumours and wonder what has happened.

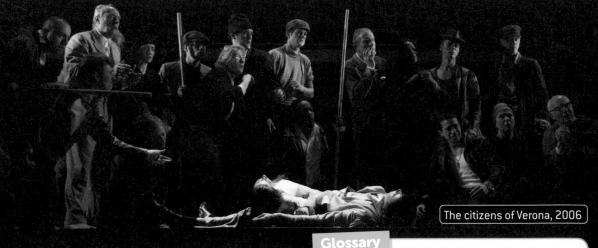

The citizens of Verona, 2006

Activity 7: Exploring staging

a. On a sheet of paper, draw the Prince in the centre (a stick-man is fine). Then draw all the characters who appear in Act 5 Scene 3 wherever you think they should be placed in relation to the Prince at this moment.

b. Choose a word or phrase from page 245 (or previous pages in the scene) for each character you have drawn and write it in a speech bubble over their head.

c. Make a list of all the **verbs** on page 245.

d. What do these verbs suggest about the mood of this moment?

e. With a partner, compare your pictures and your lists of verbs. Discuss what effect you think this scene might have on the audience.

f. How are the play's themes of love, loyalty, friendship, family and fate reflected in the relationships between the characters?

Glossary

179 **the true ground** the real cause, with a **pun** on the actual ground where the bodies lie

180 **We cannot without circumstance descry** without detailed knowledge we can't know what has happened

187 **misadventure** misfortune

194 **Sovereign** This is a respectful address to the Prince

Did you know?

The stage management team are responsible for making notes in a **prompt book** about decisions made in the rehearsal room. In a scene like this, with lots of characters and action, they might sketch out who is where on the stage.

Key terms

Verb a 'doing' or action word, such as *jump*, *shout, listen*

Pun a play on words

Prompt book a copy of the script kept by the stage management team with space for notes and sketches about staging

	We see the ground whereon these woes do lie,	
	But the true ground of all these piteous woes	
	We cannot without circumstance descry.	180

The Watch bring in Balthasar

Watch 1	Here's Romeo's man. We found him in the churchyard.

Constable	Hold him in safety, till the Prince come hither.

The Watch bring in Friar Laurence

Watch 2	Here is a friar that trembles, sighs and weeps.
	We took this mattock and this spade from him,
	As he was coming from this churchyard side.

185

Constable	A great suspicion. Stay the friar too.

Enter the Prince with attendants

Prince	What misadventure is so early up,
	That calls our person from our morning rest?

Enter Lord Capulet, Lady Capulet and others

Lord Capulet	What should it be that they so shriek abroad?

Lady Capulet	O the people in the street cry 'Romeo',
	Some 'Juliet', and some 'Paris', and all run
	With open outcry toward our monument.

190

Prince	What fear is this which startles in your ears?

Constable	Sovereign, here lies the County Paris slain,
	And Romeo dead, and Juliet, dead before,
	Warm and new killed.

195

Prince	Search, seek, and know how this foul murder comes.

Constable	Here is a friar, and slaughtered Romeo's man,
	With instruments upon them, fit to open
	These dead men's tombs.

200

Lord Capulet	O heaven! O wife, look how our daughter bleeds!
	This dagger hath mista'en, for lo his house

Lord Montague arrives and explains that his wife has died of a broken heart. The Prince demands to know what has happened and the Friar begins to tell him.

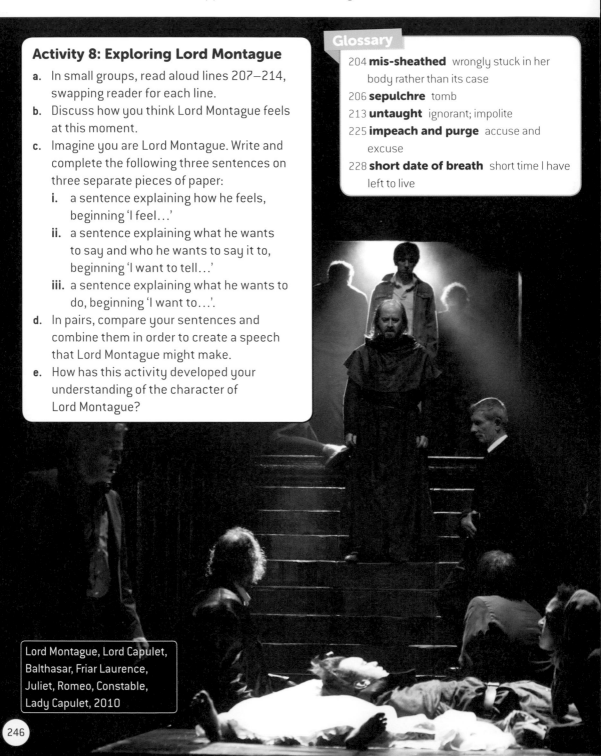

Activity 8: Exploring Lord Montague

a. In small groups, read aloud lines 207–214, swapping reader for each line.
b. Discuss how you think Lord Montague feels at this moment.
c. Imagine you are Lord Montague. Write and complete the following three sentences on three separate pieces of paper:
   i. a sentence explaining how he feels, beginning 'I feel…'
   ii. a sentence explaining what he wants to say and who he wants to say it to, beginning 'I want to tell…'
   iii. a sentence explaining what he wants to do, beginning 'I want to…'.
d. In pairs, compare your sentences and combine them in order to create a speech that Lord Montague might make.
e. How has this activity developed your understanding of the character of Lord Montague?

Glossary

204 **mis-sheathed** wrongly stuck in her body rather than its case
206 **sepulchre** tomb
213 **untaught** ignorant; impolite
225 **impeach and purge** accuse and excuse
228 **short date of breath** short time I have left to live

Lord Montague, Lord Capulet, Balthasar, Friar Laurence, Juliet, Romeo, Constable, Lady Capulet, 2010

Is empty on the back of Montague,
And is mis-sheathed in my daughter's bosom.

Lady Capulet O me, this sight of death is as a bell   205
That warns my old age to a sepulchre.

Enter Lord Montague

Prince Come, Montague, for thou art early up
To see thy son and heir now early down.

Lord Montague Alas, my liege, my wife is dead tonight.
Grief of my son's exile hath stopped her breath.   210
What further woe conspires against mine age?

Prince Look and thou shalt see.

Lord Montague O, thou untaught, what manners is in this?
To press before thy father to a grave?

Prince Seal up the mouth of outrage for awhile,   215
Till we can clear these ambiguities,
And know their spring, their head, their true descent,
And then will I be general of your woes,
And lead you even to death. Meantime forbear,
And let mischance be slave to patience.   220
Bring forth the parties of suspicion.

Friar Laurence I am the greatest, able to do least,
Yet most suspected, as the time and place
Doth make against me of this direful murder.
And here I stand both to impeach and purge   225
Myself condemnèd and myself excused.

Prince Then say at once what thou dost know in this.

Friar Laurence I will be brief, for my short date of breath
Is not so long as is a tedious tale.
Romeo, there dead, was husband to that Juliet,   230
And she, there dead, that's Romeo's faithful wife.
I married them and their stolen marriage-day
Was Tybalt's doomsday, whose untimely death

Activity 9: Exploring the Friar's story

a. In groups, read lines 230–263, swapping reader at the end of each sentence.

b. Now two or three people in your group become the Friar, taking it in turns to read aloud a sentence at a time. As they read, the others in the group act out the story as the Friar narrates it. The actors should respond quickly to whatever is described using their best over-the-top acting.

c. Discuss why you think Shakespeare has the Friar tell the story in this way at this point in the play.

d. As a group, decide on the three moments you think are the most important to the Friar's story and why.

e. Create a freeze-frame for each of these three moments.

f. Write a paragraph for each of the three moments your group chose, describing the moment and why you believe it is important to the action and the themes of the play.

Glossary

237 **Betrothed** engaged to be married

242 **by my art** through my skill

244 **it wrought on her** it worked on her

254 **keep her closely** keep her hidden

265 **is privy** shared the secret

265 **aught** anything

266 **Miscarried** went wrong

The citizens of Verona, Friar Laurence, Romeo and Juliet, 2006

Banished the new-made bridegroom from this city;
For whom, and not for Tybalt, Juliet pined.   235
You, to remove that siege of grief from her,
Betrothed and would have married her perforce
To County Paris. Then comes she to me,
And with wild looks bid me devise some means
To rid her from this second marriage,   240
Or in my cell there would she kill herself.
Then gave I her, so tutored by my art,
A sleeping potion, which so took effect
As I intended, for it wrought on her
The form of death. Meantime I writ to Romeo   245
That he should hither come as this dire night
To help to take her from her borrowed grave,
Being the time the potion's force should cease.
But he which bore my letter, Friar John,
Was stayed by accident, and yesternight   250
Returned my letter back. Then all alone,
At the prefixèd hour of her waking,
Came I to take her from her kindred's vault,
Meaning to keep her closely at my cell,
Till I conveniently could send to Romeo.   255
But when I came, some minute ere the time
Of her awaking, here untimely lay
The noble Paris and true Romeo dead.
She wakes, and I entreated her come forth,
And bear this work of heaven with patience.   260
But then a noise did scare me from the tomb,
And she, too desperate, would not go with me,
But, as it seems, did violence on herself.
All this I know, and to the marriage
Her nurse is privy. And if aught in this   265
Miscarried by my fault, let my old life
Be sacrificed, some hour before the time,
Unto the rigour of severest law.

Prince We still have known thee for a holy man.
Where's Romeo's man? What can he say to this?   270

The Prince reads Romeo's letter, which confirms the Friar's story. Lord Capulet and Lord Montague promise to bury their hatred and create golden statues of Romeo and Juliet to remember them by.

Activity 10: Exploring the themes of family and loyalty

a. In small groups, read lines 290–303.
b. Create two freeze-frames: one of line 290 and the other of line 303. Each freeze-frame should show clearly how each character feels at that moment.
c. Discuss how you think each character might feel at the end of the play. Do you think Lord Capulet and Lord Montague really want to be friends?
d. Choose one phrase spoken by each character from lines 290–303 that you think best represents how they feel. Explain your choice.
e. Rehearse a sequence that begins with your first freeze-frame, brings the scene to life as the characters speak the phrases you have chosen and then ends on the second freeze-frame.
f. Now each character in the freeze-frame speaks aloud their true thoughts.
g. How do you think the themes of family and loyalty are reflected in this moment?

The citizens of Verona, 2006

Balthasar	I brought my master news of Juliet's death,
	And then in post he came from Mantua
	To this same place, to this same monument.
	This letter he early bid me give his father,
	And threatened me with death, going in the vault,
	If I departed not and left him there.

275

Prince	Give me the letter, I will look on it.
	Where is the County's page, that raised the watch?
	Sirrah, what made your master in this place?

Page	He came with flowers to strew his lady's grave,
	And bid me stand aloof, and so I did.
	Anon comes one with light to ope the tomb,
	And by and by my master drew on him,
	And then I ran away to call the watch.

280

Prince	This letter doth make good the friar's words,
	Their course of love, the tidings of her death.
	And here he writes that he did buy a poison
	Of a poor 'pothecary, and therewithal
	Came to this vault to die, and lie with Juliet.
	Where be these enemies? Capulet, Montague?
	See what a scourge is laid upon your hate,
	That heaven finds means to kill your joys with love.
	And I for winking at your discords too
	Have lost a brace of kinsmen. All are punished.

285

290

Lord Capulet	O brother Montague, give me thy hand.
	This is my daughter's jointure, for no more
	Can I demand.

295

Lord Montague	But I can give thee more,
	For I will raise her statue in pure gold,
	That whiles Verona by that name is known,
	There shall no figure at such rate be set
	As that of true and faithful Juliet.

300

Activity 11: Exploring the final moment

a. In groups, look closely at the photo on this page and identify which character you think is being portrayed by which actor.

b. Write a line in modern English to express how each character feels at this moment.

c. How do you think an audience will feel watching the play at this moment?

Glossary

304 **glooming** gloomy

Lord Capulet, Balthasar, Friar Laurence, Juliet and Romeo, Constable, Lady Capulet, 2010

Lord Capulet   As rich shall Romeo by his lady lie,
Poor sacrifices of our enmity.

Prince   A glooming peace this morning with it brings,
The sun, for sorrow, will not show his head.   305
Go hence to have more talk of these sad things,
Some shall be pardoned, and some punishèd,
For never was a story of more woe
Than this of Juliet and her Romeo.

Exeunt omnes

Exploring Act 5

Activity 1: Exploring fate

a. Look at the Friar's line in Act 5 Scene 3 (line 136): 'I fear some ill unlucky thing'. Other references to fate include:

- Before going to the Capulet party, Romeo said: 'my mind misgives/ Some consequence yet hanging in the stars/ Shall bitterly begin his fearful date/ With this night's revels' (Act 1 Scene 4, lines 104–107).
- When he killed Tybalt, Romeo said: 'O, I am fortune's fool!' (Act 3 Scene 1, line 126).
- When he heard of Juliet's death, he said: 'I defy you, stars!' (Act 5 Scene 1, line 24).

What other moments are there in Act 5 when a character has mentioned fate, luck or being governed by the stars?

b. In small groups, list all the examples of bad luck that happen in the play. Discuss how far you think that bad luck might have been prevented if characters had behaved differently. Do you think bad luck or characters' actions are most to blame for Romeo's death?

c. Write your own response to the question in task b, making your argument clear and persuasive.

Romeo, 2010

Activity 2: Exploring the ending of the play

a. How far did Act 5 provide the ending you expected to the play? Give reasons for your answer.

b. Write an essay explaining how one or more of the key themes of the play is concluded in Act 5. Include in your answer any final developments to the theme (or themes) in this final act. Don't forget to include some specific detail and quotations from the play in your answer.

Juliet and Romeo, 2006

Exploring the play

Activity 1: Exploring the play as a whole

a. In groups, discuss what the citizens of Verona might be thinking about recent events.

b. One of you takes on the role of producer of a news channel, while the others are journalists on your team and people of Verona. Together create a five-minute TV report that focuses on this tragic outcome of the Capulet–Montague feud in Verona. The producer is responsible for creating the shooting script, which details what happens and when during the report. It should include timings for each item in the report.

c. The report should include: film footage of key events (which you could enact live or film), interviews with key witnesses, interviews with experts and a summing up of what will happen next.

Juliet and Romeo, 2010

Activity 2: Assessing the importance of the play

Look at the photo on page 256, taken from the last scene of the play. In this production, the director chose to have Romeo and Juliet in modern dress and everyone else in Elizabethan dress. However, in the last scene of this production, the costume choice is reversed – Romeo and Juliet are in Elizabethan dress while everyone else is now in modern dress.

The director wanted to convey to his audience the idea that Romeo and Juliet are just like teenagers in any time and any place when they are alive, but when they die they become frozen in time and the world moves on.

a. Discuss the following questions:
   i. How far do you agree with the director? In what ways are Romeo and Juliet like teenagers you know and in what ways are they not?
   ii. What do we learn about relationships within families and between friends through studying this play?
   iii. What do you think is the main message of this play?
   iv. Why do you think the play is considered to be worth studying in this day and age?

b. Following your discussion, write an essay with the title 'How is Shakespeare's play *Romeo and Juliet* still relevant today?'
   Think about the following when writing your essay:
   • themes
   • plot and structure
   • characterisation
   • use of language.

Balthasar, Lord Capulet, Lady Capulet, Romeo, Juliet, Benvolio, 2006

Shakespeare's life

William Shakespeare is probably the most famous playwright of all time. Here's a summary of his life, his work and important events at the time.

1564
William Shakespeare is born in Stratford-upon-Avon.

1595
Romeo and Juliet and *A Midsummer Night's Dream* first performed.

1593
Shakespeare's first published work, the poem *Venus and Adonis*.

1592–3
The London theatres close for several months because of a plague outbreak.

1596
The Merchant of Venice first performed.

1596
Hamnet Shakespeare dies and is buried in Stratford-upon-Avon.

1597
Shakespeare buys a large house, New Place, in Stratford-upon-Avon.

1608
Death of Shakespeare's mother, Mary.

1606
Macbeth first performed.

1605
The Gunpowder Plot, a threat to blow up the king in Parliament, fails. ➤

1611
The Tempest first performed.

1611
The *King James Bible*, or *Authorized Version*, is published.

1613
Shakespeare's last plays, *The Two Noble Kinsmen* and *Henry VIII*, both jointly written with John Fletcher, are performed.

1582

He marries Anne Hathaway.

1583

Susanna Shakespeare, William and Anne's first child, is born.

1585

Two more children, the twins Hamnet and Judith, are born.

1592

By this date Shakespeare had begun his career in London as an actor and playwright. A rival, Robert Greene, described him in print as an 'upstart crow'.

1588

◄ Spanish Armada is defeated.

1598

Much Ado About Nothing first performed.

1599

Shakespeare's theatre company builds the Globe theatre in London. ➤

1603

Death of Queen Elizabeth. The new king, James I, takes over the patronage of Shakespeare's company and they are renamed the King's Men.

1601

Death of Shakespeare's father, John.

1616

Shakespeare dies in Stratford-upon-Avon and is buried in a local church.

1623

The first collected edition of his plays, the *First Folio*, is published in London. ➤

Shakespeare's language

Shakespeare's language can be difficult for us to understand for two different reasons. One is historical: words and their meanings, and the ways people express themselves, have changed over the four hundred years since he wrote. The other is poetic: Shakespeare's characters don't speak like ordinary people, even in the Elizabethan period, would have spoken. They speak in a heightened, poetic language full of repetition and elaboration.

Verse and prose

Most Shakespeare plays are written in verse with a small proportion of prose included. You can tell verse from prose on the page because verse lines are usually shorter and each line begins with a capital letter, whereas prose lines usually begin with lower-case letters (unless it is the beginning of a sentence) and continue to the very edge of the paper. Verse is a more formal way of speaking and is often associated with higher-status characters, whereas servants or other lower-class figures more often speak prose. Comic scenes are sometimes in prose, where the language is more relaxed and natural.

Romeo and Benvolio, 2008

Shakespeare's verse is often called blank verse – blank means it does not rhyme. But occasionally he does use rhyme, sometimes in a couplet (two rhyming lines) at the end of a scene to signal that it has come to a conclusion. For example, here's the end of the first scene of *Romeo and Juliet*:

Romeo	Farewell, thou canst not teach me to forget.
Benvolio	I'll pay that doctrine, or else die in debt.

At other times, Shakespeare uses rhyme to suggest formality. Rhyming lines were probably easier for actors to learn.

Iambic pentameter

Poetry — like music — is words ordered into rhythm. The metre of poetry is like its drumbeat. Most of Shakespeare's verse lines are written in iambic pentameter. A pentameter means that there are five beats to the line (and usually ten syllables); iambic means that the beats are alternately weak and strong, or unstressed and stressed.

An example from *Romeo and Juliet* is the first line of the Prologue, below. The numbers below the line count the syllables; the marks below the numbers show that the syllables alternate between unstressed (signalled with -) and stressed (/). It looks more complicated when you write it down than when you read it aloud.

Chorus	Two households, both alike in dignity
	1 2 3 4 5 6 7 8 9 10
	- / - / - / - / - /

As with music, the sound of Shakespeare's language would get repetitive if he never varied the rhythm. So sometimes he changes the arrangement of stressed and unstressed syllables, and sometimes lines can be read with different emphases depending on the actor's interpretation. Reading Shakespeare's lines aloud often helps.

One clue: often Shakespeare puts important words or ideas at the end of his lines, rather than at the beginning. If you look down a speech and look at the last word in each line you can usually get some idea of the main point of the speech. One additional clue: with longer speeches, often the beginning and the end are the most important, and the middle says the same thing in different ways.

Shakespeare's world

Knowing something about life in Shakespeare's England is often helpful for our understanding of his plots and characters, and of the assumptions that members of his audiences would have had when they went to see his plays. But it is also important to remember that he was an imaginative playwright, making up stories for entertainment.

Just as we wouldn't necessarily rely on modern Hollywood films or television drama to depict our everyday reality, so too we need sometimes to acknowledge that Shakespeare is showing his audiences something exotic, unfamiliar or fairy tale.

London and the theatres

At some point in his early twenties, Shakespeare moved from the country town of Stratford to London. Thousands of people at the time did the same, moving to the city for work and other opportunities, and London expanded rapidly during the Elizabethan period. It was a busy, commercial place that had outgrown the original walled city and was now organised around the main thoroughfare, the river Thames. Shakespeare never sets a play in contemporary London, although many of his urban locations, particularly Venice, seem to recall the inns and streets and bustle of the city in which he and his audiences lived and worked.

17th-century engraving of London by Claes Jansz Visscher

As a port city, London was a place where people from different places mixed together, although its society was much less racially diverse than now. Jews had been banned from England in the medieval period, although there were some secret communities in London, so almost no one in Shakespeare's England would ever have met a Jewish person. A visit of Arab ambassadors from North Africa to Queen Elizabeth's court in 1600 must have seemed very exotic indeed.

The audience for Shakespeare's plays was quite mixed, but probably tended to be younger rather than older and male rather than female. Types of entertainment such as romantic comedy, that are now mainly associated with female audiences, were then directed at male theatregoers. Entry to the theatres was cheap – one penny, the cost of two pints of beer – so a relatively diverse social mix could attend. We don't know how well-educated the audience was, although educational opportunities were expanding during the 16th century and historians think that the number of men who were able to read and write in London at this point may have been as high as 50%. Literacy was connected to social status: wealthier individuals were much more likely to be educated than poorer ones. Laughing at unlearned people and their mistakes in language is a common source of comedy in Shakespeare's plays: we don't know how many of the people laughing were themselves not well-educated.

The Watch

Elizabethan England had no police force. Instead, the Watch was an amateur force of local men who agreed to serve their community for a fixed term, to keep order and patrol the night streets. Their job was to look out for thieves, to stop fights and to keep a watch for fires. Shakespeare's father John served as a constable in the Stratford Watch when his son was a child.

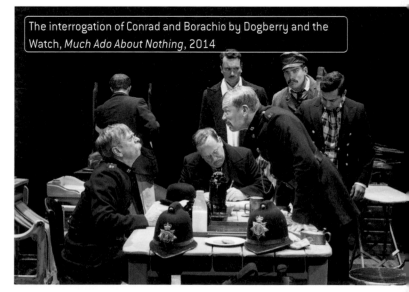

The interrogation of Conrad and Borachio by Dogberry and the Watch, *Much Ado About Nothing*, 2014

Comedy and tragedy

For us, a comedy is something funny. In Shakespeare's time, comedy had those associations too, but more importantly it was defined by the shape of the story. A comedy had a happy ending, in which characters were united, social bonds reaffirmed and things were better than they were at the beginning. A tragedy was the opposite: the central tragic character (often the play is named after them) becomes more and more isolated and is destroyed in a plot where things are definitely worse at the end than at the beginning. One of Shakespeare's fellow playwrights, Thomas Heywood, defined comedy and tragedy: 'comedies begin in trouble and end in peace; tragedies begin in calms and end in tempest'.

Mercutio in disguise, *Romeo and Juliet*, 2006

Masks

We don't know how popular masked parties or balls were in Elizabethan England, but Shakespeare makes use of them in his plays because they allow usual social conventions to be lifted. Under the cover of a mask, characters can speak their true thoughts or can have unusual access to other characters (particularly of the opposite sex) in disguise. In combining disguise with music and costumes, the masked ball is like the play itself: a space for characters to find out new things about themselves and each other.

Fate and the planets

Many people in Elizabethan England believed in horoscopes and the idea that the position of the planets at the time of birth influenced the child's future life. Astronomical events like solar or lunar eclipses or comets visible in the sky were often understood to be signs or portents. The planets were also thought to have a role in disease: the word 'influenza' (from which we get the abbreviation 'flu') comes from the Latin for 'astrological influence'. These older, more superstitious attitudes to the planets co-existed in Shakespeare's lifetime with new scientific discoveries, including Galileo's telescope and observations of the planets by other astronomers.

Don Armado and Moth, *Love's Labour's Lost*, 1946

Love

Claudio and Hero, *Much Ado About Nothing*, 1950

Romantic love had been a prominent literary theme for centuries. Courtly love traditions tended to present an idealised female figure who ignored her suffering admirer; romantic stories tended to end in disappointment or worse. Love was considered to be a random emotion (in contrast to the arranged marriages discussed under 'marriage and courtship' on pages 267–268). The symbolism of the blindfolded god of love, Cupid, was clear: Love did not care where his arrows fell, creating mayhem in the world by making people fall in love with each other. The goddess of sexual love, Venus, was well-known in Elizabethan literature: one of Shakespeare's earliest works is a long poem, *Venus and Adonis*, which flips the usual story for comic effect and shows the goddess longing for a young man who is not interested in her.

A person in love was often thought to show symptoms of melancholy or depression, and to withdraw from company, particularly of the same sex. Enjoying love poetry or other romantic literature, or the company of women (for men) might also be a sign of being in love.

Women

Ideas about the ideal woman are current in many societies, including modern ones. Just as we know that most real women now do not conform to the thin, beautiful, youthful ideal of modern advertising, so too probably Elizabethan women were different from the models given to them in conduct books, sermons and literature. The ideal woman, according to writers on morality in Shakespeare's England, remained meekly at home. She was chaste, honest, silent and obedient to her husband's will.

A moral double standard meant that women's behaviour, especially their chastity, was much more policed than that of men. Unmarried women were expected to obey their fathers and conduct themselves modestly. Women did not attend school or university, although wealthy ones might be educated at home. Except for widows, women could not hold property in their own right. But alongside these stereotypes there were many exceptional women, from Queen Elizabeth to the writer Mary Sidney and the pirate Mary Killigrew, as well as ordinary women living, working and running their households.

Rose Oatley, Sir Hugh Lacy and Rowland Lacy, *The Shoemaker's Holiday*, 2014

Marriage and courtship

Elizabethan marriages tended to be seen as alliances between families, as much as between the couple themselves. In wealthy or noble families, a suitable marriage arranged between the parents of the couple was common; for ordinary people, there may have been more possibility to choose a partner, although parental permission was still important. Marriage was a practical commitment rather than, or as well as, a romantic partnership: perhaps couples then did not place such high emotional expectations on their married relationships as in modern western societies. Some high-born people might be engaged as children, but the age of consent was 21 (Shakespeare needed his father's permission to marry aged just 18). Most Elizabethan brides and grooms were in their mid-twenties when they married.

Romeo and Juliet with Friar Laurence by Mather Brown, c.1805, Royal Shakespeare Company Collection (oil on canvas)

Weddings could happen in church, but they also could be legally contracted if the couple promised to marry each other in front of a witness and then consummated their relationship. A betrothal or engagement might precede the formal marriage service: this was a legally binding commitment between the couple. The Elizabethan church marriage service suggested that marriage had three purposes: children, the avoidance of fornication, and the comfort and companionship between husband and wife. Bible verses in the service instructed husbands to love and cherish their wives, and wives to submit to their husband's authority. The couple would wear their best clothes (the tradition of a bride wearing white came later) and afterwards there would usually be feasting.

Marriages were subject to the same problems and stresses then as now, although there was almost no divorce allowed in the Elizabethan period. Cheating on your husband or wife or being married to more than one person were seen as sins to be punished by the church courts; a clergyman who broke the rules on the correct forms of marriage would also be in serious trouble. A man whose wife was unfaithful, or rumoured to be unfaithful, was ridiculed and disrespected. He was known as a 'cuckold' and it was said that horns grew on his head.

Illegitimate children were often acknowledged within noble families – they were thought to have dark and negative personalities because they were born outside of marriage, which was considered immoral – but poor women who gave birth outside marriage were often left homeless and penniless. Lower-status women were the most vulnerable in Shakespeare's England: if a woman was thrown out by her family her prospects were very harsh indeed.

Children

In the Elizabethan period, children were expected to obey their parents, wives their husbands, and servants their masters. Consequences of disobedience could be very serious. Children in higher-class families often lived with relatives or were quite distant from their parents; for lower-status families, young children would be expected to work in the household. It is likely that the young Shakespeare would have helped out in his father's workshop. Young children in noble families wore the same clothes for both sexes until a ceremony called 'breeching' when boys began to wear breeches (trousers), aged about 7.

Duelling and sword fights

Being able to handle a sword was the mark of a gentleman in Elizabethan society (servants were not allowed to carry swords). Noblemen were often quick to take offence if they were insulted, and defending their honour was sometimes a justification for a challenge to a duel – a single combat with weapons. However common it might have been, duelling was actually illegal in Elizabethan England. Shakespeare's sword fights are more to do with the theatre than with real life. They play the same role for his audiences as action sequences in modern films do for us now, placing characters in an intense encounter, often where we want one particular individual to triumph. Sword fights also give fit male actors an excuse for impressive physical display.

Edgar duels with a masked opponent, *King Lear*, 2007

Health and medicine

The Elizabethans believed in an ancient theory that saw four elements — fire, earth, air and water — reflected in four parts of the body. These were known as 'humours': yellow bile, black bile, phlegm and blood. The balance of the humours was felt to be necessary for good health and when Shakespeare uses the word 'humour' he means something like 'temperament' rather than, as now, something funny.

Elizabethan doctors — physicians — treated only the wealthiest members of society who could pay for their services. Lower down in society, surgeons might deal with injuries and barbers were licensed to take blood (to balance the humours) and pull out teeth. The most common medical practitioner for ordinary people would have been an apothecary, who sold drugs and potions. Many people made their own remedies — known as simples — from herbs and other ingredients. There was little understanding of the relationship between health and sanitation, and, when outbreaks of plague happened in London, the main response was to ban gatherings of people at the theatre and to close up or quarantine infected houses.

Honour

Behaving honourably was an important element of male and female behaviour. But male and female honour were differently understood. For men, honour was about status and about being judged by others: keeping up appearances, looking brave and manly, not being ridiculed or made to look foolish. For women, honour was about sexual conduct: to be honourable was to be chaste and to be seen to be chaste. Honourable behaviour for women was to be beyond reproach.

The Apothecary, *Romeo and Juliet*, 2004

Death

Representations of death in the Elizabethan period often used a skeleton or a skull to suggest mortality. The image of the skeleton who is part of everyday life was key to a famous set of illustrations called the *Dance of Death*, which show how Death, complete with a scythe or other weapon, waits in every situation to take his prey. Monuments in churches often used a skull to symbolise death.

The dead were buried in the churchyard, with a Christian service that emphasised that the living returned to the earth from which they had originally been made: 'earth to earth, ashes to ashes', and prayed for eternal life at the day of judgement. Richer families would pay for a coffin and there might be a procession of male relatives and others following the body. The poor would be buried in a shroud or sheet. One disturbing element of the plague was that mass burials in plague pits were required to dispose of all the dead.

'The Abbess' from the *Dance of Death* by Hans Holbein

Mourners wore black and it was common to buy mourning rings or other mementoes to remember the dead. In his will, Shakespeare left money to three fellow actors to buy rings in his memory. Suicide was considered a sin, and those who had taken their own life were not allowed to be buried in the holy ground of the churchyard or according to the church rites.

Key terms glossary

Adjective a word that describes a noun, e.g. *blue*, *happy*, *big*

Anachronism something wrongly placed in the time period represented

Antithesis bringing two opposing concepts or ideas together, e.g. hot and cold, love and hate, loud and quiet

Aside when a character addresses a remark to the audience that other characters on the stage do not hear

Atmosphere the mood created by staging choices

Banter playful dialogue where the speakers verbally score points off each other

Blank verse verse lines that do not rhyme

Body language how we communicate feelings to each other using our bodies (including facial expressions) rather than words

Casting deciding which actors should play which roles

Choreograph create a sequence of moves

Clown an actor skilled in comedy and improvisation who could often sing and dance as well

Dialogue a discussion between two or more people

Dramatic climax the most intense or important point in the action of a play

Dramatic irony when the audience knows something that some characters in the play do not

Emphasis stress given to words when speaking

Extended metaphor describing something by comparing it to something else over several lines

Falling action the part of a play, before the very end, in which the consequences of the dramatic climax become clear

Feeding the lines reading lines aloud a few words at a time so that the actor can repeat them without holding a script

Freeze-frame a physical, still image created by people to represent an object, place, person or feeling

Gesture a movement, often using the hands or head, to express a feeling or idea

Iambic pentameter the rhythm Shakespeare uses to write his plays. Each line in this rhythm contains approximately ten syllables. 'Iambic' means putting the stress on the second syllable of each beat. 'Pentameter' means five beats with two syllables in each beat

Imagery visually descriptive language

Improvise make up in the moment

Irony saying the opposite of what you mean

Monologue a long speech in which a character expresses their thoughts. Other characters may be present

Objective what a character wants to get or achieve in a scene

Obstacle what is in the way of a character getting what they want

Paraphrase put a line or section of text into your own words

Personification giving an object or concept human qualities

Plot the events of a story

Prompt book a copy of the script kept by the stage management team with space for notes and sketches about staging

Pun a play on words

Quatrain a stanza of four lines

Repetition saying the same thing again

Rhyme scheme the pattern of rhymes at the end of lines of a poem or verse

Rhyming couplet two lines of verse where the last words of each line rhyme

Shared lines lines of iambic pentameter shared between characters. This implies a closeness between them in some way

Soliloquy a speech in which a character is alone on stage and expresses their thoughts and feelings aloud to the audience

Sonnet a poem with 14 lines. Shakespearean sonnets are written in iambic pentameter and include three quatrains and a rhyming couplet at the end

Statue like a freeze-frame but usually of a single character

Syllable part of a word that is one sound, e.g. 'dignity' has three syllables – 'dig','ni','ty'

Symbol a thing that represents or stands for something else

Tactics the methods a character uses to get what they want

Theme the main ideas explored in a piece of literature, e.g. the themes of love, loyalty, friendship, family and fate might be considered key themes of *Romeo and Juliet*

Tone as in 'tone of voice'; expressing an attitude through how you say something

Verb a 'doing' or action word, such as *jump*, *shout*, *listen*

Vowels the letters a, e, i, o, u